What an absolute gem! *A River Between Us* brought me on an emotional journey that produced both hope and tears. Truly a beautiful story about loving our enemies and seeing beyond our divisions to the humanity in all of us. A swoon-worthy hero and a strong heroine who surmounts impossible circumstances make this one of Jocelyn Green's best yet!

Heidi Chiavaroli, Carol Award-winning author of *The Orchard House* and *Hope Beyond the Waves*

A River Between Us carries currents of hope, courage, resilience, and restoration into a war-marked world. With Jocelyn Green's trademark combination of impeccable research and masterful storytelling, prepare for an immersive read, and to fall in love with characters who are as relatable as they are inspiring. Cora Mae, Ethan, and June will pull you into a tale both tender and strong; one that will fill your heart with the best of things, and linger there long.

Amanda Dykes, bestselling author of *All the Lost Places*

Jocelyn Green returns to her signature century with a richly researched historical novel that transports you to the tumultuous Civil War era. *A River Between Us* has all the hallmarks of Green's bestselling fiction - history, romance, suspense, faith, and a seamless blending of the American north and south. A moving story of bravery, hope, and love that outlasts the pages.

Laura Frantz, Christy Award-winning author of *The Rose and the Thistle*

A River Between Us kept me enthralled to the very end. Memorable characters, scenes that made me feel I was right there, never sure if this story would end the way I hoped; highly recommend both *A River Between Us* and Jocelyn Green. Well done, Jocelyn.

Lauraine Snelling, author of The Leah's Garden series, The Red River of the North series, and more than 100 others

Jocelyn Green pens a tender story of redemption and love in *A River Between Us*. I highly encourage my readers to pick up a copy today. Jocelyn is fast becoming one of my favorite authors to read.

Tracie Peterson, bestselling, award-winning author of more than 100 books

A layered and captivating journey that grips the heart and keeps the pages turning, *A River Between Us* is one historical romance fans will not want to miss! Green does a phenomenal job weaving together the nuances of the complicated issues of the Civil War with beautifully developed characters. With her signature masterful storytelling, the lives of ordinary people from both sides of the divide come to life with this tale of faith, discovery, and resilience. Be ready to settle in. You won't want to put this one down!

Stephenia H. McGee, FLH Award-winning author of *In His Eyes*

Filled with beautiful turns of phrase and immersive world-building, *A River Between Us* shares hope in the desperation of the Civil War. Themes of loving your enemies and found family are artfully woven into these well-crafted pages. Green's historicals are an experience not to be missed.

Heather Day Gilbert, two-time Christy Award finalist and author of the Tavland Vikings series

A RIVER BETWEEN US

Books by Jocelyn Green

A River Between Us

ON CENTRAL PARK

The Metropolitan Affair
The Hudson Collection

THE WINDY CITY SAGA

Veiled in Smoke
Shadows of the White City
Drawn by the Current

The Mark of the King
A Refuge Assured
Between Two Shores

HEROINES BEHIND THE LINES CIVIL WAR

Wedded to War
Widow of Gettysburg
Yankee in Atlanta
Spy of Richmond

A RIVER BETWEEN US

A Civil War Novel

JOCELYN GREEN

A River Between Us
 First edition 2017.
Second edition 2023.

Published in the United States of America by Credo House Publishers,
a division of Credo Communications LLC, Grand Rapids, Michigan
credohousepublishers.com

ISBN: 978-1-62586-255-6

Cover design by Bookfly Design
Interior design by Believe Book Design

Printed in the United States of America
Second edition

To all the Christian Mommy Writers,

and

To all those in need of hope.

Chapter One

ROSWELL, GEORGIA
WEDNESDAY, JULY 6, 1864

Water roared over the dam behind her, an echo of the blood rushing in her ears. Dropping to her knees, Cora Mae Stewart plunged a trowel into the earth.

The Yankees were coming. Everyone but the preacher and the mill workers had deserted town weeks ago. Yesterday, the Southern army had burned the bridge over the Chattahoochee River and retreated south, too. Cora Mae had nowhere to go, but at least the few valuables she and her mother possessed would not fall into pillaging Yankee hands.

In dawn's pearly light, Cora Mae carved away enough soil to make room for a cigar box wrapped in oiled paper. It rattled with dented silverware, a pocket watch, and jewelry. Of a sudden, she recalled the ruby ring on her finger and twisted it off, adding it to the hiding place.

Heart thundering, she tucked the box deep and refilled the hole. Spray from the waterfall beaded on her pinned-up hair. She brushed dirt from her apron as she rose, but her bare feet were hopelessly coated with mud.

Movement flickered in the corner of her eye. She whirled toward it, trowel thrust out. "Hello?"

A man stepped from between the trees and doffed his straw hat.

Relief rushed through her. "Why, Mr. Ferguson!"

The war had carved his face gaunt and sprinkled his black hair with gray. "I do wish you'd call me Horace."

She knew she ought to. That was his ring she'd just put in the earth, after all. Still, he had thirty-five years to her twenty and had been her loom boss longer than he'd been her betrothed.

Cora Mae dropped the trowel into her apron pocket. "I was—"

"I saw. Getting ready for the bluebellies, that so? Elsewise, I'd be afeared you changed your mind about our arrangement." He nodded toward her bare finger.

She rubbed the skin between her knuckles. "My mind ain't changed. I aim to marry you. And soon." It didn't matter that she felt nothing for him other than loyalty. Though he was a fair bit younger than her father, the two men had been good friends.

"There's no disrespect in hitching our wagons now," he said. "It's been a year, and then some."

It had been one year and four days since her Pap and seventeen-year-old brother Wade died, and nearly that long since Horace Ferguson had paid a call, his own face streaked with grief. He'd offered to marry Cora Mae and take care of her and her mother Matilda in addition to the stepdaughter his late wife had left him to raise. It was practical for all parties. Still, Cora Mae had asked for a year's time to mourn Pap proper, and he agreed.

Mr. Ferguson shifted, spinning the brim of his hat. "I told your pap I'd look out for you and Matilda. I promised Mavis that June would be cared for, too, and raised up with a Christian woman's influence. I aim to keep those promises, and our marrying answers both."

"I know that's so." She curled her toes beneath the fraying hem of her skirt. Were it not for the fact that she was deeply in debt, Cora Mae might have suggested they simply continue the way things stood now. Since all agreed that June needed a woman's care, she'd come to live with Cora Mae as soon as Mr. Ferguson put that ring on her finger. After all, Cora Mae would be her stepma in a matter of time anyway. She and Mama saw no reason to put off loving and caring for the child as their own. The apartment had been far too quiet since Pap and Wade enlisted, anyhow.

"Well then," Mr. Ferguson said. "I'm ready when you are."

Words stuck in her chest like dry cornbread. Her heart may not be ready, but her mind was made up to keep her promise, and that mattered more. He was a decent man, and they did have need of him. She pulled in a breath of misty air. "I'll talk to Mama, and we'll pick a day."

He worried his brim some more. "Is the least 'un already to work, then?"

"She is, and I best hurry if I'm to get there on time, too." She walked past him, but his strides matched hers as they headed toward the cotton mill just beyond the dam that powered it. Her gaze scaled the red bricks of the four-story factory as she approached.

Mr. Ferguson beckoned her to the side of the building until they were half in shadows again. "You, uh . . . want a fancy dress? If you have need of one, you can wear Mavis's. I still have it and the rest of her clothes. Might need some altering to fit you right. But you don't need to fuss with that if you don't want to. The dress don't matter none to me. I just thought . . . well, it mattered to Mavis. So I didn't know."

She studied on this. It was a kindness of him to offer, but it was also a reminder that she'd be stepping into a hole created by another woman. The ring that had marked her engagement had been Mavis's. The dress, the house, Mr. Ferguson, and especially June, had all been Mavis's. Cora Mae would be one more substitution in a time of war.

"If you don't mind, I'll wear my own dress." She wiped her hands on the apron that covered her hoopless, homespun skirt. It was plain, but so was she. Dressing up a practical marriage wouldn't make it romantic.

The bell tower in the mill yard sounded.

"We'll talk more later," she promised.

Inside the mill, she dashed up the stairs as the bell finished calling the hour. She hurried to the weaving room where she drew patterns for Confederate uniforms on special gray cloth.

Cora Mae didn't understand the war except in generalities. At the start, Pap had said he wanted no part of it, since the main freedom the South was fighting for was the freedom to own other folks whose skin was darker than their own. Pap didn't hold truck with that. War had been a far-off story fought in a place she'd never been by men she didn't know. It didn't touch her, she thought.

She thought wrong.

When rich men offered to pay Pap and Wade to be substitute soldiers, they went. Wade wanted to go more than Pap, but Pap went to keep his son safe and out of trouble. The money they'd been paid was the first cash Cora Mae had ever seen that wasn't mill company scrip.

She smoothed the scratchy gray wool on the table. Like as not, she'd drawn and cut their uniforms herself.

As she worked, the millhouse rattled and boomed with its own kind of battle noise. Up on the fourth floor, spinning girls spun thread from raw cotton. Their machines whirred so loudly that bobbin girls like June had to watch for hand signals alerting them it was time to deliver another empty bobbin or take away a full one. Brass-tipped shuttles fired across looms to weave the dyed thread into cloth, and the mill wheel on Vickery Creek chugged with the power of a locomotive.

The floor shook beneath Cora Mae's bare feet, and the table trembled beneath the cloth she worked. Her limbs thrummed. Her stooped back ached, but the Confederacy needed the uniforms, tents, and rope the Roswell mill produced. Their instructions were to stay and work until Yankee soldiers drove them out.

By half past six, the sun had lifted its bright head in the sky. Thirty minutes later, the bell rang for the breakfast break, and with a lurch, the mill shut down. She fell in line with the other girls trickling outside and waited for June.

The child appeared, dressed in brown homespun, and slipped her small hand into Cora Mae's. Her pink bonnet covered hair the color of a dark copper kettle, pulled into a bun to keep it clear of the factory machines. "I'm ready," she said.

Cora Mae tied the bonnet strings the little girl had left dangling. "So am I, Junebug."

Together, they hurried back to the apartment on Factory Hill. With a yank, the back door unstuck from its frame, and the pair entered the kitchen.

Mama was already at the table with glasses of watered-down milk and a plate of cornbread. As Cora Mae sat, Mama coughed into her handkerchief, staining it brown. More than twenty years of inhaling cotton dust and lint in the mill had taken its toll. Her smile seemed brave. "Grace, please."

The three bowed their heads, and Cora Mae thanked God for the daily cornbread in a Southern rendition of the Lord's Prayer. "Amen."

June ate and drank her share too fast to be mannerly, but on this occasion, Cora Mae didn't mind dismissing her to play outside while she shared words with Mama.

Mama broke off a small piece of bread and ate it. "You look troubled."

Wind blew under the door and ruffled Cora Mae's skirt. "I think it's time, Mama. To marry."

Mama stopped chewing. Her fingertips rippled over the persimmon seed buttons on her bodice, the way they always did when she gathered her thoughts. The irregular shapes spotted the unevenly black fabric Mama had dyed for mourning Pap and Wade. "My land. A wedding. How very fine."

Cora Mae swallowed. "Yes, ma'am, it's fine."

Mama cleared her throat. "You knew it was coming. Yet you ain't pleased."

"I'm pleased enough." She dredged up something akin to a smile and prayed her mother had forgotten everything Cora Mae had ever said about wanting to quit the mill and move away. "Maybe in time I'll grow fond of Mr. Ferguson, the way a wife should." At the moment, she barely felt anything at all, except the grit between her toes. It seemed far too much to wish for even half the love her parents had shared.

"Oh, darlin'." Mama placed one hand on Cora Mae's cheek. Her blue eyes crinkled at the edges. "Before your pap left for the war, he told me that if he should die, I should let Mr. Ferguson—a bachelor at the time—head our home. It's what he wanted."

Cora Mae's throat tightened as she clasped Mama's hand and leaned into it. "It solves our worries."

"He knows about the debt?"

"He knows." Cora Mae leaned back and sighed. Mr. Ferguson had sent vittles right regular throughout the past year, but the rent had gotten to be too much for her to handle. They'd lost two wage earners when Pap and Wade left, and when Mama's poor health forced her to retire, Cora Mae couldn't keep up. June's wages were so small they barely counted. They'd never been this far in debt before the war. Now, they were on the brink of eviction.

"And what does he say?" Mama pressed.

"That it won't matter once we marry. We'll combine our wages, and we can all live in his cottage on Mill Street together. The sooner the better. There's no use in putting it off."

Mama regarded the small space they'd called home for as long as Cora Mae could remember. "Well, if the Yankees really are coming, it'll be a comfort to have a man in the house once again."

"Yes, ma'am." Her chest constricting, Cora Mae rose and kissed Mama's silvery-blond hair.

When she and June returned to the mill, she was not surprised to find Mr. Ferguson waiting at the front gate. "Are you ready to move back into my house, June? You could have your own room again. I've made a new bed for Sissy, complete with a blanket and pillow." Cora Mae was impressed he'd remembered the name of June's doll, let alone built furniture for it.

But June clutched at her. "Leave you? But why? I want to live with you, Cora Mae! And with Miss Matilda, too!" Water filled her brown eyes. "You said we'd be together for always."

Mr. Ferguson took a knee and looked at her straight on. The child had already endured her father's death and then her mother's. Then she'd been sent away from her stepfather three months after her mother died. One more broken connection was not to be borne. "That's not what I mean," he said. "I mean that we're fixin' to make ourselves into a real family, the lot of us, all under one roof. Mine."

"So we're moving to his house? All of us?" June fixed her questions on Cora Mae.

"That's the plan," she replied. "Together for always."

"Here, step away a bit." He led them away from the stream of mill girls returning from breakfast and stopped near the dam on Vickery Creek.

"You talked to Matilda?" Mr. Ferguson half shouted over the roaring falls.

Water tumbled down thirty feet before crashing into the creek below. The spray misted Cora Mae's face, and she licked it off her lips. "Yes."

"You choose a day, then?"

She caught herself shrugging. "This one's good. After work."

His chin bobbed in a nod. "I'll get Reverend Pratt, God bless him. He and his wife and daughter are the only ones still here aside from the mill workers. June can stay the night with Matilda at the apartment, and then we can move them over with all your things tomorrow. Tonight, let's not fuss with all that. Tonight, let's just you and I . . . get settled."

Her stomach dropped. She didn't expect to feel settled any time soon. But if the Yankees were truly so close, she'd much rather all of them be under Mr. Ferguson's protection. She'd heard tell of their depredations. "June and Mama can come tonight, too. In case the Yankees come by dark. Horace?"

But he had already turned back toward the mill, leading her over the water-slicked path. She grasped June's hand as they both struggled to keep from slipping.

Chapter Two

Back at her post at the drawing table, the reverberations of the mill shook Cora Mae from the inside out. She couldn't stop her hands from trembling. The fact that Horace had been a faithful friend to the Stewarts did nothing to loosen the knot in her middle at the thought of the night ahead.

Suddenly, the mill heaved, then stopped. She turned toward the door to the stairs just as a blue-uniformed officer came striding through it. "Everybody out."

A Yankee. Here. And where there was one, there would be more.

Dread closed around Cora Mae, and sweat filmed her skin.

She gritted her teeth, fear churning into something hotter, sharper. It was one thing for soldiers to engage on the battlefield. They had no business here with unarmed women and children. Yet for all the defiance boiling within her, she couldn't bring herself to disobey him.

All around her, wide-eyed mill girls looked askance before following the order. Together, they filed down the stairs, their fear so thick it was a thing that could be felt, heavy on her shoulders.

Once outside, she stood in the dappled sunshine and listened to the eerie silence of a factory stilled during work hours. The sound of rushing water pulsed in her ears as the rest of the four hundred workers poured through the doors. When June appeared, she drew the child near.

"What's happening?" June cried.

The answer unspooled as two Yankees fled from the nearby storehouse carrying cans of oil, then turned back to watch. Crackling from the top floor, fiery-orange tongues lashed out the windows. Timber creaked, then crashed as the top floor fell into the one below it.

A woman next to Cora Mae cried, while one behind her laughed bitterly, cursing the city patriarchs who had fled Roswell weeks ago. Another set of soldiers had gone into the cotton mill, and from the smell of smoke, Cora Mae judged it would soon be up in flames as well.

Each moment beat against the flint her heart had become, until sparks caught and billowed hot through her body. Last winter the Confederate dollars paid to Pap and Wade to be substitute soldiers had been more valuable as kindling than money. The money burned to keep the apartment from freezing. Cora Mae felt its fire still, and what she felt against the Yankees also turned against the rich men who wanted this war but refused to fight it, sending her kin to their deaths instead.

The mill shuddered and collapsed.

She bent herself over June to shield her from cinders and flying pieces of their livelihood. She should not have lingered here, matching her fury to the flames. She ought to have pulled the child away to spare her from the scene. But even if she had, she couldn't shelter June from the war that had come to Roswell. Whatever anger she felt was only the ugly scab over her deep and abiding powerlessness.

Yankee soldiers, some mounted on sleek black horses, began filtering in and among the mill hands. "Clear on out of here," one called out. "Every last one of you is to come to the town square within the hour for further instructions."

Half the girls broke into a run as smoke and soot blackened the sky. Yankees followed them, making it clear they were under guard even now. Cora Mae stood rooted in place, craning her neck to find Horace as June melted into her skirt.

He lunged through the crowd to reach them. "I have to run. You'll not see me for a spell."

"What?"

A fierceness lit his eyes. "I heard talk. They're saying that any able-bodied men working in the mills are to be treated the same as if we were Rebel soldiers caught as prisoners of war, lest we take up arms and fight. I'm not sticking around to be arrested and sent away to die in some Northern camp. You women and children won't be harmed. They wouldn't dare do nothin' to you beyond making you quit work in the mill."

"But without work, how will we survive?"

The question leapt ahead of her concern for Horace's escape. Only a dozen men managed the hundreds of female mill workers. But so far, there were even fewer Yankees here, and they had their hands full burning buildings and rounding up a scattering crowd. If Horace aimed to slip away before more arrived, she had no doubt he could do it. He knew this land, its rivers, creeks, trees, and waterfalls far better than the bluebellies. But he was leaving her with the enemy in town, with June and Matilda depending on her alone.

After all his promises to provide and protect.

Then reason ruled. If he tarried, he'd be caught and sent away, and he'd be no help to them anyway. And going with him now was out of the question. There was no way her mama or June could keep pace with Horace while he fled. It was best to wait until the path was sure, the destination certain.

"I'll send for you through Reverend Pratt once I've found somewhere safe for all of us." Horace knelt before June. "Stay with Cora Mae. She's your mama now, wedding or not. Just do what the soldiers tell you to do, and you'll be all right. Don't you fret."

"You're leaving us? Now?" June's voice trembled. "But—"

He cupped her shoulder. "I'll send word soon," he whispered.

Rising, he kissed Cora Mae on the cheek and June on the forehead. He blended back into the current of mill hands flowing from the mill yard, past the tannery, past the picking and dyeing buildings, out the front gate, and toward their homes.

The row of apartments on Factory Hill swarmed with panicked mill workers by the time Cora Mae and June arrived. Union soldiers had multiplied. In and out of slamming doors they marched, their faces tanned and their sky-blue trousers freckled with fine red dust.

Holding fast to June, Cora Mae pushed past some soldiers and entered her home to find it already occupied by the enemy.

"You live here?" she heard one soldier say.

Ignoring him, she hoisted the hem of her skirts and bounded up the stairs. "Mama?"

June followed her into the bedroom where Mama sat, white-faced, in her rocker. "Yankees?" Mama whispered. "In my apartment?"

Cora Mae nodded, the instinct to defend their home rearing up within her.

The soldier from downstairs entered the room. "Are you mill workers?"

Trouble pressed in around Cora Mae until she thought it would crush the air right out of her. "The child and I are. Not my mama, though."

"Then you two are to report to the town square."

"I'm not leaving my mother with you." Cora Mae clenched the back of the rocker. June hid behind her skirts.

He held up his hands. "If this apartment is occupied, we'll leave her be, so long as she doesn't work at the mill. Our orders are to take vacant homes only. And from what I've heard, there are far larger homes on the other side of town anyway, all of them empty."

Those were the founding families' homes. They'd skedaddled with the parting instruction that the mills should keep running at full capacity as long as they were standing. Apparently no thought had been given to what would happen to the workers after the factories fell. "So you're not moving in here?" Cora Mae clarified.

"I already told you we aren't. We do, however, need you and the girl to get yourselves to Town Square."

Mama's breathing rattled before she coughed something fierce into her handkerchief. "What do you mean to do with them?"

"We're awaiting orders," the soldier replied. "All I can tell you is that all mill workers are to stay in the square until we hear what their consequence will be."

"Consequence?" Cora Mae blurted. "For doing our work? For minding our own business?"

"For aiding the enemy of the United States of America. The mills made cloth for Confederate uniforms, did they not? Tents, rope, sheeting?"

Any reply turned to sand in Cora Mae's mouth.

"Look." The soldier took a swig from his canteen. "The worst part, I'm sure, will be the waiting outside in this heat. I predict you'll get a warning not to work for the Rebel government again, and that will be the extent of it."

Mama wheezed, her fingers finding her persimmon buttons once more. "The town square has little shade. Will you set up tents?"

"We've none to spare, ma'am. They won't be held for long, though."

Cora Mae glanced at June, already flushed, wisps of hair dark with sweat framing her face. "If you've been here any time at all, you know what the Georgia sun can do in July."

"We're just following orders."

"Water, then?" Mama asked. "Food for—?" A bout of coughing cut her off. June reached out and patted her back.

The soldier's face softened, the stern lines shifting to concern instead. "I'm Dr. Ivanhoe. We're turning unoccupied homes into hospitals. Ma'am," he said to Mama, "the girls have got to go, but you'll be safe here."

Defiance fought against hope. The idea of Roswell homes being used to treat Yankee sick and wounded turned Cora Mae's stomach sour. But at least Mama wouldn't be out in the sun, and she'd be close to a doctor.

"You mean, she'll be your patient? She has cotton lint in her lungs. Could you—could you help her?" The question sprang from Cora Mae before she could consider whether she'd trust her mama to a Yankee's care.

"Not officially, no," Dr. Ivanhoe admitted. "But she will not be harassed or evicted. Neither will any other civilian residents who are not—*were* not—employed by the mills."

That left a few neighbors for Mama, at least. They were all her age or older, worn out by millwork and years past their employment. All of them dependent on their children to survive.

"We'll check on each other," Mama said. "But you'll come back afore long, anyhow."

Cora Mae hated to leave her. She also couldn't pretend that Mama belonged anywhere else but right here. "We're staying with her," she insisted.

"That isn't an option, miss."

"What's going on in here?" A second Yankee burst into the room, a pistol in his hand, and the small space shrank tighter. "Get to the square, the lot of you."

"Not her." Dr. Ivanhoe gestured to Mama. "She stays. You're trespassing in an occupied home, Lieutenant. Take your leave."

"I'll leave when those two do. Say your goodbyes and get out. Orders." The armed soldier's voice brooked no argument, but the doctor, at least, persuaded him to wait in the hall to give the women privacy.

June flinched at the slam of the door. Her breath came hard and fast.

Cora Mae knelt by Mama's rocker, mind spinning. "We'll come back just as soon's we can." She cut her voice to a whisper. "Horace has gone to find a safe place for all of us. He'll send word through the preacher. June and I will go to the square for our warning and be back to wait with you for word on where to go from here."

Mama's smile wavered. "You hold on to hope, child." She cleared her throat. "June, darlin', this day isn't turning out like we planned, but we're a family just the same. Remember that. Stick close to each other. I'll be praying you both home, you hear?" She wrapped her soft arms around the little girl and stroked the tendrils of hair at her neck.

When June scooted back, Cora Mae embraced Mama, inhaling the chinaberry soap scent of her hair. Despite her own brave words, this felt wrong. She was supposed to get married tonight. Horace was supposed to protect them all. They'd been fixing to come together all legal and proper, and now they were being ripped apart.

And what did this Yankee doctor really know about what would happen to them in the square? Was he even right that Mama could stay here without the enemy under her roof?

He was guessing.

He was a Yankee.

Yankees couldn't be trusted.

"Cora Mae." Mama's voice firmed. "I know you're powerful scared behind that fierce face of yours. Don't let it turn into hate." It was an echo of what she had said the day they burned the useless bills that Pap and Wade had died for. "The good Lord says we are to love our enemies and pray for those who bring us pain."

"I do recall that, Mama."

"You're the mama now," Mama whispered. "She'll do as you do. Lead her true."

Cora Mae took June's hand and squeezed it, her mood darker than a crow's shadow. She'd been separated from Pap, Wade, Horace, and now Mama. She would die fighting before anyone took June from her, too.

~

Her feet felt leaden on the short walk to the square. A ring of bluecoats parted to let her and June slip inside the already packed area. The noonday sun beat down upon her faded yellow bonnet.

"Let's find a spot to sit," she said to June, whose bonnet gapped at the sides of her face.

"Right in the dirt?"

"If they're going to pen us in like hogs, we may as well act like hogs to keep cool."

June managed to smile at that as they claimed a small patch of the square.

When Cora Mae caught a flash of red-gold hair, she stood again and waved. "Fern!"

Fern McGee turned and wove her way through the crowd to join them. "Is Matilda to home? I wish my Aunt Shannon knew to go check on her." Fern was eighteen years old and had been sweet on Wade before he'd joined up. The day he left, she'd sewn a star-shaped patch of Confederate gray wool onto her sun-bleached bonnet, and she wore it there still.

"I guess we'll all go home soon enough," June piped up, "and check on our kin ourselves."

"I reckon that's right." Fern smiled at her, but it was tight-lipped with brackets of worry.

"Sit with us if you like," Cora Mae offered.

But Fern only shook her head and moved on to sit with her older sister, Cynthia. With their mother long ago passed and their pa gone fighting, the two were closer than moss on a log. Besides, Cora Mae reminded her of Wade, and June reminded her of the week they learned he'd died, since that was when the child had come to live with the Stewarts. No wonder Fern didn't want to press on that bruised place in her memory.

Time seeped by at the pace of cold molasses, while smoke from torched buildings choked the air. Some folk in the square fainted from the heat, and so did a few of the soldiers standing guard. Those who needed to use the privy did so with a Yankee escort, who yelled at them to hustle. Some girls shouted that Confederate soldiers would come rescue them. But even if the Roswell Battalion had stayed to defend them instead of retreating right after burning the bridge, they'd have buckled against this force. Cora Mae couldn't count them all, but she'd heard there were some three thousand men here.

"Ain't we gonna go home before bed?" June asked. "Miss Matilda might worry. And Sissy needs me to tuck her in."

Cora Mae licked her parched lips, tasting smoke. "At this point, I don't reckon we will. But Mama can put Sissy to bed tonight, so don't you fret over that."

Mama might also try coming to the square to see if the mill hands were still there. But with all the dust in the air from people and horses, such a visit would only do her harm.

Twilight faded to ashy gray. Northern accents barbed her from all sides. "Next stop, Atlanta!" one soldier hooted. "But did you ever see so many girls all in one place before this? Think I might see about keepin' one or two of 'em warm!"

Cora Mae didn't know if this particular soldier or any of these others had taken up arms against Pap and Wade. But Yankees were all the same, anyway. They'd have killed her menfolk if given the chance.

Lying flat in the dirt, she listened to mothers hush their crying children and wondered again how Mama fared. Beside her, June sniffed.

"Junebug," she whispered, "I'm glad we're together. You're right courageous."

"Well, I'm eight years old now."

Cora Mae smiled at the girl's solemn nod. "And just as brave as you ever could be." She stretched out her arm, and June nestled into it, curling into her side.

"When will Mr. Ferguson send for us?" June whispered.

"Soon." Cora Mae prayed it was true. "Or at least, the soonest he can."

The next day, everyone in the square was damp with dew, sore, and hungry, though the soldiers did pass around cornbread. But when one Yankee made an announcement later that day, Cora Mae wished she'd left her stomach empty.

"By order of General Sherman," he hollered, "commanding officer of the United States Army, you are all under arrest for making cloth and rope for the Confederacy. Aiding the rebels with this wartime manufacturing is treason, making each of you traitors to your rightful government. You will all be deported to Indiana, where you can no longer assist the Rebellion."

Stunned silence. Then a wail rose up from the crowd. Cora Mae felt as if she was going to be sick. Indiana? She'd never have left Mama if she'd had any idea the Yankees would go this far.

"You'll be taken by wagon to Marietta and will continue your journey from there."

If he said anything else after that, Cora Mae didn't hear it. Kneeling, she gathered June close and felt the girl's arms wrap her neck. "We'll stick together. We'll find a way home. We'll hold on to hope."

But on the inside, she felt like she was falling.

Chapter Three

The wagons didn't come that day for the mill girls, or for the next three, but more Yankees did, and so did a passel of Roswell men. Just as Horace had said, they were arrested and sent north on a horse-drawn cart. At least Horace was not among them.

Cora Mae and June spent the rest of that week in the town square with four hundred others, forcing themselves to eat the rations. They worked their way to the perimeter, watching in case Mama might look for them despite the dust, waiting while one hour bled into the next.

She didn't come.

On Saturday, however, Reverend Pratt did. Cora Mae waved at him until he came as close as the guard would allow.

"Do you have word for me, Reverend?" she asked, though she couldn't guess how he would pass on Horace's message in the presence of the enemy.

"From your mother," he said. "I've just come from your apartment."

"Did the Yankees take it?" June asked, eyes wide.

He shook his head. "They've let her be. If her lungs allowed it, she'd be standing beside me, with a basket of cornbread for you. But all these tramping boots and hooves have stirred up so much dust that she's worse off than usual."

"How much worse?" Cora Mae asked.

A grim silence left little room for doubt. "For her own health, I haven't told her yet that you're being sent away. She'd die trying to get to you, and that's no exaggeration."

"I have to go see her." None of them could have guessed their parting would be for so long, that so many miles would come between them. "I have to see my mother!" she called to one of the guards.

The reverend spoke to the soldier on her behalf, but the Yankee was unmoved.

Cora Mae swallowed, mastering herself for June's sake as much as for her own. She'd find a way to get home again, even without Yankee cooperation.

"Your mother said you were expecting another message," the reverend told her.

"I'm afraid I don't have any other to deliver, Miss Stewart."

Horace had promised to send word. She wouldn't be able to meet him now, but she'd at least like to hear he'd escaped. She'd like to hope he might be able to rescue them, too, and help them all reunite as a family. But that was foolhardy. He'd be arrested before he could get close.

She and June were on their own.

Darkness fell, and a thunderstorm soaked everyone to their bones. By morning, the ground was a red clay soup, and their damp clothes steamed in the fresh heat of a new day.

When a Yankee general congratulated his troops with whiskey, new devilment wormed into the square. Unclaimed rations were quickly guzzled by those who'd already had their fill. Cora Mae shuddered as the alcohol did its work. Guards previously content with ogling the mill girls now came in among them, all hands.

"I can do what I want with you, spoils of war!" One soldier reached for Fern, a couple of yards from Cora Mae. Full of fight, Cynthia lunged forward, her blonde hair wild and unpinned. She stomped on his foot, took Fern's hand, and ran off. He stumbled after them.

Drunken Yankees hooted and hollered as if at a greased pig chase. Cora Mae hunched her shoulders, trying to be less visible. Keeping June close, she backed away from the space where blue coats mixed with homespun.

"*Oof!*" She bumped into something solid and turned to find a bearded soldier with bloodshot eyes leering down at her.

"Well, make it easy on me, Secesh!" His chortle reeked of whiskey. The top buttons of his coat were unfastened, his undershirt plastered with sweat.

Cora Mae's heart jumped into her throat. She turned and pulled June away with her.

"Well, looky what we have here!" He tramped after June. "Ain't she a beauty!"

"Don't touch her." Cora Mae's voice was a growl, alarm a drum against her ribs. She reached into her apron pocket and grasped the trowel that had been there since she'd buried the box by the dam. When the soldier moved closer, she whipped it out and pointed it at his gut.

"Who do you think you are?" He lunged for her, and she darted from him.

June slipped away, and in her panic to flee, barreled into another Yankee. He gripped her shoulders. "Lost?" he asked, his smile sloppy and wet from drink.

June squirmed and screamed. Her bonnet slipped off and was lost to the mud.

"Let her go!" The fury of a wildcat flooded Cora Mae. Leaving the bearded bluebelly behind, she clawed her way toward June's captor instead. But frantic mill girls ran between them, cutting June from view.

"Cora Mae! Cora Mae, help!" The child's voice reached a fever pitch before muffling.

"June!" Cora Mae called for her again and again, wielding her trowel to part the throng. Her dread was so thick she could taste it. "June, where are you?"

But the little girl's cries were swallowed by the frenzied crowd.

Cora Mae's head was jerked back, and she felt her bonnet rip away. A soldier gripped her braid and clasped her around the middle. His breath was hot in her ear, but the alcohol slurred his words to an unrecognizable mess. She jammed her elbows into his ribs to push away. "Let me go!" she shouted and heard the same plea all over the square. *Lord, have mercy!*

Galloping thundered in the distance, but she barely registered the noise, so intent was she on breaking free and finding June. Then the cavalry crashed into the square, whipping sharp tones at the drunken soldiers. Scabbards and bridles jangled amid the pounding hoofbeats, and in the commotion, she wrested from the hands that held her. Wildly she spun, calling for June, but she could barely hear her own voice.

Then she saw the little girl rising up out of the crowd. A mounted soldier had pulled her onto his dark bay horse, seating her in front of him.

The trowel dropped from her grip. "June!" Cora Mae screamed in the midst of terrified girls and intoxicated Yankees. "June! June!" All was confusion. Throughout the square, mill hands were being swept up on horses.

"Take my hand." The voice turned Cora Mae's head. "My name is Sergeant Ethan Howard, Seventy-Second Indiana Mounted Infantry. I'm here to take care of you.

Come on." Green eyes pierced hers. Sun flashed on the crossed gold sabers above the brim of his black forage cap.

She grabbed his forearm, and he gripped under her elbow. Almost before she knew what was happening, she was straddling a dapple gray horse, tucking her skirts around her legs.

The horse lunged forward, and she flung her arms around Sergeant Howard, clutching his leather cross belt lest she fall.

On a nearby horse, June bounced in the saddle, terror in her eyes. "June!" Cora Mae chanced to let go and wave before clasping her hands above her soldier's belt buckle once again. "Hang on tight! It's all right!"

But it wasn't. They were heading west, and every step took her farther from everything she knew. As they rode past the white-columned homes of Roswell's wealthy, Cora Mae bristled. Those residents had all gone somewhere safe weeks ago, and they could all come back when they chose to. But when and how would she get home now?

On the rust-colored dirt road outside of town, the horses slowed and formed two columns. By her estimate, close to two hundred Roswell girls were being carried away with their Yankee riders. The air was thick with dust and hoofbeats. She released her hold on Sergeant Howard and gripped the back of the saddle instead. All around her, bedraggled girls cried or scolded or moaned, while others simply stared blankly. On the other side of the road, riding parallel to her, June slumped in front of her Yankee, who had fiery shoulder-length hair.

Sergeant Howard nodded toward the pair. "Ease your mind about the girl. Lieutenant Dooley's a good man. He's a blacksmith for our regiment who volunteered to help us get you all safely to Marietta. He'll not see harm come to her."

Cora Mae eyed the blacksmith who had taken June, and he saluted her with a broad hand she could well imagine gripping a hammer. Beneath the brim of his hat, blue eyes sparkled, and his cheeks flushed almost as bright as his hair. At a forge, he must turn livid.

"Where are you taking us?" Cora Mae asked.

Sergeant Howard coughed, then turned his head to the side to speak. "Marietta." He smelled of coffee and leather and balsam. "Where you should have been taken as soon as the order was given."

"The order should not have been given at all." She braced herself for a lecture about her treasonous activity.

"This is the army. We have to follow orders, even the ones we dislike." A muscle bunched in his jaw.

"Even when it hurts women and children?"

Sergeant Howard faced forward again. If he replied, she couldn't hear it over the din of two hundred distraught mill hands.

Dust rose in great clouds from the road, fading the trees and sky. "You and Lieutenant Dooley turn around and take us home." Before and behind her, other girls on horseback echoed Cora Mae, pleading with their captors to be free.

"You know I can't do that, Miss—"

"Stewart. You mean you won't do it. That's not the same as can't."

He twisted in his saddle to look at her. "The mills are gone. The Yankees are encamped all over the place, and not all of them as well-behaved as yours truly. So tell me, what would you do?"

She leveled her gaze at him. "I'd see to my mother, who is sick and surrounded by the enemy. The same enemy as killed her husband and son."

Ethan trapped a strong word for Sherman behind his teeth. The frustrated general was growing desperate, especially since the disaster on Kennesaw Mountain almost two weeks ago. It had cost three thousand Union casualties to only seven hundred fifty killed, wounded, or captured Rebels. More than once on that sweltering day, Ethan had narrowly escaped death himself. If they'd won that battle, or if they'd at least not suffered such heavy losses from it, he wondered if Sherman would have given such harsh orders for these civilians in his quest for Atlanta.

He searched for something to say. But with Miss Stewart staring at him, a fire lit behind those hazel eyes, words dropped into his belly like hardtack. He knew what it was to care for an ailing parent, to watch a loved one suffocate. He could only imagine what it must feel like for Miss Stewart to be absent when her mother needed her most.

"As you say, the mills are gone." Venom threaded her tone. "What harm could we possibly bring you Yankees by staying with our families?"

Ethan caught Seamus Dooley's eye, but the Scots-Irishman only shrugged and glanced at the small charge astride his Morgan horse. Looking ahead once again, Ethan shifted the reins. "I'm real sorry about your parents and brother." He coughed again, the dust in the air irritating the coal dust still in his lungs.

Swinging his leg over the pommel in front of him, he dismounted and patted the saddle. "Have a seat." He looked the opposite direction while she maneuvered herself into place. "We've got sixteen miles to Marietta. Just thought I'd give Reckless here a break." Up and down the mounted infantry columns, other soldiers did the same.

Lifting her chin, Miss Stewart straightened her spine, though her walnut-brown hair hung in an unkempt braid down her back and mud caked her dress and apron. Dangling above the stirrups, her bare feet were stained red with the land she might never see again. The ache in her eyes cinched his chest.

She didn't deserve this. She was only doing her job for the company that kept her family alive.

Fumbling a bit, Ethan drew a handkerchief from his pocket and wet it with water from his canteen. "Truce?" He offered it up to her, a soggy white flag, and the mill workers in line ahead of him whipped around to glare at him. One woman with tangled yellow hair cussed at him with as much skill as any soldier he'd met.

Miss Stewart gasped. "For shame, Cynthia!" She gave a quick, disapproving shake of her head, surprising him far more than the cussing. "That kind of talk ain't fit for children's ears."

Ah. That explained it.

"Yankee lover!" the girl spat. "I reckon this is a real dream come true for you, Cora Mae. You finally get to leave Roswell." She turned back around in a huff.

Miss Stewart reddened. After a hesitation, she took his handkerchief and wiped her face and neck, then used the other side to wipe her hands and her arms before laying it over the pommel to dry. "Doesn't make us friends."

"Noted." He cleared his throat. "Care to explain that very interesting remark? You *wanted* to leave Roswell?"

"Not now. Not like this."

Ethan let the matter drop. Between sweat-lathered horses, heat from the midafternoon sun undulated in waves off the road. He felt as though he were baking inside his scratchy wool uniform. Unslinging his canteen from over his shoulder, he held it up.

With a whisper of thanks, she drank. After handing it back to him, she cast another glance toward June, who he could only guess was her sister.

Guilt coated him. These were no frivolous planter's daughters, waited on by slaves. Their pale complexions bore witness to long hours of indoor work. Before the war, his skin was just as untouched by the sun as theirs, his world as narrow. He guessed their anger had more to do with the North invading their homeland than with any preference for slavery.

Loblolly pines scrubbed the sky. A mile passed, maybe two. All around them, shrill complaints jabbed the humid air, and lower-pitched voices barked after them, yet Ethan's mind drifted.

"I lost my brothers, too." He didn't know why he said it, for he didn't expect her to care that, at twenty-five years old, Ethan was the only one left in his family. Reins in his right hand, he rubbed the heel of his left over his stinging eyes. "I'm not saying I know how you feel."

She nodded. "Your loss is still loss." She could have praised the Rebels that killed his brothers, yet she didn't.

Reckless slowed his pace. Across the road, Dooley noticed and matched Toledo's gait to keep June near Miss Stewart. The horses had reason to be worn out, and as they were in no hurry to get back to Marietta, Ethan let other mounted infantrymen and their charges pass them. When Reckless began limping, however, he halted.

"What's wrong?" Miss Stewart asked.

"We'll see. But come on down first." He reached up for her.

Careful to keep her skirts tucked modestly around her legs, she let him help her to the ground.

"Mind holding the reins?" Ethan passed them to her, then laid his buckskin gloves across the saddle. Facing the rear, he slid his hand down Reckless's front leg, pinching the back tendon. Reckless bent his knee. His shoe was clogged with mud that had dried into rock-hard dirt. While cradling the hoof, Ethan drew a jackknife from his pocket, opened it, and picked out the mud. Dooley would need to replace a missing nail in the shoe at Marietta. When he came to a rock wedged near the frog, he knew he'd found the source of the horse's limping. He dislodged it and let Reckless place his hoof back down.

"Dooley," he called, "check Toledo's shoes, just in case."

"Aye," Dooley grunted. "Already doing it."

For good measure, Ethan cleaned the rest of Reckless's hooves and shoes. "That should do it." He patted the horse's powerful haunch and put his gloves back on, then took the reins from Miss Stewart.

She scanned the road. "We're at the rear of the line."

"So we are. But we'll catch up. Reckless is in good shape now." He offered his hand to help her back up into the saddle.

She didn't take it. Instead, she walked over to June. "If you won't take us home, let us go. No one will notice."

Ethan tossed his reins to Dooley, who stood between the two horses. In three strides, he stood before Miss Stewart and her sister. "I can't let you go."

The two mill workers backed away from him, putting distance between themselves and the horses. "What does it matter to you?" Miss Stewart asked.

He approached as he would a skittish horse, calm but firm, searching for words to persuade. This entire matter left a rotten taste in his mouth, but it was out of his hands. "I told you. Orders are orders."

"My mother needs me!" Wind ruffled Miss Stewart's skirt about her legs and her hair around her face. She backed farther down the road, one slow step at a time, with June at her side. She had to know that if they ran, he'd catch them.

"Easy, Miss Stewart. You know Roswell's crawling with Union soldiers. If you go back, you'll be right here again in no time."

Her lips pressed into a grim line. "I am sick and tired near to death of other people making my choices for me. I didn't want this war. I sure didn't want to lose my menfolk to it. I didn't set out to aid the Rebel army, but I was working in the mill when somebody else decided that's what we would do."

June tugged on her skirt. "We ready yet?"

Miss Stewart touched the girl's shoulder, but it didn't seem to calm her much. "Fact is, if I'd ever been given a choice about where to live and where to work, I wouldn't choose a mill that makes a body old before it's time. It stole the breath from my mama, and if it hadn't burned to the ground, it would take mine, too."

Ethan cleared his throat but couldn't clear his lungs. If he'd met this woman under different circumstances, he'd tell her he knew exactly how she felt.

June paced back and forth beside Miss Stewart, her silent impatience louder than a bugle. She looked about ready to bolt.

He took a step toward them.

They backed up three.

Dagnabit. He did not want to chase and tackle them, but he would. And Dooley would help him. He caught the lieutenant's eye to signal he ought to be ready.

"I had no say in being rounded up and penned like livestock in the town square," Miss Stewart went on, "or about being hauled away from it. You may tell me I've got no say about going to Marietta, either, but I see a chance here to make my own decision, and I'm taking it."

"Come *on*!" June yanked on Miss Stewart's hand, pulling her off balance.

In trying to catch herself, the woman's bare foot came down hard on the side of a sun-baked wagon wheel rut, twisting that ankle. With a sharp inhale, she winced and hopped on the other foot.

"I'm sorry!" June covered her mouth. "Oh no, I didn't mean to!"

Miss Stewart paled. "I know you didn't." She tried some weight on it, muffled a groan, and stood on one leg.

"Well. That's that, then." Ethan slipped one arm around her willow-reed waist, the other beneath her knees, and scooped her up.

"I thought we were going home!" June cried.

"You will," Ethan said. "Just not today."

He felt the fight leave Miss Stewart's body as she wilted against him. Her face, so close to his, reddened from pain or embarrassment or both. Not that he blamed her. It had been a fine speech, right up until the end.

"It doesn't seem quite right, does it, for all these horses to have four shoes each when you mill hands have none." Leave it to Dooley to lighten the mood. He pointed at Reckless's legs. "He even has four white socks!"

This earned a begrudging smile from June, but then she went right back to scowling. Chuckling, Dooley swept her up into his saddle, then rubbed the white blaze on Toledo's nose.

Ethan helped Miss Stewart mount Reckless again, confident the Thoroughbred-Arab mix would not tire from her thistledown weight. Her jaw clenched, and she didn't look at him, but he spied tears glittering with anger or disappointment of a foiled plan. It wasn't a *good* plan, but it had been hers, and her pride seemed mighty hard for her to swallow.

With long strides, he led Reckless to close the gap between them and the rest of the cavalry. Dooley traveled next to him with Toledo and June.

Quiet reigned, as if Miss Stewart had spent all her words and had none left. A couple of times Ethan almost spoke to her but decided against it. What could he say? What was the use? He was a Yankee, she a Rebel—by geography, if not ideals. More importantly, he was dying, as surely as her mother was. It was only a matter of time, if a bullet didn't take him first.

Pines spiced the air with their sap. A journey that should have taken four hours stretched into five, and they still weren't in sight of Marietta. As shadows lengthened, Ethan's charge dozed. When she listed to one side in the saddle, he considered waking her before she fell, then stopped himself. She'd been sleeping on the ground for four nights, and there'd be no feather bed awaiting her in Marietta. If she could sleep sitting up, she should.

With an apology to Reckless for the extra weight, Ethan stepped into the stirrup and mounted the horse. Sitting behind the saddle, he reached around Miss Stewart, guarding her from toppling over the side. She swayed, then nestled back against him.

A protective instinct flared in his chest.

Chapter Four

MARIETTA, GEORGIA
SUNDAY, JULY 10, 1864

With a start, Cora Mae awoke to find herself braced between Sergeant Howard's arms. She sat bolt upright, embarrassed, and he dismounted to walk alongside her. A few yards away, Dooley walked Toledo with June quietly in the saddle. Ahead of them, the rest of the Roswell girls rode on their captors' mounts, too.

Fern turned around, pushing twists of hair off her face. "We'll be rescued yet, you'll see. Our boys won't let this stand."

Cora Mae wasn't as confident.

They passed Yankee guards as they entered Marietta. She'd heard this was a charming resort town, with natural springs and fancy hotels. The road they traveled was marked by abandoned homes with columned breezy porches, gingerbread trim, and picket fences. She could easily imagine the Southern belles who lived there, wearing frothy dresses over wide hoops to dance with cadets from the nearby Georgia Military Institute. She wondered about the slaves that laundered and pressed those gowns and helped the ladies get into them. She wondered about the slaves who'd kept up the grounds, chopped firewood, carried water, groomed the horses—and where they'd gone when their owners fled.

As the street broadened and they approached the center of town, she gained some idea. Aside from the swarms of Yankees, dark-skinned folks proved busy unloading wagons, leading horses, cooking, or doing laundry. Crates of army supplies crowded the sidewalks. The smell of manure and sweat-soaked wool overpowered her.

But not everyone sweltered in wool uniforms. One tall man was bare to his waist as he chopped wood for fire, his ebony back thatched with raised scar tissue. She had never seen the like. In fact, she'd never been this close to anyone who'd been a slave before. In Roswell, only the rich owned servants, and they lived on the other side of town.

Sergeant Howard must have noticed her staring. "That's Scipio."

"What happened to him?" she whispered.

"He ran away. Or tried to."

Her own back itched beneath her homespun as she imagined a whip cutting into it. Unsettled, she looked away and noticed a woman whose skin was so light she must have had one white parent. Her hair bound up in a bright yellow turban, she labored over a washboard and a steaming cauldron that smelled of lye.

"Have they traded their old masters for new ones?" Cora Mae asked. Men and horses tramped through the street, some of them pausing in the shade of maple and oak trees to stare at the Roswell girls now.

"They're free," Sergeant Howard said. "They're employed by the army and are paid twelve dollars a month. They can quit and walk away if they choose."

Cora Mae hid her surprise at the figure, silently wondering at this place called the North, which had so many healthy soldiers, sleek horses, and money to afford such wages.

The woman with the yellow turban looked up from her work, her eyes glinting with intelligence and determination, before scrubbing the laundry once more.

Sergeant Howard lowered his voice. "That's Venus. She won't walk away. She's already made it clear that when our army moves south, she's coming with us."

"But why would she do that?" Cora Mae figured that if recently freed people traveled anywhere, it would be away from the land where they'd been enslaved.

"Her mother, if she's alive, is south of here. She aims to find her. Her best guess is Savannah, since that's where they lived when Venus was sold away from her at the age of five."

Five years old. That was three years younger than June. Cora Mae looked at the little girl, so small in the saddle, and felt a tearing grief for any child and parent separated like livestock at an auction.

"I've heard dozens of similar stories in the last week," he went on. "I mean no disrespect for what you mill hands are going through. But you aren't the only ones who have been forced away from your family."

The truth of this—and the fact that she hadn't thought of it herself—singed her cheeks.

~

At the rear of the Seventy-Second Indiana columns, Cora Mae and June were the last to reach the town square, defended by a Union cannon. The square was packed with white army tents and more Yankees churning the red clay mud. Covered wagons lumbered through the street, and other tents crowded up against a drugstore, the Cole Hotel, a three-story Masonic Hall, and other buildings so obscured she couldn't tell what they were.

"We're here." Sergeant Howard's hands encircled her waist, helping her down. Pain still pulsed in her ankle, and she was mindful to favor it. Mill girls dismounted all around them.

Lieutenant Dooley lifted June down from the saddle, his face florid from the day's heat. She hurried to Cora Mae's side.

The sergeant pointed behind them. "This is the Cobb County Courthouse, where you'll be staying until you continue the journey north." The brick building rose up on the east edge of the square, facing the lowering sun. The Stars and Stripes snapped from the pole at its top.

With June's hand in hers, Cora Mae joined her former coworkers and climbed the building's steps. Sergeant Howard and Lieutenant Dooley tied their horses to the hitching post at the street's edge, then followed them up the stairs.

June paused to point at the tents. "What are all these for?"

"Those in the square are where the Second Ohio Cavalry and the Twentieth Connecticut Infantry are camped." Dooley gestured to the tents surrounding the buildings on the outside edge of the square. "All of these are hospital tents. For the sick and wounded."

June wrinkled her nose. "There must be a hundred of them!"

Sergeant Howard chuckled as he surveyed the grounds. His short, dark blond hair curled at the nape of his neck. "Try a thousand. There are five Union army corps here in Marietta, with more than four thousand sick and wounded. They've taken the churches and hotels for the patients, but obviously that's not enough room."

The courthouse's double doors swung open, and a bearded Yankee in spectacles strode through them. "All right, men, I'll take over from here. Inside, all you girls." He motioned to the mill girls lingering on the street.

"We'll sleep inside tonight, Junebug." Cora Mae forged a smile as a gust of wind, laden with heat, swept over her.

"As long as I stay with you."

"You Secesh will go where I say you go." The provost guard rocked back on his heels.

Sergeant Howard and Dooley looked at each other, brows furrowed. "These two stay together," Sergeant Howard said.

"Says who?"

"Says decency," Dooley chimed in. "Ain't no cause for separating kinfolk just to prove you can."

The provost guard grunted. "Come on, let's get you locked up." Fern and other Roswell girls straggled up the steps and into the courthouse as he spoke. "You'll find combs, soap, and tooth powder inside, compliments of the Christian Commission that's set itself up here in Marietta."

Sergeant Howard touched her sleeve so lightly she almost didn't notice. "Do you need a doctor? For your ankle?"

"No." She didn't care to see any more bluecoats than she had to. "It'll mend quick enough."

"I pray it does."

When she frowned, he added, "Didn't anyone tell you? Not all Yankees are devils." His lips slanting, he tipped his hat to her, then returned with Dooley to their waiting horses.

The room to which Cora Mae was assigned was crammed with girls and not much else. The mill hands took turns at basins of water set in the corners, eagerly using the soap and pocketing new combs. For dinner, they broke Yankee hardtack.

June teased a piece of hair from her braid and sucked the end of it. "I been chewin' on something. Do you reckon I ought to call you Mama, seeing as you almost are? You were fixin' to marry Mr. Ferguson before he had to run off. The mean Yankees might keep us together if they think we're relations."

Cora Mae's nose pinched. She still couldn't imagine being married to Horace, but she could surely imagine loving this little girl as though she were her own. "Call me Mama if you like," she whispered.

"I'm sorry about your ankle, Mama."

With a half-smile, Cora Mae pulled the end of June's braid away from her mouth. "It'll mend. And I hate to say it, but we wouldn't have gotten far without being caught again." It had taken the larger part of the journey to admit that to herself, but it was the truth.

As the mill girls claimed patches of the wooden floor and one blanket each, guards paced outside the windows. There was even a pair standing watch at the door to the hallway.

"I never did see so much blue in all my life," June whispered, then rolled onto her side. Her breathing grew slow and steady.

Outside, twilight banked the blazing sun, taking the fever from the air. Every few seconds, a soldier with a musket on his shoulder paced by, dissolving any plan to sneak out and run away.

"*Psst.* Miss Stewart." A whisper sounded at the window. "It's Sergeant Howard. I've got news for you."

A few mill girls closest to her stirred with low murmurs of disapproval. "Cora Mae? Are you sneaking a tryst with the enemy?"

It was Cynthia, again, her question so ridiculous it didn't deserve a reply.

Cora Mae rose and went to him.

"You weren't sleeping, were you?"

"Not yet," she said, leaning on the windowsill. "And neither are a handful of others, so we best keep this quick and quiet. What do you want?"

He straightened his hat and lowered his voice further. "General Dodge—the Union general commanding the sixteenth corps here—he thinks Sherman's order is absurd."

Hope flickered. "So will he let us go home?" She leaned farther out the window to better hear him.

"I told you. You can't go home, not yet."

"Well, then, what use is Dodge's opinion?"

"Dodge told the chief surgeon here to hire as many of you girls as he can. You could be a nurse, paid in greenbacks, with rations to eat, and stay here in Marietta."

She held his unblinking gaze. The sharp smells of illness and ammonia poked from tents and trenches outside. "Work for Yankees."

"Stay here in Georgia," he countered. "A half day's journey from Roswell. You'd be as close to your mother as you could possibly hope to be."

"Could I visit her?"

"Cora Mae!" Cynthia called loud enough to wake the room. "Hush up! Some of us are trying to sleep!"

Fern shushed her, but Cynthia did have a point. Cora Mae shoved the window open farther. She sat on the sill, swung her legs around, and hopped to the ground without landing on her injured ankle.

Sergeant Howard steadied her. "Trying to escape again?"

"Not without June. Just trying to have a decent conversation." She lowered herself to the ground in the shadows of a nearby magnolia tree. It was far enough away from the window that they wouldn't be overheard.

He leaned his rifle against the courthouse wall and sat with her on the damp earth. The soldiers patrolling the perimeter didn't notice.

"I asked if I could visit my mama," she reminded him. "If I work for Yankees."

"You'd have to stay here or go where the army goes," he whispered. "Do you think you could nurse wounded Yankee soldiers, Miss Stewart?"

Fireflies blinked against the lavender sky. She cupped one in her hands, and it glowed yellow between her fingers. "So they could heal up and go on out and kill more Johnny Rebs?" She rebelled against the notion.

"It's the only way to stay."

She opened her hands and let the firefly take wing. "I can't do it," she whispered. "I can't support the Yankee army."

"You're looking at it backward. Let the Yankee army support you."

Cora Mae shook her head, incredulous. "I can't understand why you care."

Ethan swiped the forage cap off his head and crushed it against his knee. "Look past my uniform for one second and recognize that I'm not your enemy."

She raised an eyebrow. "You sure look like one." But her tone lost its black-coffee bitterness. "So I'm supposed to love you."

His pulse skidded. "What did you say?"

"'Love your enemies.' It's one of the last things my mama said to me. Heard of it?" The corner of her mouth tilted, and a dimple pressed into her cheek.

Caught off guard, Ethan stifled a laugh. "Just so happens I have. Didn't notice?"

She tucked a loose strand of hair behind her ear. "Well. Personally, I haven't mastered it yet. But I know being mad won't change anything for the good. It won't help June." She looked away. "That doesn't mean I'll stay and nurse."

Ethan tamped down a smile. His gaze skimmed her silhouette, from her lashes to the tip of her delicate nose, over lips shaped like Cupid's bow, and down her slender throat. He wondered if she knew how entrancing she was. Proximity to death—especially his own—had made him more aware of beauty and life around him. Even when that beauty was cloaked in struggle. Even when life was hard. That rendered it no less precious.

Campfire smoke drifted through the heavy air, and with it came a lift of music. Voices, deep and rich, entwined as one in song. As he did every night since they'd first encamped here a week ago, Ethan turned toward the sound and listened.

"What is that?" Miss Stewart whispered.

"Former slaves, now free," he answered, "singing together at the end of a very long day. They aren't all from Marietta, either. Many have come to us from surrounding areas."

If she asked him what they would do with their freedom after the army could no longer support them, he'd have to tell her he didn't know. Instead, she simply listened to their words.

"I never heard anything like this," she confessed.

Neither had he until recently. But before he could tell her that, he felt a spasm in his lungs, coughed into his elbow, and silently cursed the dust that would not leave.

Miss Stewart watched him. "That sounds familiar."

"Coal," he explained simply. But that wasn't what he wanted to discuss. He swallowed, and the music faded with a shift of the wind. "Miss Stewart, what did that mill hand mean when she said leaving Roswell was a dream come true for you?"

A white-winged moth fluttered between them before flitting away. "It was a long time ago."

"What was a long time ago?"

Cicadas ticked above the moans of the sick nearby. She looked beyond him, and he suspected she saw more than the hospital tents spilling into the street. "By the time I was fifteen, I'd already pined for years to be anywhere else but Roswell. All I knew was the inside of the cotton mill, my family's apartment, and the path we beat between the two. Then a textile engineer from New York came to fiddle with our machinery. When he talked about places he'd been, I longed to see it all for myself. The ocean. Mountains. Prairie grass higher than my head. Wide open spaces where the sky feels close enough to touch." A smile, slow and beautiful, broke over her face like a sunrise. "The more I realized I was stuck in Roswell, the stronger my urge to leave. I just felt—" She spread her hands.

"Trapped," Ethan finished for her. "I know."

Miss Stewart peered at him. "Do you?"

"For me, it was books. It wasn't easy, learning to read while working in the coal mines. The minister's wife, who also happens to be Dooley's grandmother, taught me on Sundays after church. Then the world opened up and beckoned. Every place I read about, I wanted to visit. An impossible dream. I don't mean to compare myself to these men and women who were literally enslaved." He gestured toward the far-off voices singing of deliverance.

"Of course not." She waited for him to continue. "Tell me more."

Laughter turned Ethan's head toward soldiers passing by. When their footsteps receded, he faced Miss Stewart again. "I was twelve when my mother died of cholera. My father couldn't bear any reminders of her, so he moved us from Kentucky to a town in Indiana, where he and my two brothers and I found work in a coal mine. Samuel and Andrew were ten and eight. We broke the mined coal into pieces by hand and separated it from whatever we didn't want, like rock, slate, clay, and soil. The coal dust was so thick sometimes we could barely see what we were doing. I hated it. We were paid in company scrip that could only be used at the company store, so we couldn't save up and move because our wages were no good anywhere else. We couldn't leave. In the end, my father was the one who left us. Black lung."

She didn't respond right away. "I'm sorry." Wind rattled the trees above the courthouse, and she chafed her arms, though the night was warm. "Do you have other siblings? Besides the two brothers killed in the war?"

"Just Sam and Andrew," he told her. Ethan hadn't even been with them when they died. They were killed in battle while he was delirious with typhoid fever in a field hospital away from the fighting. "You're blessed to have June, you know. And your mother, too." Eager to change the subject, he asked, "You told your friends you wanted to explore?"

With her fingertip, she traced a seam in her apron. "They laughed at my foolishness. So I stopped talking about it and just worked at the mill like everyone else. The mill pays in scrip, too, keeping us tied to the company. But even if I had the means to leave, I wouldn't have abandoned my family."

"I understand." Hadn't he done the same, year after year, until an army recruiter showed him the way out of life underground? In her soulful eyes, he saw himself: loyalty to family; commitment to provide; and deep down, an ember of hope for a better life. He knew the ache of forfeited dreams, the sting of wishing for something different when everyone else was content with the same. "Do you still dream, Miss Stewart?"

"I really shouldn't." Her voice trembled. "My family needs me."

Darkness gathered around them, blotting out Marietta and its thousands of troops and horses. For a fleeting moment, even the war fell away. All he saw was Miss Stewart's moonlit face. "I understand you," he said again. "We're not so different, you and I."

A sad smile bent her lips. "Said the guard to his prisoner." She picked up his forage cap and placed it on his head in a gesture so endearing, he hardly knew what to make of it. "Good night, Sergeant Howard," she whispered. Her Southern drawl gentled his name.

"Miss Stewart—if it weren't for the war, we'd get along fine."

"I reckon we would. But there is a war. And we're on different sides."

Proving her point, she limped to the window. He lifted her so she could sit on the sill once more, and marveled again at the slightness of her frame. It wasn't vanity but hunger that had whittled her down so. This she held in common with the rest of the mill hands here. The North experienced nothing like the scarcity on the Southern home front.

Miss Stewart ducked back into her prison, then turned around to face him.

"I'm on *your* side," he whispered. A revelation, even to himself.

"You mean *our* side—all of us mill girls? Feeling guilty?"

He shifted and accidentally knocked his rifle to the ground. Snatching it up, he slung his weapon over his shoulder and lowered his voice. "I mean you. You and June."

"Why?" She leaned forward, braid swinging in the musky breeze.

Why, indeed? Any guilt was eclipsed by something more. Hearing her talk had been like looking at his own reflection, the recognition so complete, it was like coming home. The woman he'd captured this morning was beginning to seize his heart instead.

It made about as much sense as a blizzard in July.

Chapter Five

MONDAY, JULY 11, 1864

Cora Mae had fallen asleep last night to the haunting lullaby of the freed men and women and with visions of Scipio and Venus searing her mind's eye. She hated war. She hated that so many had died, and that the Yankees had invaded and torn the mill hands from their home. But she could not deny that others had been treated far worse for generations upon generations, and that freedom was a thing worth fighting for.

"Mama!" June tugged Cora Mae's apron.

It was a prime wonder how much energy a girl of eight years could hold, and a blessed relief that at least some of it could be spent outside, prisoners though they were. In groups of forty, the mill girls were allowed to have twenty minutes out of doors once in the morning and once in the afternoon before being locked in for the night again at five o'clock.

"Can I play with Tabby?" June pointed to a ten-year-old girl whose black hair was sandy with dust. "We're going to do a skipping contest."

Cora Mae readily agreed, suggesting they compete with jumping jacks and hops, as well. "Mind that you stay away from the soldiers. And don't go where I can't see you." So far as she could tell, this regiment had far more discipline than those drunken rogues in Roswell.

Blue-clad soldiers guarded the yard behind the courthouse, tasked with making sure no one tried to run off. Beyond the yard, hospital tents rose up between buildings as far as she could see. The frequent chugging of trains was so loud, she figured the tracks could not be more than a few blocks away.

Sunshine warm on her neck, Cora Mae took her place at the end of the line for the well, behind Damaris, Tabby's older sister. The magnolia's waxy leaves rustled, releasing the sweet perfume of its flowers. June scampered about, collecting fallen white petals, unburdened by the thoughts burrowing into Cora Mae.

Then June stopped short and pointed. "That's my Yankee!" She waved and shouted again, "My Yankee is back!"

Almost of one accord, the women in line ahead of Cora Mae swiveled to glower at June. Tabby poked out her tongue at Lieutenant Dooley, who stood behind a table stacked with boxes of hardtack for the mill hands. He tipped his hat and bowed to both girls, a smile lifting his ruddy cheeks.

"Oh, look!" June cried. A coonhound had scampered into the yard, so skinny that Cora Mae could count his ribs. Tail between his legs, he followed his nose to the crackers.

"Get!" A soldier raised a hand, but the dog dodged, leaving tracks in the dust as it dashed away. "Have some pride, dog! Hunt your grub like the hound you are!"

But the dog only sat on his haunches in a patch of shade, watching with a worried expression. Maybe his family had all gone south and left him behind. Maybe he'd meant to travel with them and got lost along the way. Either way, he was hungry, lonely, scared, and at the mercy of Yankees. Cora Mae could relate.

Lieutenant Dooley poured water from his canteen into a pail and set it near the animal before returning to the table.

"That's a good boy," June told the dog. "What a good little feller you are." She returned to playing with Tabby, casting a smile at the dog every so often. "I think he likes me," she called to Cora Mae.

As if in response, the dog paused from drinking to look at her, his head cocked and a dripping grin on his face.

"I think he does." Smiling, Cora Mae shuffled forward with the rest of the women.

At last, she neared the well and saw Sergeant Howard filling every girl's pail. "That should do it, ma'am," he said.

Damaris took her pail without a word and spat at him. Strands of black hair swaying by her jutting chin, she pivoted and stalked away to a ripple of approving laughter. Fern dared to cluck her tongue at the unseemly behavior, but Tabby whooped with glee.

Cora Mae felt her cheeks bloom scarlet as she stood before Sergeant Howard.

"Good morning," he said. Sweat ran in rivulets from his temples to his wool collar.

"Is it?"

"Getting better." He smiled as though pleased to see her, then lowered his voice. "She missed, by the way. No harm done. She ought to know, though, that if she tries that with just about any other soldier, it won't be overlooked."

Cora Mae reckoned as much. "I'll tell her, although I doubt it'll do any good. Her dander's up, and she's not the only one."

He turned the handle, and rope creaked as it unwound from the rod to lower the bucket into the well. "Can't say as I blame them. Still, antagonizing us won't earn her gentler treatment."

"So I figured." She glanced around the yard. June and Tabby crouched together, drawing pictures with sticks in the earth.

"What's that? A dragon?" June asked.

"It's a Yank. Can't you see the horns and tail?"

Gripping her knees, June looked at Lieutenant Dooley. "That ain't so." She rubbed out the tail in the dirt, and then the horns, but Tabby was already drawing another.

Cora Mae bit her lip, unsettled. Tabby was learning from her sister and the other girls here to hate, to think on their enemy as something other than human. Was June learning the same?

They might be powerless in what had happened to them, but they could choose how to respond. Hatred didn't make a body righteous. It made a body bitter and empty as a rotten walnut shell. No matter what had befallen them thus far, Cora Mae could choose to set a better example than that.

An idea forming, she turned back to Sergeant Howard. "I need to borrow your knife," she blurted. If it were for herself, she wouldn't ask anything of him. But this was different.

His green eyes arrested hers. "I'm pretty sure there's at least one rule against giving a prisoner a weapon."

"Not a weapon, a tool. June left her doll back in Roswell. It wasn't anything fancy, just a rag doll I made from some scraps of fabric. I thought I'd make her another one. If I could borrow your knife, I could cut a piece from my apron and make it into something she can play with." Something to nurture and take care of, which would be a far sight better than what the girls were doing now.

He turned the handle the other way, bringing the bucket back up. "How big a piece do you need?"

She held up her hands to form a square in the air. "About like this. That's for the body. I'd need smaller scraps to fashion a skirt and bonnet, too, so I'd take those from my hem. Homespun won't make for the prettiest wardrobe, but at least it'll be patriotic."

"I see. There must be another way to go about it that doesn't involve you cutting sizeable holes from your only dress and apron."

"Name it."

Others were starting to notice her talking with the sergeant. Their features crimped with suspicion.

The bucket rose out of the well, and Ethan poured water into her pail. "Come back to me this afternoon, after four o'clock. I'll have a solution for you by then."

At four-thirty, she positioned herself at the end of the line once again so that when she reached Sergeant Howard, no one else was there to overhear them.

Before he drew her water, he pulled a wrapped bundle from his pocket and gave it to her. "Will this do?"

She unfolded a large white handkerchief, the perfect size for the doll's body. Tucked inside was a wad of cotton she could use for the head, plus two squares of mint- and lavender-colored calico, the right sizes for the doll's skirt and bonnet. Amazed, she inspected the fabric and found that slits had already been cut in the right places so she could tie the skirt.

"Will it do?" Sergeant Howard asked again, lowering the bucket into the well. "I told the chaplain's wife what you wanted to do. She helped straight off, saying she had a good idea what you needed. That's where the flowered bits come from."

Smiling, Cora Mae grazed the "flowered bits" with her fingertip. "It'll make a finer doll than the one she left at home, that's certain. I'm obliged to you and the woman who gave you these. That was a kindness."

"I can't say as I can picture what you have in mind, but I'm glad it suits."

It would have been easier had she been at a table, but she managed to fashion the doll with a few folds and knots by the time the bucket came back up.

June ran over to Cora Mae as soon as the bonnet had been tied in place. Eyes round, she touched the skirt with one finger, then withdrew it. "I ought to wash first."

Chuckling, Sergeant Howard poured a little water into her cupped palms before emptying the rest into the pail.

Cora Mae sent him a warm smile of thanks, then placed the doll in June's arms. "It turns out," she said quietly, "that Sissy has a sister right here in Marietta. I do believe you're the one to keep her safe until she can reunite with Sissy back in Roswell. What do you say?"

"I believe that's so. Her name is Sassy." She looked up and thanked Cora Mae. "I've never seen such a fine dress. Did your Yankee help you find such?"

"He's not *my* Yankee, Junebug, but yes, he did help."

"I thought so. Then I thank you, too. Sassy needs me." She dipped in an awkward curtsy, the sergeant bowed gallantly, and then the little girl ran off.

Damaris came striding over, face aflame. "Just what in tarnation are you doing, Cora Mae, to be getting gifts from the likes of them?" She pointed a finger at Sergeant Howard.

"Easy, ma'am." He stepped out from behind the well.

"I ain't talkin' to you, so shut your trap, or I'll shut it for you."

"Damaris!" Cora Mae gasped, aware that both June and Tabby now looked on. So did Lieutenant Dooley. "That's no way to talk."

"Whose side are you on, anyway?" Damaris drew back her hand as though to strike, but Sergeant Howard was faster. He caught Damaris by the wrist, and just as quickly, she turned her wrath on him, twisting around and biting down hard on his hand.

At once, Lieutenant Dooley and another soldier were prying Damaris off and marching her away, Tabby screaming after them.

Cora Mae's attention didn't follow. Blood dripped from Sergeant Howard's fingers to the ground. "Where's your handkerchief?" she asked.

He winced. "Wearing a dress over yonder."

A smile tugged. Scooping water from her pail, Cora Mae dribbled it over his injury to rinse it. With a jerk of the strings at her waist, she whipped off her apron, wrapped it around his fingers, and held his hand fast with both of hers, pressing the muslin against the wound.

His thumb came to rest on the back of her hand. "And you said you wouldn't nurse Yankees."

She clucked her tongue against her teeth, that he should jest while grimacing in pain.

He cleared his throat of the dust she knew would never leave him alone. "You'll not make friends this way, Miss Stewart. Are you sure you want others seeing what you're doing for me?"

She lifted her gaze to meet his, then sought out June's. The little girl stood rooted with her doll, watching. Learning.

Cora Mae nodded toward her. "Maybe I do."

Chapter Six

TUESDAY, JULY 12, 1864

Darkness draped Marietta. The incessant clamor from the depot had paused after the last of twenty daily trains arrived with supplies from Chattanooga and went back again carrying the severely injured. Ethan patrolled one side of the courthouse full of mill girls, while three other soldiers patrolled the other sides.

Crickets and cicadas pulsed in his ears, and his uniform felt thick and heavy, still holding the day's heat. Riding the breeze that brushed his skin were harmonies of freed men and women joined in song.

A quiet voice, much closer, turned his head to an open window. A little girl leaned out of it. Making haste to reach her, he held up a hand to make sure she didn't somehow topple out.

"Sergeant Howard!" June whispered. "Did you bring what we asked you to?"

"Careful, now. Don't you think you ought to be sleeping?" The room behind her was quiet.

"I will, but first—did you bring it?"

"I did." In the yard this afternoon, while Miss Stewart had brought her pail for water, she had asked him to bring sewing scissors, borrowed from the chaplain's wife, if necessary.

June held out the end of her braid and whispered, "Cut it."

"What?"

"We aim to send locks of our hair to home, if you'll help us."

"For the fine birds of Roswell to line their nests? My, that's generous of you. You'll be making many, many birds happy." Ethan reached high on her braid, but she jerked it away.

"It's not for the birds! Cut a smidge off the end. Look here. We already tied thread around a little piece. So cut above that. You see it? It's just a bitty piece. Hurry!"

"I see." After slinging his rifle over a shoulder, he snipped the lock of fine hair from the end of June's braid and made a show of inspecting it. "Well, it's enough for one lucky sparrow, I suppose."

She shook her head. "You are the silliest Yankee I ever did see."

A grin edged his lips. He'd been called worse. "I brought you something else. Hold out your hands." After he tucked the lock into his pocket, he lifted the canteen from where it hung on a strap by his hip, then overturned it until blackberries tumbled into her palm. "You heard the story about Jesus turning water into wine? I tried that, but I keep getting berries."

"You *are* the silliest Yankee! You couldn't put them in your pockets or they'd smash and stain your clothes!"

He could hear the smile in her voice, and it warmed him. He'd wanted to make her laugh, but he supposed that was asking too much, considering the circumstances he was trying to distract her from. "I should have known such a clever girl like you wouldn't be fooled. In any case, this one here is for Sassy." He pulled one tiny section from the top of one berry and handed it to her, a doll-sized black pearl of fruit. Then he capped the canteen and let it rest against his hip once more.

"Thank you. She's much obliged, I'm sure." June disappeared from the window, and Miss Stewart took her place.

She sat on the sill and swung her legs around, keeping her skirt wrapped around them. Ethan reached up and helped her down, his hands about her waist. She left her hands on his shoulders only a moment, but it was long enough for him to notice how natural it felt.

He stepped back.

Moonlight traced her features in silver. She cocked her ear toward the singing and listened, though he doubted she could make out the words. This late at night, they were fading away as the singers retired to sleep. But the mournful sound still carried. It was enough to remind him why he fought. Lincoln's Emancipation Proclamation hadn't really freed them. Only a Union victory could do that.

From inside the courthouse, someone poked her head out the window. "Is that you, Cora Mae Stewart, with your very own special Yankee? I would slam this window shut so hard right now if it weren't so blasted hot. You better let the rest of us decent Southern girls sleep or so help me—"

"Shh! That's enough," Miss Stewart whispered. "I'll take care not to bother you."

Ethan, too, could be reprimanded for allowing a prisoner outside after curfew and lingering with her too long. But that wasn't enough to stop him. Not when he was so close to her and so close to the end of his life. The certainty of his impending death was a presence circling above him. If he shooed it away, it only came back later to perch upon his shoulder.

A finger to his lips, he led Miss Stewart to the same spot they'd shared the first night of her imprisonment. Leaning his rifle against the brick wall, they sat.

"I expect June told you we're fixing to send locks of our hair to my mother." She kept her voice so low, he had to lean in to hear her. "When we left Roswell, we had no idea we'd be apart for so long. Since we can't go back ourselves yet, I thought it would be fitting to send at least a piece of us both. It'll set her at ease some." She drew her own braid over her shoulder and held the end of it toward him. "I tore off some thread from the unfinished side of my hem and used it to tie off a piece already. Cut it, please? Right there, above that knot."

Wind stirred through trees and swept a wisp of hair in front of her eyes. Before he could tell himself not to, he pushed it back with his thumb, tucking it behind her ear, then ran his hand down the length of her braid until he cradled the end of it in one palm.

He shouldn't have done that. Touching her face, her hair, made this meeting seem more personal than it had any right to be. He tried to summon a tease, as he had with June, and failed. All he could do was cut the lock and try not to think about how soft it was as he placed it in his pocket with June's.

"Please fetch my thanks to the chaplain's wife," Miss Stewart said. "Do you have an envelope? Could you write a note with this that says we're unharmed? Mama can't read, but she'll ask the reverend to tell her what it says."

"I can get an envelope, and I'd be happy to write a note," Ethan said. "But you know the mail between here and Roswell isn't running right now, don't you?"

Her shoulders slumped. "I forgot about that."

"Dooley could take it." Ethan leaned back against the wall, his arm touching hers.

"Are you sure? All that way?"

"There's not a man alive I trust more than Dooley, and he's already going to Roswell tomorrow to repair a wheel and fit new shoes to several horses that need them. I'm pretty sure he can handle two feathers' worth of extra weight."

"But would he take it directly to my mother? I wouldn't want him passing it off to another soldier."

"I'll tell him. I can be very convincing—at least, with him. Clearly, my powers of persuasion are lost on you, or you'd stay in Marietta and nurse Yankee soldiers instead of getting on a train for the North." He watched her, waiting for a response. Willing her to say she'd changed her mind.

The canopy of leaves overhead threw shadows over Sergeant Howard's face, but she could see the gleam in his eyes. Cora Mae looked away, afraid that if she rested in his gaze too long, he might, indeed, persuade her against good sense. "My mind ain't changed."

Instead of quarrelling, he simply nodded, then reached for his canteen. "Brought you something."

"More water?"

"Better than that."

"Heaven help me, soldier, but if that's your whiskey ration, you can put it away right—"

The low rumble of his laughter stopped her short. He shook the canteen over his palm. "Blackberries," he said. "The trees around here are full of them, or they were. They'll be picked clean before long with this many soldiers about." He held out his hand, offering.

Heat stole over her face, and she was glad he couldn't see her blush. "And you're sharing them with me?"

He chuckled. "Well, seeing as I don't have any extra whiskey to spare, sure."

"I'm sorry I said that." She took a berry. The ripe flesh burst with flavor in her mouth, a welcome change to the crackers they'd been living on for days. "Thank you."

He ate one, too. "You're welcome. We best eat them now. I fear they'll be spoiled tomorrow. I already gave some to June. Here." He took her hand and turned it up, and a soft, silky weight filled her palm. "That's for you alone."

An owl gurgled in the branches above them. Quietly, they ate until the last blackberry was gone. Then the sergeant reached into a pocket and presented her with its contents.

"I can't see a thing," she admitted, "but it sure feels like my apron."

"Scrubbed clean of all but a trace of its former life as a bandage. And I was raised too much the gentleman to return it to you empty."

She smiled at that, silently agreeing that being a lady or a gentleman wasn't just about your blood and breeding. It was about manners, kindness, respect, and honor. You didn't have to be rich to have those.

Across the square, most campfires had burned out, yet the air held the scent of woodsmoke, salt pork, and beans. Cora Mae probed the folded apron until she detected something in its pocket. With care, she drew out what felt like a scroll tied with string. "What is it?"

"A change of scenery," he told her. "Wide open spaces."

"Tell me plain," she urged, too tired to solve his riddle. "It feels like a book without a cover, rolled up tight."

"You're close. It's not a published book but pages I stitched together years ago. I filled them with poems copied down from other books too expensive for me to buy. You'll find my handwriting much improved by the end. You'll also find a few coal dust smudges, but they fade as soon as you start reading."

Cora Mae fingered the string around the rolled-up book, wondering at the beauty inside set down by his own hand. She could not account for this. "You're giving this to me? Why?"

He leaned away from the wall and looked both ways. "Figured you could use it more than me. I've got them all memorized by now, anyway. You did say you wanted to see the mountains, the ocean, the prairie and meadows, right? The lines in that little book will take you there and show you other places, too."

"Like what?" she said. "Could you tell me a piece now?" It would be hours until she could try reading by daylight.

He stretched out his legs, crossing one ankle over the other. "'Earth's crammed with heaven, every common bush afire with God, but only he who sees takes off his shoes; the rest sit round and pluck blackberries.' Elizabeth Barrett Browning wrote that."

She stared at him, this coal miner turned soldier, reciting poetry under the stars. "Blackberries? Really?"

"Really."

She chuckled before coming back to the more important point. "Earth's crammed with heaven," she repeated, then recited the rest, savoring the lines as much as she had those berries.

"The world is so much bigger than this." Sergeant Howard gestured toward the courthouse and then the square, encompassing the homeless mill girls, the cannons and crates of weaponry, and the invading army bent on destroying the Confederacy. "What I mean is, the war hasn't taken everything. The world is still beautiful. I hope you can see that. This little book of reminders seems the best way, at least for now."

A book of reminders, he called it, but Cora Mae saw it for all the gift truly was. It was hope and vision. It was a record of his learning, of his capture of light during years he spent in the dark mines. He was giving her a piece of himself.

"Thank you." Her throat squeezed around the words. "It will be a comfort."

"You are most welcome." He shifted again, leaning into a patch where starlight reached the earnest lines of his face.

She felt a quickening inside her, like something small but miraculous was growing. A friendship, she reckoned, but one that would be over before it was even born.

Sighing, she returned the book to the pocket of the apron she'd used to bind his wound yesterday. "Does it still hurt?" She reached for his hand, grazing her fingertips over the place he'd been so viciously bitten.

"It's fine."

"No, it isn't fine. Where I come from, it is not fine to behave the way those girls have been behaving toward you." Lots of women here were just plain sorrowful—too sorrowful, even, to fuss. But again today, a few of them had hurled insults at Sergeant Howard, spit toward him if not exactly on him, and displayed an embarrassing variety of terrible manners. Common courtesy had grown scarce as hen's teeth. "They think they have cause, but if they call themselves ladies or Christians, they ought to be rising above the instinct to repay wrongs with wrongs. That's no way to live."

She didn't want this sergeant to remember all women of Georgia that way.

"Bring out those scissors again," she said. While he did, she ripped another thread from inside her skirt's hem and tied it around a small section of her hair. "Cut it."

He did. "Who's this for?"

She folded his fingers over the lock of hair in his palm. "For you. Remember me." She glanced at the window, wondering if anyone was trying to listen. But he had given her a piece of himself, after all. It felt right to do the same. "Remember that not all of us are as mean and nasty as some have been to you. Remember me and June."

"Always." Rising, he reached down to help her do the same.

Cora Mae tried to ignore the ache spreading behind her ribs as she placed her hand in his. She'd not forget him either.

Chapter Seven

WEDNESDAY, JULY 13, 1864

Raindrops fell, forming penny-bright spots where they landed on the earth behind the courthouse. Ethan studied the sky. At least there was no sign of lightning this afternoon.

With someone else taking a turn at the well, he stood behind the long serving table and handed boxes of hardtack to the Roswell women and children shuffling by. Those who didn't have all their teeth didn't need to be told to soak the crackers to soften them. Some women wore vacant expressions, and others looked at him with eyes that showed how sad, or confused, or worried they were. Aside from a few surly exceptions, they accepted the rations without trouble.

Well. Without trouble for *him*. This whole ordeal was a vast mountain of trouble for the prisoners.

He clenched his jaw, still at odds about treating women and children this way. His commanding officer had challenged Sherman on the policy of sending them north, but Sherman had replied that sending them farther south would put them in the path of two battling armies, keeping them in harm's way, and that with hundreds of thousands of other refugees fleeing that direction, they'd have little chance of finding shelter or food for themselves. He also pointed out that he intended to destroy every mill and factory in the region, and that the women could find work in Indiana instead. Sherman had made it sound like sending these mill hands away from everything they knew was akin to a favor.

It would not feel like a favor when they were dumped on northern soil. And it certainly didn't feel like a favor now.

"Hey!"

Ethan turned as the coonhound snatched a box of hardtack from the table and dashed off. One soldier pelted the animal with a rock, while another lifted rifle to shoulder and took aim.

"Private!" Ethan shouted. "Do not fire!" He marched over to the man, keeping only a tenuous grip on his temper. "We are already keeping women and children as prisoners, and you want to shoot an innocent animal, too?"

"One bullet would teach it not to come back," said Private Aldridge. Unkempt brown hair nearly reached his shoulders. "It's just a mangy dog, and a Rebel dog at that."

"Might not be sportin', but it would sure be fun," added Weston, the soldier who'd hurled the rock. Teeth stained with tobacco made for a yellowed grin.

Ethan should have expected such an attitude from these two. Zeke Aldridge had shared a hometown with Ethan and Dooley before the war. He'd been foolish before enlisting almost three years ago, but he'd been fifteen then, so Ethan had credited it to youth. Instead of maturing under army discipline, however, Zeke had found his equal to run with instead.

Stepping closer, Ethan lowered his voice. "If you discharge your weapon against anyone other than the enemy, you will be court martialed, is that clear?"

Thunder rumbled, competing with the sound of trains moving in and out of the depot on the other side of town square. "Do you understand?" Ethan repeated.

"Yes, sir," they said at once. But he knew that they didn't take him seriously. These two didn't take much of anything seriously, which made them not only a nuisance, but a liability.

"Now do your job and open that crate." Ethan kicked the wooden slats. A few yards away, near the perimeter of the yard, flies droned among a scattering of tin cans some soldiers had purchased from the sutler and discarded after eating the peaches inside. "We've got hundreds more to feed."

Maple leaves danced in the pattering rain as Ethan returned to his station. Drops rolled from the brim of his forage cap every time he looked down to distribute more rations. A tent would be a help out here, but with four thousand wounded soldiers in and around this town, not to mention the healthy troops, not a yard of canvas could be spared.

"Sergeant Howard." June appeared before him. "Did Lieutenant Dooley get off all right this morning? To do for us? Is he back yet?"

Behind the child, Miss Stewart placed a hand on her shoulder, her wet sleeve sticking to her arm. Hair that slipped from her braid lay against her face and neck, calling to mind the lock she'd given him last night, the one in his breast pocket now. Rain misted her face and glistened on her collarbones. Below that, Ethan wouldn't allow himself to look.

"It's a long ride," Miss Stewart said. "Muddy roads will make it longer."

Ethan agreed while passing them their share of hardtack. "He'll be back before tomorrow just the same, God willing, and we'll hear his news." He ought to move them along, but he couldn't resist trying to make the little one smile. "I see you've developed some kind of growth since yesterday, June. Maybe we should fetch the surgeon to take care of that."

A grin spreading on her face, the girl poked the lump inside the shoulder of her dress. "It's only Sassy," she told him. "She didn't want to be left alone inside, but I couldn't let her get wet either, could I?"

He nodded. "Just so. What a good mother you are."

Thunder boomed, and June startled before blinking up at the sky, her wet eyelashes spiked. Then she took a deep breath and whispered to the hidden doll. "That's not a battle you're hearing, it's just weather. Don't you be scared. You're all right."

His mouth pressed into a firm line, Ethan bent to her level. "Mind if I talk to her real quick?" When she did not object, he went on. "Miss Sassy, I sure am sorry we don't have nicer lodging for you and your kin here, and better food. Sorry you have to be here at all. I'm most sorry you have to wonder whether that thunder is cannon fire. But the fighting is south of us. It'll not touch you here."

The words, meant to comfort, rang hollow as soon as he said them. The fighting *had* already touched them, reaching its long fingers to Roswell and pulling them from their homes. It had made them prisoners and refugees, and very soon it would make them outcasts in the north.

Even so, June patted the lump at her shoulder. "We'll be all right," she said, and Ethan prayed with all his might that was true.

Straightening, he returned Miss Stewart's sad smile, and served those waiting in line behind them.

"What are you doing to Little Feller?"

June's voice snapped Ethan's attention to the place Aldridge and Weston should have been. A second later, he found them crouched in the mud with the dog, who had apparently returned to try his luck again.

Not trusting the pair farther than he could spit, Ethan double-timed toward them. Aldridge had looped his belt around the animal's neck to hold it in place while Weston tied a string of tin cans to its tail.

These two were more children than men, a disgrace to the army. Seething, Ethan reached for his knife to cut the string from the dog's tail, but as soon as Aldridge noticed him, he removed the belt from the coonhound's neck and slapped his haunches to set him running. The clanging cans spurred him to a frenzied, terrified speed.

Ethan must be growing soft, because the sight of that pitiful, panic-stricken dog put a stone in his stomach. It sank deep.

"You ought to be grateful," Aldridge said on a laugh. "I didn't even waste a bullet. I wager he won't bother us again."

"Why'd you go and do a thing like that?" June cried.

Miss Stewart pulled her away from the rogues, but her blazing eyes held as much censure as anything she could have said.

Weston glanced at the child, then allowed his brazen gaze to travel the length of Miss Stewart, whose dress clung to her figure. His appreciative smile shot fire through Ethan's veins.

He stepped between Weston and Miss Stewart. "Latrine duty, both of you," he growled. "Now."

THURSDAY, JULY 14, 1864

Breathing inside the courthouse felt to Cora Mae like pulling air through boiled wool. It hadn't rained since yesterday, but the mill hands' dresses hadn't dried completely. When the sun made the brick building an oven, steam lifted from their threads and settled in tiny beads on their skin. The odor of unwashed bodies ripened to an offense.

"We passed by a pond on the way here," Fern said. "I don't know why we can't take turns rinsing off in it."

"And give all the bluebellies 'guarding' us a nice little show?" Her sister Cynthia huffed. "I'd rather rot inside this dress and hope they get sick on the smell of it."

After the way that one soldier had looked at her yesterday, Cora Mae agreed. "Maybe we'll at least dry out in the sun," she said. "The only thing worse than wearing our clothes this long without washing is having them stick to our skin."

She couldn't wait for their time as prisoners to end, but neither was she eager for what would come on the other side of it. What would happen after they left Marietta? How could she take care of June in the North? When could they return to Roswell?

Questions collided in her mind with the screeching of the trains rolling in and out of Marietta twenty times a day. Any that touched on Sergeant Howard she quickly derailed. He was a flash in the pan, as Pap might have said. Here for a moment, shiny and bright, and then gone.

But he wasn't gone yet.

When it was finally time for Cora Mae and June to take their turn outside, he was standing guard on the perimeter, the dog sitting beside him.

While the rest of their group divided into lines for water or hardtack, June took off running toward the coonhound, then slowed to walk a few yards away, holding her hand out as she approached. "Hey, Little Feller. You sure found troubles, didn't you?"

Nodding a greeting to Sergeant Howard, Cora Mae ignored the lift she felt at the sight of him. Ignored the slant to his lips, the gentle warmth in his manner, and how smartly his uniform fit his shoulders.

Instead, she bent to get a closer look at the dog licking June's hand. There were cuts and puncture wounds all over his skinny hide, and his left eye wept. "Poor boy," she said. She scratched behind one floppy ear before standing again. "What happened since we saw him last?"

Wagons trundled by, heavy with crates of ammunition and other weaponry she tried not to think about. Their tails swishing, the horses pulling them seemed not to mind their burden.

"Feller has had a rough go of it," the sergeant said, and Cora Mae smiled at his adoption of June's pet name. "He lost his wits trying to run from those cans and plowed right into a thorny bramble. When I found him, he was in pretty bad shape. I'm not sure he'll ever see out of that eye again."

"How'd you get him out?" June asked.

"I offered to share my dinner with him." He paused to cough into his elbow. "Turns out he favors salt pork more than hardtack. 'Course, then I had to pull out the thorns buried in his flesh. Had to enlist some help to hold him for that, but he did fine." The streets around the courthouse teemed with people going about their business. Most Yankees didn't spare them a glance, but the freed men and women kept a wary eye on the dog, crossing to the other side of the street to pass by.

Cora Mae spied a few fresh scratches on the sergeant's hands. "And Feller hasn't left your side since?"

"Not for long, anyway." He patted an uninjured part of the dog's head.

Several yards behind him, Venus bent over the laundry tub, but she looked up every time Feller whimpered. After what seemed like the end of a great debate in the woman's mind, she let the washboard lean against the tub and crossed over to them.

Straightening her yellow head wrap, she came with halting steps, as though giving herself time to change her mind. Six feet away, she stopped, her broad face tight. "You got a hold of that dog?" she asked Sergeant Howard.

He grabbed Feller by the scruff of his neck. "He won't hurt you."

"Uh-huh." She pulled a small jar from her apron pocket. "I seen what happened. This salve will help the healing, if you can get it on him." She extended the jar but came no closer.

June brightened. "You made him some medicine? You helped dogs with wounds like this before?"

"Not dogs. Come, take it if you want to use it."

Cora Mae accepted the jar and uncorked it, releasing the thick smell of comfrey. "Thank you kindly," she said, though what she wanted to do was ask why Venus was afraid of such a scrawny, pathetic dog. Why all the other freed men and women went out of their way to avoid it. Why Scipio was marching over with thunder on his face.

"Leave that dog be," he told Venus. "He ain't got nothin' to do with you."

"But she brought the medicine for him," June said.

"That medicine," Scipio said to Venus, "is for people. It's for people like us, who been chased by dogs like that."

Cora Mae stilled, her tongue sticking to the roof of her mouth.

June's tongue, however, stayed in fine working order. "Why did they chase you?" she whispered.

Breaking off from the crowd around the table, Tabby edged closer, and June waved for her to join them. The dark-haired girl's fair skin was burned and swollen from the sun. Mill hands' voices layered on top of air already thick with the sounds of trains, wagons, horses, and men.

Someone called for Scipio to move the cart of chopped wood he'd abandoned in the street. "Tell them," he said to Venus, and left.

"Go on, use that salve, and then I best be on my way, too." Venus watched Cora Mae gingerly apply it to the dog's eye. "We wasn't just chased," she added. "We was hunted. Dogs like that was given our scent so they could hunt us and attack us."

Cora Mae's stomach rolled. She thought again of the raised stripes thatching Scipio's back. Now she imagined not only the whipping that had sliced his flesh, but the terrifying hunt by baying hounds that must have come before it.

Tabby remained silent, aside from the crack of her biting into hardtack. Mosquitoes hummed in and out of a gummy breeze.

June's brow puckered. "But why? Why did those dogs hate you so much? Feller doesn't hate you."

"Didn't need no reason. They was trained by the masters to hurt us so the masters could come and take us back. The dogs' masters was our masters, too, right up until the Union army came."

When June asked why yet again, Venus cut a look to Cora Mae, as if to say she was done explaining the way things were. When she did speak, it was to Sergeant Howard. "You know where I'll be. Just send that jar back to me when you done."

He tipped his hat to her and assured her he would.

Tabby frowned at the sergeant's respectful gesture before turning her attention back to Feller. "I seen those devil Yankees play their cruel trick on this 'un yesterday."

"I seen it, too," June said. "But this *here* Yankee is the one that rescued him from the bramble."

This here Yankee was not like the others, Cora Mae thought. He was not like any other man she'd ever met. Even without him saying a word, his nearness was a steadying hand in a world that shifted and tossed her about.

Feller leaned his head against Sergeant Howard's blue trousers. Regarding him, Tabby crunched through another bite of hardtack, a bare toe twisting in the mud. She wrinkled her nose. "That stuff smells funny."

"But it's good for Feller," June defended. "That lady was nice to share it. Especially since she's afraid of dogs like him."

"A kindness, indeed." Cora Mae's eyes stung as she continued to dab the ointment on the dog's injuries. This salve had been made for people who were treated no better than animals, and maybe worse. No wonder the other freed men and women hadn't wanted to be near Feller. The prime wonder was that Venus had shown compassion on him at all. It sparked a hope that if hatred and fear were learned, they could also be unlearned.

"I hate that you all have brought war to our doorstep," she told the sergeant. "I hate the sickness, the hunger, the fighting and dying. The ripping apart of families. The tearing up of good land. But there isn't one little piece of me that smiles on slavery. We Stewarts never did hold truck with owning people like property. You mustn't think that all of us in the South do."

He told her he knew.

Then June's questions about what Venus had shared began afresh, and Cora Mae had no good answers. She could not explain to herself, let alone to children, why some men thought it right to "own" people, to hunt and harm them.

"But she said her master stopped being her master when the Yankees came?" June asked. "She wasn't his slave after that?"

"That's what she said," Cora Mae confirmed.

The little girl grew thoughtful, dipping one finger into the salve and patting it on one of Feller's sores. She looked at Tabby, then at Sergeant Howard. "Then I guess not everyone's mad you came."

~

Cora Mae left June with Tabby, Little Feller, and Sergeant Howard while she stood in line for their provisions. When Lieutenant Dooley came into the yard, June raced to greet him, drawing stares from the mill hands who noticed. Tabby crossed her thin arms and scowled.

Anxious to hear his news, Cora Mae hurried to them as soon as she secured the hardtack. "Well?" she asked.

"Your mother is a lovely woman and says she's in better health than when you left her." Lieutenant Dooley grinned.

Relief thrummed through Cora Mae, bringing heat to her eyelids. "You found her. And you gave her the locks of our hair?"

"Aye, lassie. And she said they were more precious to her than gold. Our visit was brief, but she told me to tell you she loves you both, and she's praying you all the way home." He swallowed and wiped a shine from his forehead. "I did tell her I was sorry for the separation, and she seemed to believe me sincere."

"What else?" Cora Mae thirsted for every detail. "Was she alone? Scared? Did the Yankees take our apartment?"

As quickly as he could, the lieutenant answered her questions. The reverend had been with her. No, she did not seem scared. She was too thrilled with his visit. The Yankees hadn't taken the apartment but occupied only abandoned homes, as they'd promised. So long as Mama wished to remain there, they'd let her be. Dooley had made sure of it.

"Could you tell, did she have food?" Cora Mae pressed.

Lieutenant Dooley shifted his weight, adjusting the forage cap on his flaming-red hair. "She does now," he said, lowering his voice for her ears only. "I took her more than the locks of hair. She's got a few cans of evaporated milk, salt pork, cans of peaches, molasses, and a bag of flour."

She gaped at him. "You brought her all that?"

"It wasn't my idea, nor was it my wages that paid the sutler." He tipped his head in the direction of Sergeant Howard, eyebrows raised to finish his point.

"Thank you," she managed. The unexpected provision would not have been needed at all if the Union army hadn't invaded their town. And yet the thoughtfulness of these two near-strangers unclenched the fist inside her.

"She thought you might have need of these." From his back pocket, Lieutenant Dooley produced a roll of familiar fabric.

Accepting the bundle, Cora Mae separated three bonnets. Cora Mae's extra one, and June's, and the third was Mama's only bonnet she hadn't dyed black. She brought them to her face and caught the smell of home, the chinaberry scent of her mother.

"Thank you," she said, overcome.

Smiling, Dooley took a knee and tapped June on the nose. "I see you've still got no shoes, young lady. Shall I come by later and give you some from the horses? I'm very good at nailing them on. The horses never complain a wee bit."

"Oh no, you don't!" she cried, eyes dancing.

"No? Another time, then." Winking, the lieutenant begged his leave to get back to his traveling forge. On his way out of the yard, he stopped to visit with Sergeant Howard, then took the jar of salve from him and returned it to Venus across the street.

In the next moment, water drenched Cora Mae from the top of her head down her back, plastering her dress to her skin. Gasping, she whirled to find Cynthia McGee.

"Serves you right for doing whatever you did to earn such favors from the likes of them," she said.

Fern rushed over. "Cynthia! Was that our water? We won't get another pail of it until tomorrow!" Her voice trembled.

"She deserved it," Cynthia insisted.

"But did I?" What little composure Fern had left broke to pieces. She lowered her head, hiding her face inside her bonnet, and stormed off, her sister following her.

Water dripped between Cora Mae's shoulder blades and all the way down to her feet. She felt the ground soften to mud where she stood. Inhaling deeply, she prayed for the right response, for a way to teach June a better path.

She knelt on the ground to look June in the eye. "You see what we've been given?"

June frowned, casting a glance after Fern and Cynthia, but she answered the question she'd been asked. "Bonnets. Three of them."

"And how many are we? You think Mama made a mistake in her counting?"

June shook her head. "One's for sharing, I reckon. Lots of girls here lost their bonnets."

"That's right. Lots did. You see anyone who could use one of these?"

June's gaze found Tabby, who had been glaring at them ever since Lieutenant Dooley singled them out with his attention and gifts. "Tabby could. She's my size. I'll give her mine."

Cora Mae smiled. "I think she'd like that. I was hoping you'd see it that way, too. Her sister Damaris is my size—I'll give her mine. What should we do with the third one?"

"Let me study on it." She looked to the dozens of mill hands in the yard, then to Feller, now lying in the dirt near Sergeant Howard. Patches of his fur lay flat and shiny with the comfrey salve. She bit her lip.

"It's one thing to show kindness to a friend," Cora Mae prompted. "Seems to me it's a finer thing indeed to show kindness to one who hasn't been kind to you. What do you think?"

June faced her again, lifting her chin. "I think you're about to give Cynthia your mama's bonnet."

"I think you're right. I think I'll share our water with her and Fern, too, seeing as she misplaced hers." When June's eyes rounded, Cora Mae squeezed her shoulder. “I reckon we all feel lost and abused, like Little Feller. Let’s pray a little kindness will ease their sting.”

Chapter Eight

"Howard. Howard, wake up."

Ethan jerked awake, chest heaving and catching.

"Another nightmare?" Dooley asked.

Nodding, Ethan covered his mouth to cough, then scrambled from the tent so as not to bother the other soldiers trying to sleep, or the coonhound snoring among them. In the scant blue light of the moon, he stumbled several yards away and clutched his knees, clearing his lungs the best he could.

A canteen materialized. He took it from Dooley and drank, and though it helped calm the cough somewhat, it did nothing to remedy the real problem.

Ethan Howard was dying.

Cora Mae Stewart made him want to live.

Therein lay the trouble.

Dooley sat on the ground. "Was this one any clearer?"

"It was." After swallowing another drink, Ethan lowered himself beside his friend and welcomed the breeze on his skin. He gazed up at the stars. In the mines, he grew to hate the dark. But this was different. Constellations scattered stories across the sky, unlocking a world so much larger than his own. Reminding him there was more out there—so much more—than what he could see by day.

He imagined he was on the moon, looking at Earth. From that distance, it would be beautiful. It would be whole, and green and blue, with swirls of pure white clouds. It would not appear to be the broken place he inhabited, where men came apart or died from the inside out. It would be beautiful, he told himself again. The world *was* beautiful, just as he'd told Cora Mae. It was only a matter of perspective. Right now, he had a hard one.

But that would change, soon enough.

"Well?" Dooley tossed a twig at a mosquito landing on Ethan's bare foot. "How did you die this time?"

"Gunfire. So close I was staring down the barrel. There were trees all around me, but the trunks were so thin no man could take cover behind one. It was an uphill battle, and so hot, I thought I'd faint dead away. In my dream, Scipio was there, too, and all the freed men who've joined us were fighting alongside us. But we were mowed down like wheat before the scythe."

Dooley's fingers roved his neck, most likely checking for wood ticks out of habit. "That's Kennesaw, from what you've told me. That's not prophecy, it's a memory."

"Except for the minor details of me getting killed and the freed men fighting." The former slaves had been hired to build fortifications and trenches for the battles at Kennesaw Mountain, Kolb's Farm, New Hope Church, Pickett's Mill, and Dallas. But Sherman wouldn't let them take up arms for fear of losing the loyalty of Union sympathizers in northern Georgia.

"You're dreaming of the past, not the future," Dooley insisted. "Although I daresay you'll be staring down another rifle before long. You're a soldier. It's what you do."

He had a point.

Still, Ethan couldn't shake the feeling that he was racing toward his last breath. He'd always figured he'd die of the black lung disease that took his father, if he had the good fortune not to be buried alive in a mine cave-in. To be taken in war, instead, would be a mercy. And Ethan felt in his core that for him, it was also inevitable.

He turned in the direction of Kennesaw Mountain, roughly five miles in the distance. He couldn't see it from here in the dark, but he felt its presence daily. Thinking of the June 27 battle there made him break out into a sweat, not just because it had been one hundred ten degrees in the shade that day. What he couldn't get over was how Sherman had ordered the men up a fortified mountain in columns so thick the Rebels couldn't possibly miss. The general was tired of flanking, so he made a mad dash that felt like suicide. Entire brigades had been wiped out. If Ethan was going to die in battle, he wanted it to count. But those lives had been utterly wasted.

Worse, since then Sherman had said the worst of the war was yet to come. That it would begin, most like, with Atlanta. And Atlanta had been sighted by the extreme advance from the bluff of the Chattahoochee River. They'd be marching toward it soon.

"I'm living on borrowed time since Chickamauga," he muttered. "I should have been on that battlefield with my brothers." Night flattened the landscape. Without Kennesaw Mountain visibly looming over him, it was easy to imagine himself back in camp before the battle of Chickamauga last September. "I should have died with them." His time was coming, though. No one cheated death for long.

Dooley heaved a longsuffering groan. "We've been over this. You know my view of the matter."

Ethan did. As a designated blacksmith, Dooley hadn't fought at Chickamauga but had stayed back to repair vital equipment. Upon hearing that Sam and Andrew had been killed, he'd insisted on being the one to break the news to Ethan. His face smudged black, and still wearing his leather apron, he had fallen to his knees at

Ethan's sickbed, smelling of sweat and crucible. Tears smeared Dooley's cheeks as he shoved a freckled hand through red hair.

"Is it Sam?" Ethan had asked. *"Or Andrew?"*

"I'm sorry, laddie," Dooley had choked out. *"It's both."*

Fever and grief blurred what happened next. But since that day, the friendship he'd shared with Dooley since they were twelve years old had forged into something unbreakable.

From the tent behind them, the sound of muffled snoring blended with the rattle of insects. "The dreams are more intense lately," Ethan confessed, "and more often."

Yawning, Dooley leaned back and folded his arms behind his head for a pillow. "That doesn't mean anything."

"It can't mean nothing. It's coming. I can feel it. Sherman said he sees no sign of remission now until one or both armies are destroyed. And between you and me, until recently I was ready for it. I've got no ties holding me to this life, present company excluded."

"Ah. And then you met Miss Stewart, aye? You care a great deal about her lot. And is she warming up to you, then, after you ruined her life?"

Ethan shrugged, unwilling to put to words the quiet moments he'd shared with her. Watching her smile and turn scraps of fabric into a doll for June had hinted at the joys to be had in giving. Providing. Even when all he had to offer felt like the two fish and five loaves that Jesus turned into a feast. And when she'd bound his wounds in her apron, then touched his hand the other night . . . . Well. He looked at the bruised and scabbed fingers and couldn't say he was sorry he'd been bitten. He could still feel the warm press of her hands on his, if he had a mind to. Which he did.

In truth, he'd asked God to take her from his concerns, seeing as their acquaintance would end soon.

But if anything, Miss Stewart and June felt even more impressed upon his mind, especially after what he'd witnessed today. The way she repaid Cynthia's outburst with good, and how she'd explained it to June, had left him speechless.

"She doesn't need to warm up to me," he told Dooley at last. "That's not my aim."

Sitting up again, Dooley scoffed. "Is that why you keep giving her presents? I've not seen you without your little book since the day you wrote your first lines in it."

"I told you, I'm dying soon. What I have isn't much, but I can't take it with me."

Moonlight glinting in his eyes, Dooley regarded Ethan. "I hate to say it, but your days meeting in the courthouse yard are numbered. As soon as a railroad car comes available to haul the mill girls north, Miss Stewart and little June are gone. I heard tell that'll be tomorrow."

Tomorrow. Ethan had trained himself not to put much stock in the concept but to live only day by day, seeing as his life was to be cut short. But God willing, Miss Stewart and June would have a train full of tomorrows carrying them into the future. It was their tomorrows that concerned him.

He coughed and took another drink, the canteen cool in his hand, the metal as firm and unyielding as the course he'd set. "I've got a plan."

"You aim to woo her, then. She's given you a reason to live."

Ethan shook his head. "She's given me a purpose in death."

Chapter Nine

FRIDAY, JULY 15, 1864

A smother of full-bellied clouds threatened rain. Humidity licked Ethan's skin. His palms grew slick on his Spencer rifle as he escorted the Roswell mill workers between camps in the muddy town square, alert to soldiers eager for mischief.

Miss Stewart trudged beside him, holding June's hand. He didn't need to glance at her to see her sun-kissed face in his mind. Nor did she need to speak for him to hear echoes of conversations they'd had. "*I'm supposed to love you,*" she'd said to him that very first night. He wasn't fool enough to think she'd meant it romantically, but judging by how the week had gone, she'd made marked progress in following the Scripture teaching on relating to one's enemy.

And now she was leaving. He'd rehearsed his case into the shaving-kit mirror this morning, but now it stayed lodged inside him like unmined coal.

The plodding of bare feet filled his ears as they passed the brick depot building and into the yard of the Western & Atlantic Railroad half a block beyond it. Sherman's headquarters, the four-story Fletcher House, towered over the tracks, and a US flag shuddered from its roof. Odors of straw and livestock wafted from the open doors of two long trains, hinting at their most recent use.

Mill workers from Sweetwater Creek and New Manchester, billeted at the Georgia Military Institute, joined the Roswell hands at the depot, bringing their number to eighteen hundred souls. They jostled and tripped toward the train in an unruly mass.

The gray sky pressed like a lid over the simmering summer day. Ethan touched Cora Mae's shoulder, and she turned to him with red-rimmed eyes. It took all his restraint to keep from wrapping her in his arms. "Cora Mae."

At the sound of her Christian name, her lips parted in surprise.

He took her hand. "You can't leave like this. You get on that train, and they'll take you up to Louisville and dump you on the north side of the river, and that's it."

"What do you mean?" Wariness edged her voice.

He wondered if she realized how firmly she returned his clasp. "No one knows what to do with all of you. Sherman's order is to send you away and drop you off. You think Kentucky or Indiana townsfolk will take to hundreds of devout Confederates suddenly in the streets? You think there will be enough jobs for all of you? What do beautiful young women do when they're desperate to survive?"

"Stop," she gasped. "Why are you telling me this?"

Mill workers swept around them like a river around a stone. "Marry me."

"What?" Cora Mae pulled back.

Ethan stepped closer, drew her near enough to hear what he had to say. "Stay here and marry me. Don't get on that train. I've got no family left; my pay can support you while I serve in the army. You'll be provided for, and you'll remain in the South. If I die in the war, you'll be paid by the US government for the rest of your life. You won't have to work at a mill."

Her cheeks flamed red. "Why are you doing this?"

He cleared his throat, annoyed by the irritation, yet resigned to the coal dust that caused it. "I'm not long for this world, I'm sure of it. All you have to do is sign your name beside mine, and then at least you'd be taken care of. My death won't be wasted if it will benefit you."

"That's plain wrongheaded to say your death will benefit me. Besides, you've just as much chance of surviving this war as not."

She was wrong, but he'd no time to persuade her. "Marry me anyway. Let my pay take care of you and June until I get back. Annul the marriage then if you decide you're better off without me."

"Why me, out of all the other mill hands here?"

Ethan did not own the time to name the ways she'd captured his affection or explain why he admired her above her peers. But she had, and he did. "If I get to be any woman's husband, even on paper, even for only a matter of weeks, I want to be yours and no one else's," he told her. "I want to die knowing you'll be all right, you and June both."

The train whistle shrieked, and Cora Mae jolted. She started to turn toward the sound, but Ethan caught her against him.

"Don't do it. Let it go without you."

She didn't pull away. "Sergeant Howard, I—"

He was losing her. Without thinking, he bent his head to hers, cupped a hand to the nape of her neck, and took her lips in a kiss that would likely be his last.

Cora Mae should have pushed him away. But heaven help her, she didn't. For one urgent moment, she forgot he was a Yankee and she a Rebel, forgot to blame him for following Sherman's orders as her own menfolk had followed Johnston's. For the span of a few racing heartbeats, Ethan Howard was just a man, and she was just the woman in his arms.

"Mama?"

And then she remembered everything.

Jumping back, she pressed her hands to her cheeks and looked from June to Sergeant Howard.

Shock registered in his eyes. "I've missed something. 'Mama'?"

"Close enough," piped up June. "She's gonna marry my step-pa, Mr. Ferguson."

"You're engaged?" Sergeant Howard's tanned complexion flushed scarlet.

"She's going to be my mama," June said. "So I reckon that makes us kin enough already."

"I didn't—you never mentioned him."

Cora Mae held his stricken gaze, so intense she felt its burn. "No. I didn't." She might have pointed out that he'd never asked if she was spoken for, but the truth was, she had not been thinking of Mr. Ferguson when in the company of Sergeant Howard. Other than a prayer for his safety at June's bedtime, she had not been thinking of him much at all. She placed a hand over her galloping heart. Horace Ferguson had never made her pulse so much as trot. He'd never truly kissed her. She'd never pined for him to.

"All aboard!" a conductor called above the humming crowd. Locomotive steam rose under wooly clouds in a sky drained of its color.

Sergeant Howard turned his head to cough, then knelt and chucked June's chin. "Don't you worry. I'm not about to take her from you. You keep each other safe until you get back to Mr. Ferguson, all right?" Rising, he grasped the hilt of the sword at his hip. "If you can get to Cannelton, Indiana, there's a cotton mill there. It has giant fans to keep the lint from getting in your lungs. Godspeed." After quickly tipping his hat, he disappeared in the teeming rail yard.

Cora Mae touched her fingertips to her lips, still warm from his kiss. Too late, she thought of his book of rhymes rolled up inside her apron pocket. She couldn't catch him now to offer it back if she wanted to. Which she didn't. She couldn't read every word of those poems, but those that she did brought comfort. She supposed they'd bring more than that, now that she'd rejected the man who gave them to her.

Wind scented with coming rain sighed over her. She climbed the ladder into the boxcar, accepted a bag with nine days' rations in it, and wedged onto a bench in the steamy, foul-smelling car.

"Did I speak out of turn?" June asked, her voice small and hunched. She clutched Sassy, another token of the sergeant's kindness. He'd given them enough. He'd been plumb crazy to try giving them a widow's pension, too. Her heart tripped even now at the notion.

Cora Mae gathered June onto her lap. "You were right. I'm engaged to Mr. Ferguson, who we will find as soon as . . ." Her voice trailed away. As soon as what? There was no timetable for her return to Roswell, or for his. But one thing she knew for sure. "You and I belong together. I *am* your mama now. We're family, and nothing will change that."

"What did the sergeant mean about not finding work? You're a good worker. Mr. Ferguson said so. So am I. Why wouldn't we get jobs?"

More mill hands loaded into the boxcar. Some of them sat cross-legged on the straw-covered floor. Soon the air became almost too thick to breathe, and this was only one car. The entire train was just as full. There was a second train, too, devoted entirely to mill hands.

"So many," Cora Mae whispered.

"So many what?"

"So many of us." Fear trickled through her. "The sergeant was saying there are so many of us, almost two thousand from three different mill towns, that he doesn't see how we'll all find work in factories once we get across the river." She scanned the hungry faces around her. There was Fern, Cynthia, Damaris, and Tabby, and the rest she knew from Roswell. Between the lot of them, she reckoned they didn't have two cents to rub together. Once they came to the end of the journey, they would no longer be fellow sojourners. They'd be competitors for a decent wage. And they would fight.

"We saw you kiss that devil Yankee," Damaris hissed while Tabby directed a scowl at June.

"Traitor." Cynthia clenched folds of her homespun skirt. "Hussy."

Even Fern did not come to Cora Mae's defense this time, her face pinched and pale in the shadows of the bonnet that still bore a patch of Rebel gray. She must have seen Cora Mae's kissing a Yankee as a betrayal of not just Mr. Ferguson, but everything Wade had fought for. Loyal soul that she was, Fern was not like to forget it. Neither was her protective older sister.

They would not be her allies in the North, even if three of them did wear the bonnets she'd given them.

The train whistle screamed again, and Cora Mae's stomach turned. The locomotive belched smoke as the Yankee in her boxcar slid the door closed almost all the way.

"Next stop, Chattanooga," he said.

"It's not going to work," she murmured. She couldn't marry Sergeant Howard, but he was right. She was a fool to think they'd survive the North with nothing but a Yankee general's order to be exiled from the South.

"Get up," she said to June, who slipped off her lap. "Stop the train!" She squeezed past gaping girls to the guard at the door.

"Ain't no way." The Yankee laughed at her.

"We're getting off. General Dodge ordered the chief surgeon to hire some of us as nurses, didn't he?"

"What of it?"

"I'm going to do it. We're going to do it." Curling her arm around June, she whipped around to face Fern and Cynthia. "Come with us. Don't leave your aunt so far behind."

Fern notched up her chin. "You know I can't stay and nurse no bluebellies. Not after everything they done to us. Are you forgetting they killed your men?"

There would be no persuading her. "Take good care of yourself, then," she told them.

"Go and good riddance!" Damaris cried. She snatched the bonnet from her head and threw it at Cora Mae. "I guess we don't need a stitch from the likes of you. Tabby." She elbowed her little sister, who slowly took off the bonnet June had given her and handed it back.

"Damaris, please," Cora Mae tried. "Don't do this."

But she only crossed her arms and looked away.

"Yankee-lovin' cowards!" Another voice, a slap against her ears.

The wheels chugged beneath the floorboards. Through the narrowly open door, she watched the tracks begin to move by.

The guard yawned. "Too late."

Stooping down, Cora Mae stuffed the bonnets into her pocket and whispered into June's ear. The girl's eyes flared wide, but she nodded.

"Oh, Billy Yank," a mill hand called from the corner, "there's a seat by me if you get tired of standin'."

He accepted the invitation.

As soon as the Yankee was out of reach, Cora Mae threw her weight against the rusty door to shove it farther open. Before the train picked up any more speed, she scrambled to sit at the edge, pulling June to sit beside her. In one breath, Cora Mae told her, "I'll help you down, be ready." Skirts bunched in one fist, she jumped to the dusty platform below.

She whirled back to the boxcar and hurried alongside it to catch up to June. The little girl leaned forward, and

Cora Mae reached under her outstretched arms. “I’ve got you!” she cried and, with a great heave, pulled a screaming June off the train.

Chapter Ten

Stumbling under June's weight, Cora Mae fell back onto bags of feed corn stacked on the platform. Still buzzing with heightened energy, she kissed the top of June's copper hair. "Anything broken?"

June stood, wiggling and walking in place. "Fit as a fiddle!" Behind her, hundreds of factory workers who hadn't fit on the train milled about the yard.

The train rolled by, and hot waves billowed over Cora Mae. A gust of wind stirred up dirt and dust. Blinking furiously, she rose and shook straw from her skirt as an older man approached.

"Found yourselves on the wrong train, did you?" The twinkle in his blue eyes disarmed her, despite the Union blue of his coat. White whiskers fluffed about his cheeks and jaw like cotton.

"We've got no cause to go north, you see." The damp wind strengthened, whipping her dress about her legs.

"I'm afraid General Sherman says otherwise, my dears." He bent and offered his hand to June. "I'm Theodore Littleton, a chaplain."

"I'm June." She shook his hand. "A Georgian."

He chuckled, and Cora Mae introduced herself, as well. "We aim to stay. The surgeon still needs nurses,

I reckon." Now she knew what humble pie tasted like. After all her resistance to the idea when Sergeant Howard had first suggested it, she was ready to beg for the job if that was what it took to stay right here, a four-hour ride from Roswell.

Chaplain Littleton eyed her. "I haven't heard anything at all about using mill hands to fill those slots. There are plenty of convalescent nurses doing the job."

A second train screeched onto the tracks. They could be thrown onto this one. "Please, sir." She raised her voice to be heard over the officers calling for order. "It was General Dodge who said we could. We need to stay here in Georgia." She craned her neck to see if she could spot Sergeant Howard. Surely he would confirm this. But all she saw were the strained faces of women and children and the backs of Yankees she didn't know. "I wouldn't lie to you, Chaplain. Please. Don't put us on that train."

Chaplain Littleton squinted at her. "I'll take you to the provost marshal."

Pebbles pressing the soles of Cora Mae's feet, she and June followed him through the rail yard to the Fletcher House as the first drops of rain splashed her face. Crates of Union army supplies stacked up outside the double doors of the hotel, smelling of damp leather and wool. Inside the high-ceilinged lobby, they waited while Chaplain Littleton climbed a broad staircase of polished cherrywood, a slight hitch in his gait. The sweet scent of tobacco puddled in the heavy air.

Rain drummed against many-paned windows, streaming down in braids. Beneath the ragged hem of her skirt, Cora Mae curled dusty toes into plush red carpet, wishing she could hide her bare feet. Opposite the staircase, Yankees lounged in armchairs between doily-topped tables, their newspapers rattling open and shut. Two soldiers burst through the front door, scabbards swinging at their hips as they planted wet footprints up the stairs.

"Think they're going to meet with Gen'ral Sherman?" June whispered, face paling. "Think they're planning new devilment for Georgia?"

"Hush, now." If they were going to stay here, they'd best not give cause for reprimand.

"I just wondered if Mr. Ferguson might have found that safe place he was talking of." Her voice quavered. "Or if maybe there's no safe place left."

A sigh feathered Cora Mae's lips. "I wonder, too."

The chaplain came down the stairs with another man in Yankee uniform. "Miss Stewart, this is the provost marshal."

"How do you do." She dropped a curtsy, though it galled her. "This is June. She's a hard worker. She can carry water or boil it, or whatever the patients need. I want to nurse."

"So I've heard." He peered over his spectacles at her. "You understand these are Union patients."

"Yes, sir."

"And I understand you and your town have suffered, from your perspective, under Union hands."

She held her tongue and gave June a silencing look as well. It would do no good to reveal their feelings now. "Sir, the suffering on both sides need care."

The chaplain stood to the side, waiting.

The provost marshal's eyes were hard. "We need that in writing. From both of you. You need to sign the oath so we know we can trust your loyalty." He produced two slips of paper and a pen and motioned for them to follow him to the reception desk.

Thunder rumbled outside. June stood on tiptoe, her hands on the brass rail encircling the desk. "I get to make my mark, too? I can letter my first name. Will that do?"

"Fine. But first, raise your right hands. The both of you. You will repeat after me. 'I do solemnly swear, in the presence of almighty God. . ."

Cora Mae's right hand shook. What would her mama say about this? What would Pap and Wade? She didn't feel like a traitor, though some would call her such. All she felt was the instinct to survive and stay in her homeland, and this here was the only way she knew how.

". . . that I will henceforth faithfully support and defend the Constitution of the United States and the Union of the States. . . ."

She repeated it but barely heard herself, so small was her faltering voice and so loud the judgment she heard in her head. But what did it matter what words she said when they kept her and June from starvation? Outside, the train hissed and shrieked, drowning out the provost marshal, but she did her best to follow along and move her lips after he did. Then it was over. He lowered his right hand, and they did the same.

June took the pen first. The tip of her tongue poked out in evident concentration. Then she smiled at the large, uneven letters of her name.

"Now, Miss Stewart, if you please." He slid a small piece of paper toward her, inked the pen, and gave it to her.

She took it. "I sign this, and I'll be paid and given rations, isn't that right?"

"If you work, you'll surely be paid."

She hesitated. It was a practical thing she was doing, and that made it fitting for her and June. But there was still a weight in her hand and spirit as her name took shape on the Yankee form. A finality heavier than so short a moment could hold.

The provost added his name to the document and waved it in the air to dry the ink.

"What was all that other writing?" She couldn't make out all those fancy loops and dips.

"The text of the oath you just took," Chaplain Littleton said.

June grasped the brass railing and leaned back as far as she could go. "I didn't understand a lick of all that."

"It was the Oath of Allegiance, young lady." The provost marshal tucked both their papers into a folder. "It means you're a true and loyal citizen of the Union. You're not a Confederate anymore."

June's chin quivered. "What?"

"It means we can stay and nurse." But Cora Mae's voice quaked as she said it, and a tear trickled accusingly down her cheek. "We're still here, still together. That's what matters." She was sick to death of North and South, Yankee and Rebel, Union and Confederate. "Our loyalty is to each other, to our family. Nothing can change that."

~

GEORGIA RAILROAD LINE NEAR DECATUR, GEORGIA
TUESDAY, JULY 19, 1864

Already roasting inside his wool jacket, Ethan stared into the flames crackling from the wooden cross ties and felt an intimate sympathy for the iron rails laid over the top. He burned with embarrassment for playing the fool at the Marietta depot with Cora Mae. He shook his head at his own recklessness. She was gone now, God help her, and he had a job to do.

General Sherman's Special Field Order No. 37 instructed General Garrard's cavalry units to destroy the Georgia Railroad. The rails were to be heated in the middle, then bent or twisted so they couldn't be used again without being hauled away, melted down, and reforged, which the Confederacy was in no position to do. With the railroad destroyed, Lee wouldn't be able to send reinforcements for the battle that would soon come to Atlanta, now that the Confederates' beloved General Johnston had been replaced by General Hood. The one-legged general was a fighting man and likely ready to brawl. The fall of Atlanta would mean a huge loss to the South in manufacturing power and transportation, and Hood wouldn't easily give it up.

Ethan and his fellow cavalrymen had started several fires along this stretch of track, at fifteen-minute intervals. Freedmen employed by the army waited along with the soldiers until the iron grew soft enough to bend. Stepping away from the smoke and the undulating heat, Ethan scanned the surroundings. Picketed away from the bonfires, cavalry horses swished their tails against flies. On one side of the tracks, a sparse thicket of pines screened a frame house and its outbuildings. Stone Mountain rose up in the distance, as bald as Garrard, who remained mounted as he patrolled the railroad line with a spyglass. If he heard or saw anything that hinted of battle, the cavalrymen would drop their special mission and reinforce McPherson's army.

Ambling back to the fires, Ethan counted heads and came up two short. "Where are Aldridge and Weston?"

Someone pointed at two figures sneaking toward the woods.

"Aldridge! Weston! Get back here. We need every man!"

"I didn't sign up for hard labor," Aldridge countered, but halted a few yards from Ethan. "Besides, that's what you brought *them* for." He motioned toward the freedmen.

"They are not our slaves," Ethan reminded them. "Your job is to follow orders, and right now, that means we all do the same work. We're all getting paid for it, too."

"Maybe," Weston said as they approached. "But we *ain't* the same, and I'll fight anyone who says different."

They were close enough now that Ethan could smell whiskey on their breath, which accounted for the loosening of their tongues. Their views toward their fellow man, however, had been apparent before this. The only reason Aldridge and Weston had enlisted was for the thrill of battle. Principles had nothing to do with it.

Ethan's blood boiled. "You are drunk in the middle of the day, while on duty. Just because your enlistments are almost up doesn't mean you're above the code of conduct."

"A feller gets thirsty, Sergeant." Weston held no respect for authority. As far as Ethan was concerned, the sooner the two men left the unit, the better.

"Rail's hot!" Dooley called.

General Garrard trotted closer to the fire. "All right, men. Five to each end of the rail."

Ethan walked to one end and wrapped gloved hands around the iron bar.

Weston and Aldridge moved so slowly that other men filled the spaces, which was likely their plan all along. "Just because I wear blue doesn't mean I got to cozy up to no Negro," Aldridge muttered.

"Every other man facing opposite directions," Garrard instructed. "On the count of three. One, two, three!"

With a heave, the ten men lifted the thirty-foot-long, five-hundred-pound rail.

"Walk it!" Garrard called, and the men obeyed, shuffling along the ground and over to a dead pine tree. As soon as the red-hot center of the rail was positioned against the trunk, the men walked their ends toward each other until the rail was bent completely in half.

"Cross the ends!" Garrard shouted.

The dry, dead wood of the pine smoked and flared where the rail looped around it. The iron was already beginning to cool. Sweat spilled between Ethan's shoulder blades as he strained to push one end of the rail over the top of the other, then pull the opposite end back toward him. When the ends of the rail had been pulled as tight as they could, the men dropped it to the ground, then went back for the rail's twin and repeated the process.

Afterward, Ethan walked over to Reckless while the next bonfire was heating its rails. He pulled off his buckskin gloves, rubbed the horse's nose, then took a swig from his canteen.

"Howard!"

Ethan turned toward Garrard. "Sir?"

"Get those men in line!" the general growled, pointing after Weston and Aldridge. The two delinquents were running back into the woods. This time they had their rifles and satchels, which Ethan could only imagine they meant to fill with plunder.

"Yes, sir." He grabbed his rifle. It was little wonder so many Southern women were terrified of Yankees. Fools like these two gave them reason.

Pinecones crunched beneath his boots as he followed them through the woods. Sunlight fell in slanting shafts through the trees. "Weston! Aldridge!" he shouted, marching double-time. "Do not trespass on that private property!" He emerged into a clearing a short distance from the house in time to see them slip inside the front door.

A woman screamed. Ethan took off running.

On the front porch, an old woman gasped from a rocking chair in the corner. "Don't hurt me, please! Oh Lord, have mercy!"

"I'm not here to hurt you," he said. "I aim to fetch the two scoundrels who broke into your home."

"Ain't we poor enough already?" she cried. "You gotta tear up the railroad, too? It's not just soldiers you're keepin' away. It's food. It's medicine. It's anything worth havin'."

Drunken laughter tumbled out the open window.

"They can have my money. I got wheelbarrows full of Confederate dollars out back. But if they steal the only things that mean somethin' to me . . ."

"They won't." With the toe of his boot, he nudged the door open farther, his hands firmly on his rifle.

Ethan lifted his gaze to the creaking ceiling, then bounded up the steps.

At the top, he caught a glimpse of a round black barrel.

So this was it. Death had come for him, as he knew it would. He just hadn't expected it to come like this.

There was no chance to shout or duck or raise his own weapon and fire a shot in self-defense. All he could do was watch the spark and smoke spew from the rifle's mouth.

Fire combusted below his right elbow. His rifle clattered down the stairs. Stunned, he stumbled backward, lost his balance. He felt himself falling, but his arm refused to catch himself. His body crashed against the hard edges of the steps, his head slammed into the wall. His right hand useless, he pushed himself up with his left. Leaning against the wall in the stairwell, he looked from the blood soaking his sleeve to the white faces staring down at him from above.

"You idiot!" Weston hissed.

"I thought he was a Reb comin' to kill us!"

The injury hadn't killed him yet, but pain was a hatchet to his flesh, a torch to his nerves. Clamping his hand over the hole in his arm, his fingers grew crimson with blood. The metallic smell filled his nostrils and turned his stomach. "Get. Out."

Rifles slung over their shoulders, Weston and Aldridge pushed past him. The last thing Ethan heard was the slam of the door behind them and the woman weeping from her chair.

Chapter Eleven

MARIETTA, GEORGIA

The bunch of wild violets pinned to Cora Mae's collar had been June's idea. The sweet scent withered beneath odors of unwell men, and they wilted before long each day. But Cora Mae wore a fresh bunch daily just the same. She figured the patients could all use a little glimpse of beauty in this place.

In the Methodist church turned hospital, Cora Mae walked down the aisle between wounded men held aloft by planks resting atop the pews. In the three days she had been nursing here while June helped in the cooking tent west of the square, the helpless condition of these patients had made it easier to ignore that they were Yankees. They didn't mock her. They needed her.

The men were placed side by side across the pews, with an empty pew between each row. Beginning her rounds with the patients closest to the altar, she climbed onto the front pew, dipped her sponge in her pail, and then squeezed it over each patient's wound to keep moist the lint the doctor had packed inside. When she was done with one row, she hopped to the floor, walked five pews up the aisle, and climbed on that one to repeat the process.

Other nurses worked here, too, but most of them were soldiers recovering from illness or injury. Weak themselves, they needed frequent breaks. Tasks they could not do fell to freed men and women, including Venus.

"You're doing well, Cora Mae." The soft voice of Anne Littleton, the chaplain's wife, drifted from the side aisle, where she held a tray recently emptied of its cornbread. "We're most grateful for your help. I hope you know that if they were Southern boys, I'd work alongside you to care for them, too."

"Thank you." Cora Mae finished wetting a patient's wound, then climbed down from the pew and walked up to the next. She smoothed her apron over the calico dress Anne had insisted on giving her.

Anne walked with her, peering over her shoulder to confirm the patients in earshot were sleeping. "I suppose you have relations in the war yourself?" she whispered.

"My pa and older brother, Wade, were killed at First Manassas, way back at the start."

"Merciful heavens," Anne murmured. "And now here you are. What a fine Christian woman you are to nurse our men."

"I do aim to be. But truth is, I just didn't want to go north."

Anne fanned the flies off the patient closest to her. "I don't blame you one bit. This is your home. You want to be near your mother, as I want to be wherever my husband is."

"That's a fact." Cora Mae stepped onto the pew, plunged her sponge into the tepid water, and wrung it out over the next wound. She would ask Anne to help her write a letter, but the mail wasn't running, and Dr. Wilcox had told her the Yankees pulled out of Roswell already, which meant Lt. Dooley had no more reason to go there, and neither did anyone else. Except, of course, for Cora Mae and June.

On the other side of the church, Venus raked soiled straw from the floor. She said nothing, and neither did she spare Cora Mae a glance. But her presence was reminder enough that families had been torn apart since the first Africans arrived in the South. The pain of Cora Mae's separation from Mama was genuine, but it was not unique. And at least she knew where Mama was.

Cora Mae moved to the next patient, wetting his bandage while he slept. "Is June doing all right in the cooking tent?"

"Real fine." Anne smiled. She and June had become fast friends when June recognized that her doll's dress matched the older woman's apron. "I best get back there now." She glided away.

Moments later, Dr. Wilcox burst into the church, commotion in his wake as a new patient was brought in. "Nurse!"

"Coming!" Leaving her pail and sponge, Cora Mae jumped into the center aisle and hastened to them.

The table that once held the sacraments had been moved to the rear of the sanctuary and now held a bleeding soldier instead, another sacrifice on war's altar. Some of the patients resting atop the pews looked over at the injured man, while others turned their heads away.

Dr. Wilcox held a napkin folded into a cone over the man's nose and mouth. He counted, then touched the patient's eyelids with his fingertip and, apparently satisfied at the reaction, took the cone away.

She sucked in her breath. Her mind whirred. *Sergeant Howard. Ethan.*

"What happened? What do we do?"

"He was shot in the forearm at close range. Bones shattered." The doctor handed her a pair of scissors. "We need his shirt and jacket off straightaway. You can do this. Consider it practice. There will be more than you can count once the battles begin."

She took the scissors from the doctor and slipped a blade under the fabric at Ethan's right wrist. *It's only another uniform I'm cutting out,* she told herself. *Just a pair of blades on wool, but blue instead of gray.* Quickly, she cut from the wrist to the place where the sleeve had already been blown away. Stifling the urge to gag, she began cutting again, from above the wound all the way up to his shoulder, until they could peel the material completely away from his arm.

"If there was no battle, how did this happen?" she whispered.

"Keep cutting. We need his torso bare so we can monitor his breathing through his chest wall."

Her own pulse hammering, she obeyed. The sight of his bare chest buckled her heart as she remembered melting against it four days earlier. Laying down the scissors, she stripped the fabric down and away from his body. His right forearm was destroyed. The hand that had cradled her head as he kissed her was bloodied and useless. Above it, shards of bone thrust from shredded muscle and skin.

"Watch his face." Dr. Wilcox positioned Ethan's arm at a right angle to his body. "His tongue could slip back and choke him before we realize he's in danger. If he turns gray, you must reach in and pull the tongue forward."

Obediently, Cora Mae watched, fighting to master her emotions. In the corner of her vision, Dr. Wilcox threaded a tourniquet strap around Ethan's arm, then turned a screw to tighten it, and she felt her chest constricting. "Must you really?"

"There's no repairing it. He'd die of infection in days."

Oh God! Tears clotted her throat. She watched Ethan's complexion for a change in color and thought she saw a twinge across his features. "Can he feel it? Is he aware?" Horror spiraled through her.

"Not if I hurry. Scipio!" the doctor called.

The freedman joined them. His sleeves were rolled to the elbows, revealing thickly muscled arms.

"Hold these linen straps," the doctor told him, "and pull snug to retract the muscle tissue away from the bone. Like I showed you before, you understand?"

"Yes." Without hesitation, Scipio obeyed.

Stomach roiling, Cora Mae kept her gaze fixed on Ethan's face. His eyes were closed, but she remembered their sparkling green. She tried to remember the shape his lips made when they smiled.

The sound of sawing turned her knees to jelly. She leaned against the table. A grimace stole across Ethan's countenance, and she nearly came undone. The possibility that he could hear, could feel, that he knew what was happening, was too terrible to accept.

Then, almost as quickly as it began, it stopped.

Ethan's right hand was no longer a part of him. The operation was over.

After working needle and thread for what seemed an eternity, Dr. Wilcox asked for a wad of lint, then for adhesive strips from his kit to be dunked in a pail of water. While Scipio complied, the doctor dismissed Cora Mae to fetch the bucket of water from the pew where she had left it. At last, he wiped his hands on his apron and pulled a pocket watch from his vest.

Cora Mae dashed the tears from her face and noticed for the first time how Scipio regarded Ethan. "Do you know him well?" she dared to ask.

"I know he joined the army to make men free," Scipio said. "And now he won't fight no more." His hands curled into fists at his sides.

"Eight minutes." Dr. Wilcox shut his timepiece and slipped it back into his pocket. "From start to finish, that took eight minutes. We'll need to get it down to five."

Cora Mae waited for an explanation. "I don't understand."

"Once the battles begin, we'll have more amputation cases than you can imagine. Minutes shaved are lives saved." He wiped the flat of his saw and knife blades against his apron and put them back in the case.

The tendons in Ethan's neck pulled taut in his sleep.

Cora Mae's fingernails dug into her palms. Straw crunched beneath her steps as she hastened outside and down the steps, where she sank to the ground and wept.

Chapter Twelve

The burning in Ethan's right hand pulled him back to consciousness. Even before he could lift his leaden eyelids, he groaned through gritted teeth and instinctively reached for the pain.

He couldn't find it.

Heart lurching, he opened his eyes. A bandaged stump ended below his elbow. Revulsion twisted his gut. His hand wasn't there, though he could feel it as vividly as he felt his left. His pulse thundered.

Ethan had been preparing himself to die. He hadn't prepared for this.

With his left hand, he pushed himself to sit up on the straw-covered door beneath his back. The blood rushed to the end of his severed limb with such force, he cried out and collapsed. Sweat coated him. There were other patients in the sanctuary, but he could scarcely hear their groans over the throbbing in his nerves. Throwing his left arm over his eyes, he tried to bear up under it, but he feared the moaning in his ears was his own.

Then relief trickled over the scorching pain. Breath suspended, he lowered his arm to see someone squeezing water from a sponge over his dressings. Remarkably, it cooled his no-longer-there hand.

"Does it help?" the doctor asked.

Ethan exhaled. "Yes, some."

"I'm Dr. Wilcox. The first few days are critical. You must lie still and not exert pressure, or you'll disrupt the healing. Understood?"

"The healing," Ethan repeated dully.

"The operation was a success, no matter how it feels to you now. You will heal, a little lighter in the arm, but no less a man than you ever were."

But the only words Ethan grasped were *less a man*. They landed on him with a physical weight and burrowed deep.

The doctor's retreating footsteps shook the pew beneath Ethan's wooden bed. He prayed for sleep to take him.

Cora Mae's face filtered through his semiconscious state. It was well indeed that she'd refused his proposal. She deserved more than he could give her now. Deserved more than he could be. It was this train of thought that carried him into slumber.

Razor-sharp images scrolled across his tormented mind, terrible pictures of war and death, until he fought to swim back to wakefulness. The drone of cavalry faded to the buzzing of flies.

Then it stopped. A miraculous coolness covered his brow, and his eyelids fluttered open. At the sight of Cora Mae leaning over him, he wondered if he was dreaming.

"You're awake." Dimples starred her cheeks as she wrung out a rag over a pail and began wiping the sweat from his skin.

"Are you—really here?" With his left hand, he touched her wrist as she passed her cloth over the depression in his chest.

"I really am." Her hazel eyes glistened. A tendril of hair swayed near her cheek. "I bet Little Feller is mighty jealous of that, too. I've seen him around some, looking lost again. I do believe he's been looking for you."

Whatever she said, he heard pity in her voice and rebelled against it. He hadn't dreamed he would see her again. Certainly not like this. Never like this. "I thought you got on the train." His voice was hoarse, a fractured thing, but less broken than his body.

"You persuaded me otherwise." She swiped the rag from his neck over his left shoulder and down his arm. The cool cloth moved to his cheek, so soothing he couldn't help but close his eyes. "Can you tell me what happened?" she asked.

Ethan turned his head to cough. "Two soldiers disobeyed orders and entered a private home with obvious intent to plunder." It was not a story to be proud of. Yet, void of glory and honor as it was, he continued with the truth. "I went after them to stop them, and one of them shot me. Said he thought I was a Rebel coming to kill them both."

"You were shot by your own man?"

He coughed again, his flat position making his lungs work harder. When he opened his eyes, he caught her looking at his bandages. Humiliation seared him. "You can go, Miss Stewart. I don't need you."

She flinched. "But I—"

"I don't *want* you here."

Cora Mae's face reddened. Her lips grew thin.

Good. Let her be angry. Maybe then she'd stay away.

~

"Did you see him?" June fairly pounced on Cora Mae as soon as she entered the small tent where a few female nurses slept. "Does the sergeant know his arm's cut short?"

"He knows." A knot tightened Cora Mae's chest as she eased herself onto the cot and pulled the shoes—another gift from Anne—from her swollen feet.

"Well, what did he say?"

Anne sat on June's cot, rubbing her back. In a secondhand nightdress bleached white, the little girl looked pure and fresh and altogether too young for a war.

"I reckon he's doing all right, considering." Cora Mae sighed, unwilling to think on Ethan's parting words, let alone repeat them. But it was the pain she heard and saw in him that wouldn't let her be.

"Well. I surely do hope he mends." June's forehead furrowed, but she closed her eyes.

When she had drifted off to sleep, Anne rose and wrapped her arm around Cora Mae's shoulders. "Do you know how long the spirit takes to heal?" the older woman asked.

"Much longer than skin and bone."

"Give him time, dear." She paused. "I didn't realize you were friends."

Cora Mae sniffed, chuckling. "He fetched me and June out of Roswell and kept us prisoner at the courthouse." Inexplicably, she confided in Anne about the rail yard proposal, and Mr. Ferguson, and jumping off the train. She did not, however, tell her about his kiss. That, she kept for her memory alone.

"Merciful heavens!" Anne fanned herself when the tale was told. "Little wonder that you care!"

"But I shouldn't. Leastwise, not any more than I care about the other patients. My future is in Georgia, wherever Mr. Ferguson finds us another mill, and Sergeant Howard's is in the North. There's a river between us, and I don't just mean the Ohio."

"That may be so. But the wonderful thing about rivers, Cora Mae, is that they can be crossed. Even after the bridges have been burned." Anne kissed Cora Mae's forehead and bade her good night.

The next day, there was no time to think of Ethan or rivers or trains. On the twentieth day of July, there was a battle at Peachtree Creek, outside Atlanta, and the wounded poured into Marietta like rain down a waterspout in a storm.

The church filled with broken men bleeding into the straw so quickly that the freed men and women who were tasked with changing it could not keep up.

The tents bordering the square swelled with patients, too. Ambulance drivers crammed wounded men together under patches of shade that couldn't cover them all. The screams that rent the air seemed loud enough to be heard in Roswell.

"You stay away from the square, June. Do you hear me?" Cora Mae knelt and grasped June's shoulders. "Do not go near them, no matter what. I don't want you in any of the hospitals, either. Say you understand." No little girl should see or hear what was going on inside.

"Yes, ma'am." June agreed to help Anne in the cooking tent.

Convalescent nurses labored to keep up with the mere forty-five Union doctors. Dr. Wilcox pulled Cora Mae from the Methodist church to assist his operations beneath a tent at the edge of the town square. While he amputated, she stood with him, her apron spotting scarlet as she held the retractor strips the way Scipio had done, separating flesh from bone. Whatever the doctor asked of her—lint, adhesives, water—she supplied. It did not matter that she felt sick. All that mattered was that she did her job.

The amputations took seven minutes now. Then six. Then five. They could not be done any quicker without unspeakable barbarity.

Day melted into night. Fireflies and moths fluttered against the lantern Cora Mae held while Dr. Wilcox performed his work in the jaundiced glow.

"No more," the doctor finally said at midnight. "We must rest." He wiped the flat of his saw on his apron as she splashed a bucket of water over the door on which the surgeries took place.

After four hours of sleep that felt like none, she awoke with muscles as sore as her heart.

"Good morning, dear." Anne smiled down at her. "I hate to rush you, but Dr. Wilcox has already sent word. He needs you straightaway."

Covering a yawn, Cora Mae nodded and stiffly rose from the cot. "How is June?" She bent and kissed the girl's tangled hair as she slept.

"Getting along, but it's all so much for her to take in. I keep her close, so don't you worry."

"That's a comfort to me. I'm obliged." There was more to say but no time for it. Instead, Cora Mae raked her fingers through her hair and bound it again at the nape of her neck.

The walk to the square was bewildering. Wind sighed mournfully through maple and oak trees while songbirds trilled cheerfully from their branches. Overhead, a cloudless blue sky hung over scenes of anguish. White hospital tents flapped in the breeze like angel wings, shielding the men from the sun, and perhaps the heavens from the hell below.

When Cora Mae found Dr. Wilcox at his table, two freedmen were already with him.

"Miss Stewart, you remember Scipio, and this is Titus. They'll be assisting us today."

She greeted each of them, then turned to the doctor. "Do you need me, then?"

"I need all of you. The fellows we'll be operating on today may put up a fight, and Scipio and Titus will need to hold them still."

She frowned. "Won't they be unconscious for the operation?"

"Too much time has passed since their injuries." He waved to the freedmen to bring the first patient to the table.

"But how can you! With nothing for the men!" Shock sharpened her tone.

"Do not pretend to care more for them than I do. If we put them under at this point, they very likely will not wake. Feel sorry about it later, but now we must work."

Disbelief paralyzed her as a young man was helped onto the table.

"Don't take my arm! Don't take it off! Oh God, help me! Get away from me, you old sawbones!" His eyes were wild with terror, his forearm crushed beyond saving. Scipio and Titus flanked him, holding him down.

"Miss Stewart!" Dr. Wilcox barked.

With a fortifying breath, she plunged into her work. "Hello, soldier, my name is Cora Mae Stewart." She took the scissors and began cutting up his sleeve. "What's your name?"

"M–Morris. James Morris the third."

She cut the sleeve from his arm all the way up to his shoulder. "Where are you from, James?"

"Chicago. Illinois." His speech slowed, likely because he'd lost so much blood already. "Please—stop."

"What's Chicago like? You have kinfolk there?" She held his gaze as Dr. Wilcox threaded the tourniquet band under his arm.

When he looked at her, she offered a soft smile, hoping to reassure him.

Dr. Wilcox set knife to flesh.

Placing her hands on James's shoulders while the freedmen stabilized his arm and legs, she forced a steadiness into her voice. "Look at me, James. Keep looking at me. You will get through this."

"Oh no, oh no no—" He struggled under their hands.

"Try not to move. It will be over soon."

The color left his face, and he soon passed out from the pain. A mercy.

When Dr. Wilcox finished minutes later, Scipio and Titus carried him off the door and laid him under a tent.

"Next!" The doctor called, and she prayed that God would be her strength and the doctor's, too.

Every operation bruised her. The screams she would carry in her mind forever, she figured. But Dr. Wilcox didn't flag, and neither did she, until at the end of the day, he declared them finished.

"I've had no time for rounds." He cleaned his spectacles on the inside of his apron. "In the morning, I'll need you to change whichever dressings are three days old. Then come back to me."

For the second night in a row, Cora Mae slept in her clothes.

Chapter Thirteen

FRIDAY, JULY 22, 1864

Pail in hand and fresh violets pinned to her dress, Cora Mae entered the Methodist church. The smell nearly knocked her back, but she walked over the soiled hay anyway. Most of the men crowded onto the pews would only need their dressings moistened. There were only a few whose bandages needed to be completely changed. Ethan Howard was one of them.

Flies peppered the foul air, along with voices invoking God's name such as this place of worship had never heard before. Sorrow threatened to drown her at seeing so much suffering in one place. She felt no rejoicing that Confederate soldiers had caused it, nor was she unaware that Yankee soldiers had likely dispatched the same amount of anguish. *How long, Lord? When will this wretched war end?*

Pushing a strand of hair off her forehead, she scanned the sea of faces. There at the end of a pew, she spotted Ethan and went to him.

As she drew near, however, alarm bells clanged inside her. His blond hair was dark with sweat. His complexion was so altered, he barely looked himself. She touched his brow and drew away. His skin was scorching hot. Quickly, she wiped a cool, wet cloth over his face, neck, and torso.

"Sergeant Howard? Ethan."

He didn't stir.

Glancing at his bandaged arm, she pulled fresh linens and lint from her apron pockets and laid them on the pew. While cradling his elbow in one hand, she unwound the dressings until only the adhesive strips were left. With a sponge, she soaked those until they loosened. She removed the sodden strips—and the ball of soiled lint tucked inside—until his skin was bare. Odor assaulted her.

The place where Dr. Wilcox had fused the skin back together was so swollen, she was sure it was the cause of his fever. A bright red hue crept upward toward his elbow. Was the unchanged dressing the cause? She couldn't help but wonder as she sponged his arm clean.

With nimble fingers, she took a pinch of lint, wadded it into a dense pack, and held it against the seam at the end of his arm. Then she wrapped it snugly into place with fresh strips, winding the bandage around and around until she finally tied a knot below his elbow.

Ethan's eyelids fluttered. "Cora Mae? Am I dreaming?" He didn't sound like himself. "This is no place for you." His chest rose and fell with his breath.

Then he was gone again, deep into a fevered sleep.

Were others not depending on her, she would have lingered, waiting for his next waking, practicing what comfort she might offer, listening for whatever he might say. She would have kept his brow cool and waved the flies away. She'd have talked to him some, even if he couldn't reply, so he'd know he wasn't alone.

But more sick and injured awaited. With a weight in her spirit, she said a prayer and moved on to the next patient in need of fresh dressings, more troubled than she cared to admit.

~

Wagonloads of casualties came pouring in again, this time bearing wounded from another battle for Atlanta. While Anne kept watch of June, Cora Mae steeled her nerves against the screams of shattered men and helped Dr. Wilcox do his job in the sweltering tents.

She feared a callus had formed over her heart, for she no longer quaked at every rasp of the saw, every snap of bone. Only sweat, not tears, now wet her face as she understood that Dr. Wilcox's efficiency was not cruel but merciful.

But once another twenty-four hours passed from the time of the battle, the anesthesia was necessarily put away and operations performed without it. Cora Mae never would get used to this. Surely, she reckoned, the doctor felt the same. The terror, the thrashing, the begging and pleading to take life rather than limb—it was enough to shake an oak tree from the ground.

"Enough," Dr. Wilcox declared at last. "Clean up, eat, rest."

She rinsed the ruined door. "Will there be more battles soon?" She could not imagine how many more men the Union had to spare.

"More battles, yes. Soon? I don't know. Too soon for my liking, at any rate."

Weary, she parted ways with the doctor she'd come to respect.

And there was June, looking lost and thoroughly out of place amidst the sea of wounded Yankee soldiers.

Cora Mae gasped and ran to her, as though there was time to protect her from all that surrounded them both. "Oh June, I told you to stay away! Why did you come?" She reached out to her, but June stepped back.

"I was lookin' for you or for Little Feller. What—what happened? Are you hurt real bad?" She pointed to Cora Mae's soiled apron.

"No, no. It's not my blood."

"Then whose—" Her gaze caught on a pile of limbs from two days' work. The child turned white as muslin. Her voice shrank to a whisper. "Is this what you been doing all day? But I thought you were making them *better*. I don't—I don't understand."

Emotion choked Cora Mae as she grappled for a response. "You're not *meant* to understand. It's a war, and wars don't make a lick of sense, even for the grown-ups."

The little girl turned and lurched away. Cora Mae called her name, following her through the square, between and around white tents that billowed in the sultry wind. But she would not take June's small hand while she had blood on hers.

Finally, June stopped and fell sobbing to the ground. She pulled her knees up under her chin and rocked back and forth.

Cora Mae sank to her knees beside her, murmuring assurances that she tried to believe herself.

Vaguely, she registered that a man with one leg, who came after the first battle, was sitting up under the nearest tent, listening intently. "What's she crying about?" he asked.

Disoriented, Cora Mae turned to him. "She saw too much. Enough to upset anyone. And she doesn't like that I had anything to do with it." She turned back to June, wishing she could lay a steadying hand on her quaking back. "But my aim was only to help."

"Liar!" The word cut through the air. "She's a liar! And a butcher!"

Cora Mae stood and whirled around. James Morris came rushing at her, waving what was left of his arm.

June screamed.

"Listen to her, she's a Secesh! One of the exiled Roswell hands with an ax to grind—or should I say, a bone saw! She helped the doc cut me apart without anesthesia! She means us harm, all right!"

June cried harder.

"Aw, shut up and leave her alone." A voice came to her defense from somewhere in the tent's shadows. "She's a saint for nursing the likes of us, especially after what we did to her homeland."

"No, no, Morris is right! She did the same to me!" called another man. "Gave me nothing for the pain. Didn't seem troubled a bit as I felt the blade slice through me."

James waved his upper arm in her face. "How would you like to know what it feels like?"

June had the good sense to flee. When Cora Mae moved to follow her, Morris blocked the path.

"Please." Her voice betrayed her dread. Union guards paced the perimeter of the square, but not here in the middle of the maze. "You'll tear your stitches. You need to rest. Go back and lie down."

"You think that'll help me feel better?" In a flash, he gripped her upper arm with bruising force.

Her thoughts scrambled. She could break free, but in the struggle, he would surely reopen his wound. He needed to release her of his own accord.

"Let her go, Morris!" Whoever yelled it couldn't do more than that. "You're a disgrace, you fool!"

"I know you're upset, but I'm telling you, you're making your injury worse," she told Morris with all the authority she could muster. Which wasn't much, especially since her accent seemed to make him angrier.

In his view, she was the enemy and had deliberately caused pain. What wouldn't he do for revenge?

A shot rang out.

"Unhand her, you rat, or the next bullet will be for your head," a man's voice boomed.

Morris relaxed his grip, and Cora Mae spun away from him. She dashed behind the officer who trained a pistol on Morris. But it was Dr. Wilcox who hooked her arm through his and marched with her from the scene, escorting her to the edge of the square, where he deposited her at her tent with a weary good night and a reprimand to be more careful where she went.

Cora Mae scrubbed as clean as she could at the nearby well, then went inside. "Junebug?" Spotting the little girl on the cot, she quickly exchanged her soiled clothes for a nightdress, then lay down beside her and fought to tame her pulse. Finally, she touched June's shoulder, her knuckles smarting from the lye soap. "Will you talk to me?"

June shook her head. But then, not a minute later, she said, "The doctor rescued you? I saw him take a soldier with him to find you. I told him to do that."

Cora Mae rolled onto her back. "Yes, he did. Thank you for fetching him." She stared at cobwebs strung in the corner of the white canvas above them. "I'm sorry for what you saw." She hated that those images would haunt them both.

Wind lifted the flap of the tent and stirred the air, bringing the smell of cookfires. June turned onto her side. "Mrs. Littleton had to go into the churches to help. She told me to stay here, but I was waiting *forever*. I got scared. I missed you. I wanted you."

"I want you too." Cora Mae's throat pulled tight around the words. "You and me. We belong together." She tucked a piece of June's hair behind her ear and thanked God again for the blessing this child was to her. A cricket chirped from beneath the cot, and lavender shadows deepened.

"I don't know why all those men had to get cut up so bad, though, even if they *are* bluebellies." Her chin quivering, tears rolled from June's eyes, and she covered them with her hands.

Cora Mae kissed the top of her head. "If those men didn't have those operations, their limbs would become poisonous and kill them. Can you understand that?"

After wiping her face, June flopped onto her back again. "I think so."

"Good. My, won't Mr. Ferguson be surprised to find you such a grown-up girl next time we see him." She tried to smile. Tried to imagine that beyond the shadows that hemmed them in, the world could be a safe place again, full of kindness and comfort, and people whose wounds had healed.

"I don't want to be a grown-up girl." June blinked tears from her lashes, but her eyes soon filled again.

"I know how you feel." Cora Mae spooned her into her arms, singing to her until she fell asleep at last.

~

Dawn touched the sky with the hues of a ripening peach. Light melted through the church windows, scattering shadows to the corners.

"Sergeant Howard. Ethan?" Cora Mae cradled his name in her voice. He'd been her first thought upon waking. Instead of the looked-for improvement, however, he seemed to be the same or worse.

She brushed the hair off his forehead before laying a damp cloth to his skin. She'd done the same for countless others, but with Ethan, even the most practical touches held an intimacy she couldn't explain.

"It's me," she told him without knowing if he heard. "I'm right here, and I'm telling you that it's not your time to go. This here isn't it, so you need to fight this fever and come on back. You've got a lot of living left to do."

His skin was dry as paper. She didn't need to be a doctor to know he needed to drink. With her thumb, she pressed down on his stubbled chin enough to part his lips, then dripped clean water into his mouth. Mercifully, he swallowed, then accepted a few teaspoons more.

"That's good," she encouraged. But it wasn't near enough. "Let's see if we can't get a little more in you."

She slipped her arm beneath his neck and lifted his head so it rested against her shoulder. The little purple flowers on her collar brushed his cheek as she brought the dipper to his lips. "Drink, Ethan," she murmured, and he did.

Other patients stirred, all of them thirsty, too. As soon as Ethan stopped drinking, she wiped the water from the corner of his mouth with her fingertip. "You must get well," she told him. Resisting the urge to kiss his brow, she left to tend other men.

The sun was high in the cotton-tufted sky before she found Dr. Wilcox at the square. "Have you checked on Sergeant Howard yet? He's got a fever and won't wake up." A basket of dressing supplies swung from her elbow, a pail of water from her hand.

"Ah, Miss Stewart." His tone held a sigh. "I'm afraid you won't be needing those anymore." He took the pail and basket from her. "Walk with me."

She followed him from the hospital tent into shade cast by the three-story Masonic Hall.

"I'm afraid there's been a change," Dr. Wilcox told her. "Howard is no longer your concern."

Her breath hitched. "I beg your pardon?"

"You won't be nursing anymore."

She tried to make sense of this. "I don't understand."

"Word travels fast, even when the messengers don't have both feet, as it happens. News of your incident yesterday evening with Mr. Morris reached Sherman's ears. He called me in to explain, which I did to the best of my ability. Turns out, he never authorized the chief surgeon to hire any mill hands to stay on as nurses."

"No, it was General Dodge," she explained.

"Sherman outranks him." He swatted a fly from his apron. "He says this disorder among the men must end. That he can't have doctors spending time guarding

Southern nurses, or patients interrupting their healing to lash out at you, or other patients growing sympathetic to the plight of Southern civilians because of you."

Her head ached with concentration. "What are you saying?"

"Not me. Sherman." His apologetic tone unnerved her. "He's ordered you north, like all the other mill workers. You and the girl in your care will be given two tickets and passes to get you through. The train leaves"—he consulted his pocket watch—"in thirty minutes. You'll both be on it."

"No."

"I realize you've not yet been paid. Take this." He stuffed a roll of greenbacks in her hand, along with two documents. "Your oaths and a letter of recommendation. They should help you find gainful employment. Lieutenant McDowell's enlistment is up, and he's agreed to escort you as far as Louisville." Chin to his chest, he muttered, "Blast this war. Blast it all to—" He signaled to someone, turned, and walked away.

Dazed, her gaze drifted to soldiers she'd cared for over the last several days. It was not a role she'd aspired to, but now that she was stripped of it, she hardly felt relief. *Go north? Now?* The gears of her mind labored to grasp this. She was breathless with the effort.

She felt a touch on her elbow, and found a soldier waiting for her. "I'm Lieutenant McDowell, ma'am. Here's your tickets and passes. I'll be riding with you. I'll make sure nothing happens to you on the journey."

The plummeting sensation inside her grew so strong, she gripped the man's arm to stay standing, to remember which way was up. Sherman's command rearranged her life and future as well as June's. Already, she felt the tearing away from all she knew. "What will I do in Louisville?"

"Papers say there's a women's refugee center a block from the depot. A thousand mill hands are there. You could find shelter and rations there, I wager." He scratched through his charcoal-colored beard. "But some reporters say there's not enough beds or blankets. Still, they have to stay there because they won't take the Oath of Allegiance to the Union."

She blinked. "You mean this?" She showed him her oath.

"Yes, that's the one. If you've signed that, you won't need to sit out the war in prison. But you'll need to find your own work and lodging."

"Cannelton." The word burst from her. "In Indiana. There's a mill there, Sergeant Howard said. Can you help me get there?"

"That's on the Ohio River. Once we get to Louisville, I'll see you onto a steamboat, and it'll be up to you to get off at the right dock. But we better hurry now."

Still reeling, she managed to carry herself toward the tent she'd called home. When she reached it, June was outside, folding linens with Venus and another freed woman. Anne was nowhere to be found.

"What is it?" June asked when she saw Lieutenant McDowell.

Cora Mae choked out an answer she could scarcely credit herself. "Get your things, June. And mine, too, please." She turned to McDowell. "I want to look for Mrs. Littleton. I want to say goodbye." She wanted one last glimpse of Ethan, too. It mattered to her how he fared. He mattered to her.

The train whistled from a few blocks away. She barely heard June's rising protests.

"No." McDowell looked in the direction of the depot. "We're going now."

Shock numbed her. Even goodbyes were stolen from her, as they had been at Roswell. She locked her gaze with Venus. "I hope you find your mother."

Without another word, she plunged into the tent and searched frantically for a paper and pencil to leave a note for Anne. Finding none, she took a tin of talcum powder and dashed a thin layer across a folding table. With her fingertip, she traced her farewell: *Thay sent us northe.*

Chapter Fourteen

TUESDAY, JULY 26, 1864

Above Ethan, a crystal chandelier caught the light and threw miniature rainbows against whitewashed walls. The air was thick with heat and flies and the smell of wounded men. Turning his head, he stared hard at the bouquet of bandages beneath his elbow until his sight overrode the sensation that he still owned his right hand.

Finally, the uncanny feeling receded, and mere pain took its place. Sweat filmed his skin as he gritted his teeth against it. Then a pitiful moan filled his ears. On the plank next to him lay a patient with one leg.

"Water," he rasped. "Oh, for the love of God! Bring me water!" The lilting accent contrasted with the more common northern twangs.

Ethan pushed himself up and surveyed the sanctuary crammed full of men. Not a nurse or doctor was among them. "What's your name, soldier? Where's home?"

"Joseph Buford, east Tennessee. Not all of us in our state wanted to secede. And you are?"

"Ethan Howard. Indiana." And although he had but one arm, he still had two legs for walking. "Let me see about that water. I'm parched, myself." Coughing, he swung his legs over the side of his plank and jumped down onto the straw-covered aisle.

Light-headedness slowed his pace, and the sun nearly blinded him when he stepped outside and sneezed. But he was up and moving. It felt like a victory. His arm throbbed beneath his bandages, but he shoved that aside as he focused on the well. Surely he could work it with one hand.

Just before he reached it, a short, plump woman swept toward him, a pail and dipper swinging from her fist. "Hello there!" A wisp of black hair sprang from her bun and coiled beside her wilting collar. "You need some water, honey? Let me get it."

Warmth flooded him at the idea that the task was beyond him. "Much obliged, ma'am." He wondered if seeing his bare chest and reduced arm made her as uncomfortable as he was. "But would you mind if I draw it myself?"

"Oh, there's no call for that, dear, I can manage it."

He rubbed his hand over his face and was surprised to find a week's worth of beard. "I don't want to sound ungrateful, but I'm itching to use the muscles I still have."

"Oh! Well!" Her cheeks flamed red. "Of course, I just—" Apparently giving up on her speech, she stepped back.

"What day is it, anyway?" He grasped the handle and turned, unspooling the rope to lower the bucket.

"Twenty-sixth of July."

"Then it's been more than a week since my injury." The fever must have erased a few days' time from his memory.

"And we've had two battles since then. I'm so sorry you had to come looking for water yourself. But there are many, many more for us to tend now."

Ethan felt sick at the idea. Before he'd been shot, there were already four thousand Union wounded in and around Marietta. The thought of more suffering men tied a knot in his gut. He wondered how many of them had been like him, willing to die of battle wounds but unprepared to survive them. He prayed for Dooley but felt some measure of comfort in knowing the blacksmith stayed in the rear during combat. He wondered if he'd see Cora Mae again or if she'd keep busy with other patients after how he'd sent her away.

"Who won the battles?" he asked. The bucket dipped into the water, and Ethan turned the crank the other way to pull it back up.

"The Union."

He exhaled, imagining the cost. In vain, he wished that his injury and amputation had at least been service to either victory.

"I'm Anne Littleton, by the way. Chaplain Littleton's wife."

"Pleased to meet you. I'm Ethan Howard."

"Sergeant Howard!" She clapped her hands together.

"Have we met?"

"No, no. Cora Mae was so concerned when you were laid low with the fever recently. She'd have been so pleased to see you up." A shadow passed over her face.

Perhaps it was merely a reflection of his own. "Well, you can tell her not to worry next time you see her."

Her expression drooped. "I'm afraid I can't."

Ethan grabbed the bucket's handle as soon as he could reach it. "What do you mean?"

"She was sent north, dear. Cora Mae and little June both. Yesterday." She lifted the pail, and with awkward compensation for his missing hand, he poured the water into it. "They're headed to Louisville now."

The news shouldn't have mattered to him at all. She was engaged. He was an amputee and on the opposite side of the war. Yet her absence carved away at him. He dropped his gaze to hide the emotion churning behind his eyes, and spied a clump of violets. Most of the ground around here was dry as dust, but stray water from the well must have been enough for them to grow. He frowned at the flowers, a memory struggling to surface. Bending, he picked one and brought it to his nose.

The smell carried comfort along with sweetness, but he had no idea why.

"June's favorite flower." Mrs. Littleton smiled. "Cora Mae wore a fresh bunch every day she nursed."

Ethan inhaled the fragrance again. This time, her voice came with it. Calling his name, urging him to drink. He could almost feel her touch.

That had been real. But Cora Mae herself was a vanishing dream.

Angry that he was so drawn to a woman he couldn't have, he nodded to Mrs. Littleton, hoisted the pail, and returned to Joseph Buford in the church.

"Sit up, will you?" Ethan walked between the pews and stood over Joseph. "I'm not putting this dipper to your lips for you. Couldn't if I wanted to."

Joseph sat up on his plank. "I see that. It's hard knocks, eh, Howard? I went home in June on furlough as a bonus for re-enlisting. I should have stayed home like Daisy wanted. This is what I get for signing up again without first talking it over with the missus, I suppose."

Ethan winced at the wretched timing. "Kids?" He lowered the pail into Joseph's lap.

"Not yet. We were only married a few months before the war started." Joseph took the dipper and drank. "But ask me again after all this fighting is over. I aim to raise a houseful. Much obliged for the water." Sighing, he lay back down.

"Bring it here!" a voice called to Ethan's right. "Please! Water!"

"I want some, too!" From his left.

All over the sanctuary, men beckoned. So Ethan went to them and helped them quench their thirst.

When the pail was empty, he returned to the well, far more fatigued than he cared to admit, even to himself. He leaned on the moss-furred edge and pulled in a breath that triggered coughing.

A dog barked.

Ethan turned toward the sound and knelt in time for Little Feller to bound into his arms. The coonhound licked Ethan's cheek and wagged his tail so hard his entire body shook.

"I missed you, too." Laughing, Ethan scruffed behind his ears, noting that the wounds on his hide had healed. The eye, however, was gone. Some kind surgeon had taken the time to stitch it closed.

Worn out from his round inside the church, Ethan sat with his back leaning against the sharp stone edges of the well. He coughed into his elbow and wondered fleetingly that he hadn't been coughing more.

The dog plopped his head on his lap, and he stroked the hound's fur. "Well, Feller. Now what?"

"Now you rest a spell with an old man who could use some company. Bring your friend." Chaplain Littleton strolled up and held out a hand, helping him up. "But cover up first. I'm blushing." He tossed Ethan a clean shirt.

Ethan slipped the loose-fitting garment over his head, threaded his arms through the sleeves, and then followed the chaplain to crates of soap, socks, and mosquito nets sent by the Sanitary Commission, waiting to be distributed. The dog sat on the ground and nuzzled his wet nose beneath Ethan's palm. They faced the town square, covered with mud-splattered canvas tents. From the depot one and a half blocks away, a train chugged into motion on its way back to Chattanooga.

"I've got something for you, son." The chaplain pulled from his haversack a round, greenish-gray metal bottle that tapered into a narrow neck.

"That's quite a flask. You thirsty, too?"

Chaplain Littleton laughed. "Actually, yes. But for something far more satisfying." He popped off the cork and turned the bottle upside down until a small scroll slid out. Setting the bottle aside, he pulled a loop of twine off one end of the scroll, and a small booklet unfurled in his brown-spotted hands. THE SOLDIER'S PRAYER AND HYMN BOOK was printed in block type on its cover. The chaplain flipped it open and began to read. "'My soul thirsteth for God, for the living God. . . . My tears have been my meat day and night, while they continually say unto me, Where is thy God?'" He closed the booklet and looked Ethan in the eyes. "Put thy trust in God."

"The forty-second psalm."

Seams creased Chaplain Littleton's face as he smiled. "You know it."

"I believe in God. I'm a sheep in His fold." A hot breeze waved the empty end of Ethan's sleeve. Feller turned in a circle and rested at his feet, chin on his paws. "But right now, my soul is thirsty, and somehow I can't seem to get a drink. I don't expect you to understand."

"Really?" The older man pulled up the hem of his trousers, exposing a wooden leg.

Ethan's eyebrow lifted, and the chaplain let the faded cloth fall back into place.

"I wasn't always a chaplain, you know. I was a soldier once, like yourself."

"Mexican War?"

"Right. That was nearly twenty years ago. During one battle, a friend of mine was hurt badly. He had this bottle on him, with letters for his wife inside. Right there on the field, he handed this to me, and before he died, I promised him I'd deliver the letters to his wife. Tucked this bottle into my uniform jacket and kept fighting. It wasn't long till I was hit, too."

"In your leg."

"And lost it. But I kept my promise to my friend."

"You delivered the letters to his widow?"

"Yes." The chaplain grinned. "And then I married her."

"You did?" Ethan laughed in surprise. "Mrs. Littleton was your friend's widow?"

He nodded.

Ethan pointed to a crunched dent near the bottom of the bottle. "What happened there?"

"I don't know. Not sure my friend did, either, but look at this." He pointed to the letters carved into its neck. "*Spero*. It's a Latin word. It means 'hope.'"

"Hope," Ethan repeated. "Well, I sure could use a dose of that."

"Who can do without it?" The chaplain rolled up the prayer book and slid the twine over it before slipping it back into the bottle. "*Hope* is on the inside. Even if the vessel is battered and scarred. Hope can live within." He turned the bottle over, smiling. "This bottle has served me well. It's high time it brings hope to someone else." He passed it to Ethan. "Be ever hopeful, son."

Ethan searched Chaplain Littleton's eyes. "You would give this to me?"

"I just did."

"Thank you." The words seemed so inadequate.

When the chaplain stood, Ethan remained on the bench, pondering the gift in his hand. *Lord, fill me with hope. Satisfy me with Your living water. Help me trust You for Cora Mae's care and focus on what You would have me do right here. Use this vessel for Your work.*

Chapter Fifteen

CANNELTON, INDIANA
TUESDAY, AUGUST 2, 1864

"This is it!" Cora Mae told June, who was leaning over the railing watching the steamboat paddle white ruffles into the river.

The last two days on the steamboat had been a welcome change after five days of train travel. They'd retraced Sherman's path up through northern Georgia, where lone chimneys stood mourning the ruins of their homes. Chattanooga was entirely surrounded by Union tents camped upon mountain slopes. Nashville, too, crawled with Yankees. Louisville had been as sooty and crowded as she'd imagined a dumping ground for exiled Southerners would be. It had seemed to Cora Mae that the entire world had turned Union blue, when a month ago, her life had been wrapped in Confederate gray.

"Ready to set foot in the North?" She poured all the calm into her voice she could find. *Please, God, let me find work.*

The steamboat docked. Slinging her satchel over her shoulder, she walked with June down a wooden plank and onto the north side of the Ohio River. People and horses and wagons flowed past her in such a great hurry, she felt like a sapling at the edge of a stream. The women's gowns swayed like bells around their footsteps, a marked contrast to the hoopless calico dresses Cora Mae and June wore.

"Now what?" June kicked at a rock in the road.

Wind pressed Cora Mae's bonnet to her cheek as she scanned the river. "There. Do you see it?" The four-story building with two pointed towers loomed large, even from this distance.

"It's a mill!" June cried. "Just like Sergeant Howard said! How did he know?"

"He didn't say this was his hometown, but I wouldn't be surprised if it is." Otherwise how would he know about the giant fans that kept the lint from settling in the workers' lungs?

It didn't take long to walk there. As they neared it, the familiar clanging and thudding sounds grew louder. The building was made of gray stone, not the red brick of Roswell's mills, but the windows looked larger and cleaner. As they reached the front gate, a bell rang from one of the steeples, and the thwacking inside grew silent.

"Quitting time, I reckon." Summoning confidence, Cora Mae tucked loose strands of hair inside her bonnet and fished Dr. Wilcox's letter from her satchel. Girls in crisp blue muslin dresses with white collars and aprons streamed out the front doors. Mostly their words twanged in the Northern way, but some of them talked more like Dooley, and a few spoke a language Cora Mae had never before heard. Then came a man wearing a dark suit and bowler hat.

"Here we go. Best behavior now, June." Cora Mae felt more like her mother with each passing day and sounded like it, too. Drawing herself up as straight as a spindle, she marched toward the man in his Sunday best and stopped him on the sidewalk.

"Excuse me, sir. You work at the mill?"

"Yes, I do." A neatly trimmed black beard and mustache shadowed his pockmarked face.

"Who would we talk to about employment?"

"You're talking to him. But we're not hiring." He tipped his bowler hat to her. "Good day."

Dismay cut through her. "I have a letter from a Union surgeon." She thrust it out, awkward and uncomfortable in her desperation. Swallowing, she tried again. "My name is Cora Mae Stewart, and this here is June. I've worked at a cotton mill for ten years, and I truly would appreciate a job at yours."

Perhaps it was only curiosity that made him reach for the letter. But as he read it, the hard angles in his face seemed to soften. "What sort of work do you do?"

"I'm a drawing girl."

The faint smell of burning coal stuck to the wind, hinting at the massive mill's source of power. A few more young women whisked out of the building, bright spots of blue and white against the limestone.

Returning the letter to her, he crossed his arms. "It's a real shame what happened to you and the other mill workers in Georgia. But I'm afraid we have more workers than work as it is. Our cotton supply is drying up. As you can imagine."

Cora Mae's stomach dropped. Horses clopped and buggies trundled by. "This is all I know, sir. I don't mean to tell you how to run your fine factory, but I surely would appreciate the chance to work for you."

His mustache twitched. "I'm sorry to disappoint you. There's simply nothing I can do." He tipped his hat to her and sauntered away, leaving her hopes on the ground behind him.

"What are we going to do now?" June's small voice lifted.

Cora Mae knelt on the sidewalk and wrapped her arms around the little girl. She was tired of placing her survival in the hands of other people. "We're going to make our own way. Just because the factory isn't hiring doesn't mean we're giving up on this town yet."

With sore feet and fraying nerves, Cora Mae stopped in front of a shop window displaying two dresses and matching bolts of fabric on a small table between them. A painted wooden sign spelled: *Aldridge Dressmakers, Fabric and Fine Notions*. A fresh wind whispered through her. She'd already tried three hotels and two restaurants, asking after work of any kind. She'd scrub dishes if they'd let her, and all other manner of labor, but no one seemed to be hiring. Leastways, they weren't hiring a travel-worn woman with a southern accent and child in tow.

All she needed was one *yes*. Just one. And so, after checking her reflection and retying her bonnet, and then June's, she entered.

Bells tinkled overhead, and from some unseen corner, a voice called, "Be right with you!"

A good sign. A shop with enough business to make customers wait was a shop that could use more help. Or so she prayed.

Ladies drifted through the displays, their voices twanging like plucked banjo strings, their skin so smooth, so pale. A woman with a passel of daughters must have been nearly as old as Mama, but she looked decades younger. They spoke of colors, fabrics, and styles as though they could afford to be choosy. Judging by the gowns they wore, with skirts wide enough to make two dresses for June in each, they were.

Though no longer wearing homespun, Cora Mae's skin pricked as though the stiff, dull fibers scratched her neck. She thought of Mama and her persimmon seed buttons and of dyeing their own mourning clothes. Choice was not something they'd had much of lately, in dress or anything else. Except, of course, the choice to be bitter, or not.

Fifteen minutes passed while the shopkeepers minded the other customers. Cora Mae used all of them to pray.

When at last Mr. Aldridge approached and asked how he could help, she said, "As a matter of fact, I was hoping I could help you." Extending her letter of reference, she explained who she was and what she could do.

The man took his time reading over the letter. "You could cut fabric from a pattern, couldn't you? Hem cuffs, sew buttons, all of that?"

"Yes, sir."

He scratched at hickory-brown side whiskers that bristled thick and wide, clear down to his jaw. The last rays of the day slanted through the windows, and shadows crept higher up the walls. "And who's this little mite with you?" Bending, he smiled at June.

She stuck out her hand. "My name's June. Pleased to meet you."

"My, what fine manners you have, even at the end of such a long journey." Still smiling, he straightened and angled toward the counter where a woman wrote in a ledger. Her blonde hair, swept into a graceful roll behind her head, faded to ash gray at her temples. "Sarah, dear, come over and meet these people," he called.

The woman carried herself as though ready to fight or defend. She stood as tall as the man, her shoulders almost as square.

June took a half-step behind Cora Mae while Mr. Aldridge made introductions and explained what he'd learned about their plight.

"You need the help," he said, "and they need the work."

"I'm getting on fine," Mrs. Aldridge countered.

"Sarah." The word held a rebuke so subtle Cora Mae almost missed it.

With pursed lips, Mrs. Aldridge at last thrust a sharp glance her way. "I don't need *her* help. She's one of them, Jeremiah. You ought to know better."

"She took an oath to the United States, and so did the little one. Miss Stewart's help will be a blessing to you, and we can be a blessing to her. See here what the doctor says about her. Why, it might have been our own son she nursed down south. Mrs. Beasley was in here yesterday with a letter from her grandson, who said their regiment has been camped at Marietta." He focused on Cora Mae. "Our boy was never good about writing home, so we get our news of his whereabouts where we can."

Cora Mae lowered her lashes, as much to give the couple a shred of privacy as to avoid being singed by the heat in Mrs. Aldridge's gaze. The moment pulled thin and tight. But she stood her ground, all the same.

At last, Mrs. Aldridge spoke. "Do you know anything of Zeke Aldridge? Ezekiel Aldridge, 72nd Indiana regiment? Maybe he isn't writing because he—can't."

"I don't know that name," Cora Mae replied. But she did know the regiment. This was Ethan's hometown, sure enough. "Could be he never had need of any nursing or doctoring." Or it could simply be that someone else had seen to his care.

Mr. Aldridge lifted his chin. "Very likely. Sarah, Miss Stewart was forced from her home, tended the wounds of boys in blue, and now she's here, in need of some of the same kindness she's shown to others."

"If you please, sir," Cora Mae said, "I'm not after charity. I'm only asking for a chance to work. Any wages, I intend to earn fair and honest. Try my work for a time and see if it suits. If not, I'll be on my way."

"A trial basis," Mr. Aldridge said. "Well, there's no risk in that. You're hired."

A somber relief threaded through her, bridled by Mrs. Aldridge's pinched brows. The stately woman would be beautiful if she weren't cinched so. The war did that, Cora Mae supposed. War clutched at women both North and South, until the waiting and the fear—or the loss—twisted the beauty right out of them.

"Do you have lodging already?" Mr. Aldridge asked her.

"We've only arrived today. I'll see to that next."

"We have a room upstairs."

"Jeremiah!"

Without acknowledging his wife's protest, he went on. "It's not being used. You're welcome to it."

"Then that's their wages, Jeremiah. At least until the trial period is over."

At this, Mr. Aldridge faced his wife. "All right. But only if we give them board as well. They won't be able to buy food without cash."

With a flounce, she turned and left.

"Will it suit, for now?" he asked Cora Mae. "Room and board for your work?"

"It'll suit us fine," she told him. "Thank you."

That night, with their bellies full of biscuits, cold chicken, and beans, Cora Mae and June readied for bed in the room of a Union soldier who was off fighting Johnny Rebs. She wondered if the young man would share his mother's feelings about this arrangement or if he had the same compassion shown by his father. A month ago, she would have doubted that of a soldier. But a month ago, she hadn't yet met Ethan Howard.

June faced the window while Cora Mae brushed and braided her hair. "I wish we could tell Sergeant Howard how things worked out for us here," the little girl said. "Not like he thought, but still."

"Maybe we can. Maybe we can tell Mama, too." If mail could pass between Mrs. Beasley and her grandson, surely Cora Mae could send something, too, so long as it was addressed to someone in the Union army.

It had been eight days since she'd left Ethan. Was that time enough to heal from the fever that had made him insensible? Or had he only gotten worse? She'd seen fevers take other men to the grave.

An emptiness pressed her ribs. *Please, God, let him live.* But for every soldier in blue or gray who had died, women had prayed that very thing. She'd not pretend to understand why some were answered and some weren't. All she knew was that the notion of Ethan dying left her more bereft than she had any right to feel.

"Are we real Yankees now?" June whispered.

Cora Mae tied a scrap of calico around the end of the braid. "You and I are the same people as we ever were."

But she wasn't. The war had changed her. It had changed everything.

MARIETTA, GEORGIA
MONDAY, AUGUST 8, 1864

Atlanta was under siege. Less than twenty miles from Marietta, the Union army shelled a city second only to Richmond in its importance to the Confederacy.

And Ethan Howard was here, on the army's payroll as a convalescent nurse attached to the Methodist Church, while able-bodied soldiers were attacking the Gateway to the South and being fired upon in return. Ethan was safe while untold numbers of civilians in Atlanta were no doubt huddling in fireplaces or dugout shelters, praying to see another day.

Ethan hadn't joined the army to be safe while others weren't. He'd aimed to make a difference with his life, or at least with his death, and he'd done neither. Zeke Aldridge had stolen his capacity for that purpose the second he pulled the trigger and shattered Ethan's arm.

Little Feller nudged Ethan's leg, earning a pat on the head and a small bit of salt pork from his pocket.

The one-eyed coonhound grinned and winked. It had occurred to Ethan that they shared Zeke's abuse in common. Only the dog had seemed to forget it.

Deep inside Ethan, bitterness festered. Aldridge and Weston had both been brought up on court-martial and found guilty, which meant six months without pay. There was no way they'd be sent home early, though. Sherman was desperate for men. In the next two months, three-year enlistment terms for entire battalions would expire. Even now, regiments fulfilled their terms and left for home on a daily basis.

Not Ethan. He might not be able to fight, but at least he could bring water to the sick and wounded who sorely needed it and keep their bandages wet between dressing changes. Other amputees and convalescents were doing the same. The constant reminders that others fared worse than he did kept Ethan's attitude in check. And the water he carried brought to mind the Living Water, the source of life Ethan prayed to for strength beyond his own.

Sunshine pounded his neck as he drew water from the well outside the church. The ground was dry and barren where violets had bloomed earlier this summer. It had been weeks since he'd seen any, but he didn't need to in order to think of the woman who'd worn them on her collar or of the little girl she mothered. But dwelling on Cora Mae and June brought no comfort. He could only worry for them and then be angry that he cared.

A shadow crept over Ethan, along with the rustle of skirts and petticoats. He looked up and found a woman he'd never seen before, likely looking for her loved one. Then he noticed the starched black dress beneath an apron trimmed in black. A matching snood blended in with her raven hair. She had to be baking in all those dark layers.

He poured water from the well bucket into the pail and stood back. "May I help you, ma'am?"

"I'm—actually, I was hoping I might be of some help to the men, myself. Mrs. Littleton said I'd be welcome here, even if all I do is bring them water or wash their faces."

He had heard that musical drawl before. He studied her heart-shaped face, long lashes bordering sunken blue eyes. She did not look strong. "This is a rough place for a lady. You're sure you want to volunteer?

"Nothing too involved, as I have no training. But I can manage small tasks. Please, I beg you. Anne said it would be all right." She twisted thin hands together. "Oh, pardon me. My name is Mrs. Daisy Buford. My husband died here, you see."

Ethan's stomach twisted. Joseph Buford was the first patient Ethan had brought water to before becoming an official nurse. But his amputation had turned gangrenous, and he perished not long after. Anne Littleton had written to his widow.

Setting the pail of water on the ground, Ethan straightened and reached out his left hand. She grasped it, and he introduced himself. "I knew him," he added. "When I woke up after a fever, he was right there beside me. He told me how much he loved you."

She rotated the gold band on her finger. The skin there had been rubbed raw. "Did he? We argued on our last visit together. I came to see where he was laid to rest and where he spent his last days. And now that I'm here, I find I'm not ready to leave. I must do something—anything—to be helpful. I don't know whether I'm coming or going half the time, you see. It would be a mercy if I could be of service here. If I could do for others what I ought to have done for Joseph."

Ethan rubbed his jaw, wrestling with the grief this vulnerable woman embodied. So far he'd avoided penning letters home to patients' loved ones and counted himself lucky for it. He hadn't relished the idea of sending a family bad news. Now he couldn't turn away from the sorrow he hadn't wanted to confront.

"Mrs. Buford, I can tell you Joseph didn't blame you for not being here at the end. God knows he wouldn't have wanted you in this place. He went so quickly, you couldn't have been expected to arrive in time."

"But I'm here now. Have you got another pail and dipper? I can bring a cup of cold water, if nothing else."

He hesitated. Cora Mae had done this and more, but this widow did not seem as sturdy. Then again, if Mrs. Littleton had already approved it, maybe she thought it would help Mrs. Buford, as it had played a role in healing him. He passed the pail to her. "They'll be grateful, ma'am." If she could help with the water, he'd take care of the bedpans himself.

She wiped her palms on her apron. "I'm obliged. Do I just go in and start anywhere?"

Ethan explained his own method as he walked with her up the front steps and through the front doors. "I'll be in and out," he told her, "so holler if you need anything. All right?"

She didn't look all right. It would be a shock to anyone, entering a church that smelled and sounded the way this one did, with broken men stretched atop the pews. Her complexion turned sickly. Clamping a hand over her mouth, she thrust the pail back at Ethan and ran outside, where she retched behind some bushes.

Poor woman. Ethan's conscience teetered between checking on her and fulfilling his duties to the men in his care. Fighting back a sigh, he decided the bedpans could wait while he showed a kindness to Joseph's widow.

Straightening, Mrs. Buford wiped her mouth with a handkerchief as he approached. He extended the pail of water, wondering if she'd mind sharing a dipper with all the men inside. Instead, she produced a tin cup of her own, dipped it in the pail, and drank.

"Thank you," she said. "I can do better."

Ethan blinked, taking in her delicate profile. "I'm not here to rebuke you, ma'am. That's a hard place in there, to be sure. I understand the need to be helpful, but there are other ways."

"If I wanted to knit socks and roll bandages, I'd have stayed home and done it there. No, Mr. Howard, I'm doing this. Now, if you'll excuse me, I have work to do." She took the pail and dipper, squared her shoulders, and marched right back inside.

He had to admire her spirit.

Chapter Sixteen

CANNELTON, INDIANA
SUNDAY, AUGUST 14, 1864

In the pre-dawn darkness, Cora Mae recognized that smell.

Jolting fully awake, she lit a candle, then crawled out of bed to kneel by the pallet where June slept on the floor. The child had wet herself. Again. This made the fifth time in the twelve days they'd been in Cannelton. Cora Mae had never known this to happen in Roswell.

Something was wrong.

The building shuddered, and Cora Mae waited while footsteps that could only belong to Mr. Aldridge trudged up the stairs and down the corridor. Down the hall, the Aldridges' bedroom door opened and closed with a quiet click. She didn't know what took him or kept him away at odd hours, and she didn't need to. She had more important things to mind.

"June, wake up. Are you sick?" She felt the girl's forehead and cheeks but found no fever there.

June sat up and groaned, but she didn't look ill. In most ways, she looked better than she had a month ago. Living with the Aldridges had been stressful at times, but the food was good, and there was plenty of it. The fact that they took meals in the kitchen with the cook suited better than dining with Mr. and Mrs. Aldridge, anyway.

But then there was this, and Cora Mae didn't know how to explain it.

"Wait, what is—not again!" Horror splayed across June's face as she realized what she'd done. "Oh no. I'm awful sorry, Mama, I'm so sorry. I don't know why I did that. I didn't mean to make a mess, honest. Are you vexed?" Her chin trembled, and tears spilled down her cheeks.

"Shh, it's all right. I'm not vexed." Cora Mae smoothed June's hair away from her face. "I know you didn't mean to. It was an accident. But let's get you cleaned up. That sun is going to peek in here any minute, and then it'll almost be time for breakfast."

June stripped off her nightgown and rolled up the bedding, which Cora Mae would clean soon. The first time this had happened, Mrs. Aldridge had found her washing the linens and declared that since Cora Mae had so much free time, she could take on the weekly laundering and save the Aldridges the cost of hiring it out. It was Mr. Aldridge who'd insisted she at least be paid in cash for the extra work. But the wage was precious little when held against the cost of train tickets home.

After a sponge bath, June put on fresh clothes and opened the window to air out the room.

"Has this ever happened before, honey?" Cora Mae asked. "I mean, before we came to Indiana."

June hugged Sassy and bit her lip. "That night after I saw—the night before we were put on that train."

That was the night after June had gone looking among the hospital tents and had found Cora Mae wearing an apron marked by patients' blood. The child had seen that pile of amputated limbs, the very thing she'd meant to keep her from.

"I had an accident," June went on, "but when I woke up, you were already gone nursing. I didn't want to tell you about it, and besides, when I saw you next, you were with that Yankee who said we had to hurry on to the train station anyway."

"I'm so sorry you saw what you did," Cora Mae said. "And I'm sorry if I ever made you feel like I'd fuss over an accident you couldn't help."

June sent her a sidelong glance. "I know that now. But I got in real big trouble before."

"What do you mean? Before you came to live with me?"

A sigh lifted the child's thin shoulders. Even though she'd been eating more and gaining weight, she remained smaller than other girls her age. Especially here in the north.

"Was it Mr. Ferguson who got vexed with you?" Cora Mae guessed.

June brushed a loose thread from her doll. "No. It was my ma. My first one. She paddled my backside good, said I was trying to punish her by making such messes when I knew she was already overburdened."

A gasp escaped Cora Mae. "Why would she think—I mean, what was she overburdened with? Was this when your pa died?" She remembered that news. He'd gone off to find work outside of Roswell, Mavis had said. But he drowned in a river crossing months later.

"No. She was burdened before he died. It was his leaving that riled her. My ma didn't tell me why or where he went. I heard them quarreling one night when I should have been abed. He left and slammed the door so hard the plates rattled on the shelf. But when I asked her what happened, she wouldn't say. She only said he was dead to us now, we'd not be hearing from him again. We were on our own. She didn't ever say his name again, nor abide my saying it neither."

Mavis had told the truth when she'd told neighbors her husband had gone to find work elsewhere. What she hadn't said—not that Cora Mae blamed her—was that he'd abandoned her and their daughter, with no intention of sending wages home.

Cora Mae pulled June onto her lap and pressed kisses into her hair. "I'm sorry, darlin.' That's a heavy burden indeed, for both of you."

"She was so cross with me." June sniffed. "She said I was much too big a girl to be making those messes, that I was doing it to get back at her, and that it was ten times worse than sass. She said I blamed her for pa leaving us, but I never said a word about it. I wouldn't dare backtalk. My backside was too sore already." She hugged her doll.

Folks weren't supposed to talk ill of the departed, but Cora Mae couldn't stay silent on this. "Your ma was hurting, that much is plain. But she ought not to have said or done what she did to you. You didn't deserve that, not one little bit." June had been six years old when her pa disappeared. Six.

This child had seen too much.

"I got better after a spell," June said, "and so did she. She did say her sorrys for what she done, and I hugged her real good so she knew how much I forgave her."

Cora Mae could not imagine the strain Mavis had been under. Or the guilt she must have felt upon realizing the fault in her reaction to June. "Was that the last time this happened, before it started again in Marietta?"

A breeze swept through the room, blowing out the candle. But dawn raised its head and chased the dark to the corners.

"Well, it happened after my ma died, too, just a few times, but I cleaned everything up myself. I don't think Mr. Ferguson noticed the laundry on the line. Tell you the truth, he didn't take much notice of me in general, except to get me a job at the mill soon after Ma died. He's not like Sergeant Howard. The sergeant even noticed Sassy more than once. When he brought us blackberries, he picked off one of those bitty little sections and said it was just for her."

"Did he?" Cora Mae imagined him doing that and smiled past the ache it brought. "Well, I notice you plenty. I notice how your hair shines like copper in the sun and your cheeks look like apples when you smile. I see you've grown so much that I'll need to let your hem out in your dress, but your heart is bigger, still. I'm proud you've not let it grow hard. I love you with all my strength."

June looped her arms around Cora Mae's neck and kissed her cheek. "Thank you, Mama. I love you, too. Now let me help with the wash."

~

From the kitchen, Cora Mae brought kettles of hot water to the backyard and poured them into the washtub while June added flakes of soap. Dawn's silver light gave way to a bashful pink that crept across the sky. The early morning air was heavy and cool, and dew beaded a spider web strung between stalks of milkweed.

With a broom handle, Cora Mae plunged the first soiled blanket into the tub.

The kitchen door opened. Mrs. Aldridge emerged, her blonde hair perfectly pinned above a collar starched whiter than goose down. Her nose wrinkled.

Cora Mae moved the rest of the bedding to the tub, but the ammonia smell told the story. She prayed her employer would not shame the child for it.

"We were fixin' to get this here laundry done before breakfast," June offered. "And then get ready for church."

Mrs. Aldridge turned to June but said nothing, so that the only sound in the yard was that of water sloshing, and birds chattering, and the cook inside closing cupboards. The chorus of homey sounds could make a body feel cheerful.

Then she spoke. "'Fixin' to.' 'This here.' Have you yet to hear Mr. Aldridge or me speak this way?"

June frowned. "No, ma'am."

"Every time you open your mouth, you mark yourself a Southerner. Is that what you want?"

Cora Mae pressed a fist to her aproned hip. "Want or not, we two *are* Southerners."

"Believe me, that could not be more clear. If you're ever going to fit in here, you would do well to amend your speech."

"Begging your pardon, ma'am, but I don't reckon we need to fit in here," June said, "so long as we follow the rules you set out for us as your guests. Isn't that so? This isn't where we're from. It's not home."

"But this is where you live, at least for now. If it's only rules you listen to, and not friendly advice, here's a new one for you: do not speak southern under my roof."

June's gaze darted to the ripening sky, and Cora Mae prayed she'd show sense enough not to point out that they currently were not under anyone's roof at all.

"It's an embarrassment to have my customers hear you," Mrs. Aldridge said, "and it casts doubt on my own loyalties. And me with a son in the army."

It would do no good to remind her that Cora Mae and June had signed oaths of allegiance to the United States of America, so Cora Mae held her tongue and focused on the wash instead.

Mrs. Aldridge moved closer to the tub, pointing at the swirling suds. In a low voice, she said, "Don't think I don't realize what's going on here. Those are ruined. That means you bought them, as they'll never be usable for anyone else again."

Cora Mae couldn't say that was unfair. As much as she scrubbed, the stains remained. "How much do I owe you for these, then?"

The sum named seemed princely indeed. "That's for the sheets, the blankets and pillow, the laundry soap, and the coal required to heat the water for washing." Mrs. Aldridge stepped back, as if even now the smell offended. "I know you don't have the money. I'll simply stop the wages I've been paying you for laundering until you've earned that much."

"Ain't you earning money in the shop, Mama?" June asked.

"Don't say ain't," Mrs. Aldridge corrected. "What your mother earns in the shop covers room and board for both of you. And you ought to be grateful for that."

"I am," Cora Mae told her. "We both are."

That ought to have been the end of the matter. Instead, Mrs. Aldridge narrowed her eyes. "Mr. Aldridge and I have noticed that you're awfully young to have a daughter this age. You must have been *quite* young when you had her. Barely old enough to marry, I'd say. Curiously, I've not heard one mention of her father. Or perhaps, that's not such a wonder after all."

Heat flashed through Cora Mae. Mrs. Aldridge might as well have come right out and called her a hussy. It would be easy enough to explain the matter, but not for all the kingdoms of this world would Cora Mae say that June was not her daughter. Not with June looking on as though her greatest secret was about to be revealed. She would not deny June as her child. Besides which, she doubted her explanation would be credited, anyway.

Dropping the sheet back into the tub, Cora Mae wiped her hands on her apron and draped her arm around June. "And ain't I the lucky one, to have a daughter so fine as this?"

"Mama!" June whispered. "You said ain't."

"I know exactly what I said." She grinned, and June giggled, and the ground felt more solid beneath her feet.

Chapter Seventeen

MARIETTA, GEORGIA
MONDAY, AUGUST 15, 1864

On his way out of the church, Ethan saw Joseph's widow bend to give another patient a drink. Mrs. Buford had worked here a few times since the day he'd met her at the well, but she had run out of the church two of those times. The other time, he hadn't seen her leave. To her credit, she kept coming back.

Little Feller wagged his tail as soon as Ethan stepped outside. Bounding from his dusty patch beneath a tree, he hustled to lick Ethan's hand.

"Sergeant Howard?" Chaplain Littleton beckoned Ethan into the shade of the church, near a knot of freed women bent over washtubs. They eyed Little Feller, but the coonhound stayed at Ethan's heels.

"I reckon Mrs. Littleton has taken Mrs. Buford under her wing?" Ethan mopped his brow and neck before tucking his handkerchief back in his trouser pocket.

"Oh yes. My wife has always been a mother hen, collecting as many chicks as she can, even though she is forever letting them go as they fly away. But we've just heard from one of them." Lines webbed from Chaplain Littleton's face as he smiled. He showed him an envelope postmarked from Cannelton, Indiana. "Miss Stewart has written me a note, asking how you fare. She is well, by the way, and so is June."

Relief and gratitude formed a knob in Ethan's throat. Looking away, he blinked the heat from his eyes before revealing how the news affected him.

"She has also enclosed a letter she would like me to take to her mother in Roswell. That's half a day's journey from here, one way. I'm afraid I can't spare a full day away from these men. I understand Lt. Dooley paid a visit to Mrs. Stewart once, but those were different circumstances. Dooley is miles away, closer to where the siege is playing out, and he can't be spared from the forge."

"I'll do it," Ethan said, and only then realized the task would require getting on a horse for the first time since his amputation. And it wouldn't be Reckless, since he was needed for the mounted infantry. Ethan had yet to ride one-handed, but he'd have to figure out how to manage sometime. It might as well be in service to Cora Mae and her mother.

"I'd appreciate that." Chaplain Littleton gave him the envelope. "When is the next time you're off duty?"

"Technically? Right now. I just had no reason to do anything else."

Until now.

After entrusting the dog to the chaplain's care, Ethan obtained leave from the site commander, then bought provisions from the sutler. Thus supplied, he headed to the southwest corner of the town square to rent a horse from a man named Sullivan.

The smells of hay, leather, and horseflesh permeated the stable. Horses whisked their tails at black flies. After coughing from the dust in the air, Ethan paid for the use of a horse, plus all its tack and feed for the rest of the day.

Sullivan saddled the horse, performing with ease simple tasks that seemed utterly beyond Ethan's capability.

Once again, he felt the painful phantom presence of his right hand and in his mind flexed the fingers and wrist that weren't there. Maybe someday he'd be able to blanket and saddle for himself again, but for bridling, he'd always need help.

All of this had occurred to him before today. But standing in front of a horse he couldn't make ready himself burrowed the sting deeper.

"This is Star," Sullivan told him, patting the white blaze on her otherwise black head. "She's older, but she's got a soft mouth. She'll do as you lead. Ready, soldier?"

Sweat slicked Ethan's skin. He coughed again. If he had both hands, he'd put foot to stirrup, grab hold of the pommel and mane, and hoist himself up without hesitation. But with only one hand, he envisioned an awkward, fumbling attempt that might land him on his back.

"Here." Sullivan set a wooden crate on the ground between Ethan and Star. A mounting block. "I know you don't use mounting blocks on campaign, but I do recommend using one when available. It reduces strain on the horse, and these horses are our greatest allies." He left unsaid that it would also reduce strain on Ethan.

Grateful for the man's consideration of his pride, Ethan climbed the block, put his boot in the stirrup, gripped the pommel, and poured his concentration into a graceless mount. Embarrassment battled exhilaration.

Sullivan smiled and stuck a piece of hay in his mouth to chew. "See there? She hardly noticed."

Chuckling, Ethan gathered the reins into one hand and worked them into a manageable position. "I'll be sure to keep her comfort in mind."

"You're all set." Sullivan stepped back, and Star responded to Ethan's walking her out of the stable.

It was a victory. The next time would be easier. And even the plodding pace of the aging mare was still movement. It was progress toward a destination, and that was something he'd not felt since the amputation. The place where his skin closed over bone still burned, but as he put Marietta behind him, the trapped feeling loosened one knot at a time. He inhaled the clean air without coughing. The relief was measurable.

Thirteen miles, one creek crossing, and four hours later, he arrived at the mill workers' village in Roswell. Aside from a handful of elderly folks he saw on a few cottage porches, the entire town was abandoned—of civilians and the army, both. Concern for Mrs. Stewart gripped him. If she was gone, what would he tell her daughter?

Weeds reclaimed gardens and choked paths. On Sloane Street, he found the brick apartment Cora Mae had specified in her note to Chaplain Littleton. No one saw his awkward dismount onto the front porch steps. After picketing Star by the nearby creek to drink, he circled back to the apartment and knocked. The door nudged open, creaking on the hinges. Calling out his presence, he entered.

The smell was of a place unlived in. It was empty except for some furniture. A table and chairs downstairs, beds and a rocking chair in the rooms on the second level. Bed linens had been taken away, but curtains remained on windows that looked over the creek where Star drank. The mid-afternoon light tinted the plain wood floors and white walls yellow.

Ethan could picture Cora Mae here. He imagined her breaking cornbread at the table, kneeling at the bedside with June for evening prayers. He could see her wrapping a shawl around her mother's shoulders as she sat in a rocker by the window. But the watercolor images in his mind quickly faded.

Above the bed, a note fluttered where it was pinned to the wall. *Cora Mae*, it read, *I've settled your mother with the widow Shannon McGee. I'm taking my family south. God bless you.* It was signed *Reverend Pratt* and included a simply drawn map to a farm north of Roswell.

Ethan exhaled a prayer of thanks and a plea that Mrs. Stewart fared well. Then he noticed a piece of linen poking out from beneath the small mattress on what must have June's bed. Bending, he lifted the mattress and found a doll made of a handkerchief or rag, the way he'd seen Cora Mae fashion for June in Marietta. This was the doll June had left behind.

A smile hooking his lips, Ethan scooped up the lost doll and tucked it into his jacket.

His dark blue, Union army jacket.

If Mrs. Stewart didn't trust him on his approach, he hoped the sight of this doll would tell her he was a friend even before he could explain.

Before he reached the McGee farm, however, Mrs. Stewart's first impression of him was the least of Ethan's concerns. On either side of the road, the grass had been pulverized, the ground churned to mud that had dried holding the shapes of horseshoes. Thousands of them. The trail they left spanned half a mile or wider. They were heading north, and by the condition of the horse droppings along the way, they had passed through here a few days ago.

It didn't take much arithmetic to figure these were the Confederate cavalry that had been set loose to make mischief in Union-held northern Georgia. From what Ethan had heard, some rail lines had been cut, supply wagons attacked. All of it had been north of Marietta. But if they passed through here, that put the McGee farm right in the path of cavalrymen bound to be hungry.

Ethan urged the horse to go faster. Rounding a bend, he rode over hard-packed clay past a few sticks in the ground suggesting a fence. The property was spacious, but no hens scratched at the dirt, and there were no pigs or sheep in sight.

A quarter of a mile later, a two-story clapboard house rose into view. On its porch stood a woman in homespun, training a shotgun on him.

"Whoa." Ethan drew rein, halting the horse. Rather than reach for the doll inside his jacket, he held up both hands—or rather, one hand and an empty sleeve. "My name is Sergeant Ethan Howard, and I bring a letter from Cora Mae Stewart."

The door behind the woman banged open, and a second widow appeared, this one coughing. It had to be Mrs. Stewart. "Shannon!" she gasped. "Don't shoot!"

"Mrs. Stewart? Mrs. McGee? I come alone," he added, "and I mean you no harm. May I approach?"

The gun lowered. Mrs. McGee speared him with a steel-tipped gaze. The hair pulled into a bun was the color of a hazy sunset.

"Did you say you have news of Cora Mae?" Mrs. Stewart asked. White streaked the faded blonde braid crowning her head. "And June?"

"I did. I do."

"Could there be a mention in there of Fern and Cynthia?" Mrs. McGee's voice was so much softer than her demeanor that it almost didn't fit.

Ethan confirmed there was.

"Please come on," Mrs. Stewart said.

After leading the horse to the porch, Ethan dismounted onto the top step. He looped the reins around a porch column and fit a feed bag over the horse's head. "Miss Stewart asked me to deliver her letter to you. I hope you don't mind I went inside your apartment to look for a forwarding direction."

The woman coughed a fair bit, then tapered off. "I'm glad you found it."

"That's not all I found. I thought you'd like to have this." From his pocket he pulled the handkerchief doll. "I believe her name is Sissy. She was hiding under June's mattress. June has a new one very like it now, a sister to this one, she says. She named the new doll Sassy."

Mrs. Stewart covered her mouth as she accepted Sissy from him, and Mrs. McGee wrapped an arm around her shoulders. "Come in, then, seeing as Mrs. Stewart here needs a sit down."

"Much obliged." Ethan grabbed his haversack and followed the widows inside.

"I'm afraid we have no vittles to set out for you." Mrs. Stewart sat at a pine table worn smooth. Ethan joined her.

"We barely have vittles for ourselves." Mrs. McGee huffed as she took a seat, leaving the shotgun leaning against an empty pie safe. On the papered wall behind her hung a portrait of herself and a man Ethan presumed to be her late husband. Her face was sober in the image but not nearly as thin and stern as she had become.

A portrait of two little girls hung beside it. "Your daughters?" he asked.

"My nieces," she corrected. "Fern and Cynthia were the daughters of my heart. Never needed more children than them two, that's sure and certain. Not that I got to see them near enough to please me. It's why I had their picture made."

Ethan tried to reconcile the image of the sweet-faced girls with the versions he had seen. For Mrs. McGee's sake, and for theirs, he wished he brought better news of them.

"I saw an army's worth of hoofprints outside," he said. "They came through here looking for food?"

Mrs. Stewart nodded. "Confederate cavalry, this time. They crossed the Chattahoochee at Roswell."

"Matilda," Mrs. McGee snapped. "It ain't our place to say such. Were it not for this bluebelly promising news of the girls, I'd say it ain't our place to trade words with him at all."

Ethan didn't blame her for the sentiment. "The cavalry left a trail easy to interpret," he said to assure them Mrs. Stewart had spilled no secret. "It wouldn't be Yankee troops heading north."

Mrs. Stewart released a shuddering sigh. "No, it wouldn't. In any case, some stopped here and pumped our water dry, took all the food they could, from cupboards and garden both."

"And you have no male protector about the place?"

His question disappeared in a fist of silence. Black flies darted in and out of the descending heaviness. "Pardon me if I've offended. I meant to ask after Mr. Ferguson. Miss Stewart told me she's betrothed to him, and I thought maybe he'd be around, watching out for you, if he's not been conscripted or taken prisoner." Or worse.

"Male protectors," Mrs. McGee scoffed. "My Matthew passed on before the war, and now the rest of the menfolk are gone, too, stranger. Roswell's sons, brothers, husbands, fathers. Killed in battle or by sickness they never would have gotten if they hadn't had to join up and fight off invaders."

Ethan removed his hat. "You do have my condolences, Mrs. McGee. Mrs. Stewart, I understand you lost both husband and son. And then Sherman's order came, taking your daughter and June, too." He stopped there, at a loss for how to comfort when it was his army that had taken her entire family, her mill, her town. What could he say that would not sound disingenuous?

Mrs. Stewart studied him, but not unkindly. "Not one of us escapes this war without suffering. I see you've had your share, too." Her glance touched the cuff of his sleeve, the space that still caused pain on occasion. How could something hurt that was not there? The doctor couldn't explain it and maybe didn't even believe it. But then Ethan thought of Cora Mae, and he knew that the pain of an absence could be true.

"And that's only what I can see," Mrs. Stewart said. "Have you lost kin, as well?"

"My parents before the war. Then, two brothers at Chickamauga, ma'am. Both younger than me." He cleared his throat of the barbs attached to the mention of Sam and Andrew.

"Oh, Mr. Howard. That's a prime sorrow."

Mrs. McGee rubbed at a stain on the table. "You asked about Mr. Ferguson," she said quietly. "He did send word a month ago that he was safe at that time but wanted to lay low a spell longer with all the Yankees about. We've not had news since."

"Well." Ethan wasn't sure how to respond to a man who hid while women remained defenseless. And this was the one Cora Mae had promised her life to? He reminded himself it wasn't his business. What he did know was that these two widows were hungry. "What I have isn't much, but it's yours."

He pulled from his haversack rations and food he'd bought from the sutler, spreading them on the table. Bread fresh from this morning's camp oven, salted beef, peas, cornmeal, rice, desiccated potatoes that would prove edible after adding water, dry beans, and ground coffee.

Mrs. Stewart's eyes misted. "Real coffee?"

"Yes, ma'am. Please eat, drink. I've had my fill already." He prayed his stomach wouldn't growl and give him away.

With a nod of thanks, or at least acknowledgment, Mrs. McGee broke the bread in two and gave the slightly larger portion to Mrs. Stewart. Then she moved to the stove and lit a small fire within before moving a kettle on top of it.

Ethan laid the letter on the table and asked if they preferred to read it alone. Cora Mae had mentioned that her mother couldn't read, but perhaps Mrs. McGee knew how.

"If you wouldn't mind telling it to me," Mrs. Stewart said. "I'd be so grateful."

"It would be my honor," he told her. He unfolded the letter, and read.

Dear Mama,

First off, June and I are healthy, and we miss you more than we can say. I wish we were there with you now, but I need to make some money first, so I can get train tickets to come back down. We'll get home to you, Mama, don't you worry about that.

I recall what you said about loving our enemies, and leading June in that path. I been trying. Some Yanks are easier to love than others. There was that one—a blacksmith—who fetched you the locks of hair, the food, then fetched word of you back to me. Another soldier helped me find fabric for a new doll for June. He gave me a fine book of verses which I read every night for the beauty of those poems. He helped me stay in Marietta as long as could be, trying to keep me near to home when all the other mill-workers were sent away northe. He's the one, too, who told me of a cotton mill in Cannelton, Indiana. So when at last we did get put on a train, that's where we knew to go.

Mrs. Stewart reached across the table, placing her hand on Ethan's sleeve. "Was that you?" she asked. "Are you the one who looked out for my girls?"

"Yes, ma'am. And the blacksmith you met was my friend."

She wrapped her fingers around his and squeezed. "Thank you. God bless you. Did you know I prayed for that very thing? For kindness in an unkind place. For care in an uncaring world."

"I did care," he confessed. "I still do." He did not tell her that he carried the lock of Cora Mae's hair or explain that it brought both comfort and ache when he felt the silky strands on his skin.

Mrs. Stewart sat back. "I know you do."

While Mrs. McGee set about soaking the beans in whatever water they had saved, Ethan shared all the reasons Mrs. Stewart ought to be proud of the daughter she raised. How she rose above her own fears and hurts and refused to repay evil with evil. How she set an example for June in trying to love the enemy.

The smile on Mrs. Stewart's face radiated beauty. "I'm right proud of that. Go on."

It was her daughter's words she thirsted for, not his. But after he read a single line telling that Cora Mae nursed among the Yankees, he couldn't help but add to it. "You can imagine that nursing soldiers, whether they're sick or injured in battle, requires strength of character, courage, and a heaping dose of compassion. Your daughter proved all three. No lady should have to even think upon that kind of suffering. But she didn't just think on it, she saw it. Heard it. Smelled and touched it. She did what she could to bring comfort."

"All that for Yankees?" Mrs. McGee said over her shoulder. "The ones what ravaged our land and kinfolk?"

"All that for her fellow man," he said, and Mrs. Stewart pressed his hand once more.

"What does she write of Fern and Cynthia, though?" Mrs. McGee asked.

That part came next, Ethan told her, and read.

The only way to stay in Marietta was to nurse the Yankees. Cynthia was madder than hornets ever since we were rounded up in Roswell, and I knew she, and Damaris and Tabby, would never do it. I thought maybe Fern would stay behind with me, and I did my best to persuade her, but she refused, too. I do believe she's still in pieces over Wade. The last I saw anyone from Roswell was July 15. They're in the northe now, only I don't know where they landed.

"Of course they wouldn't nurse bluebellies." Mrs. McGee brought a handkerchief to her eyes. "Fix them up so they could fight another day and kill more of our boys? No, sir. My girls know what they're about. I couldn't be prouder." Her forehead buckling, she marched from the room.

Mrs. Stewart watched her go. "She's hurting something powerful. But I want you to know that your coming today is a balm to my soul. I been more worried over Cora Mae and June than a God-fearing woman ought to be." She coughed again. It sounded bad, but not like his father had sounded at the end.

Ethan passed her his canteen, and she drank.

Shadows lengthened across the table as she shared how much she'd relied on her daughter, and how much joy June had been to her ever since she came to live in their household. With every story, he felt more convinced that Mr. Ferguson was to be envied above all men.

At last, Ethan read the rest of Cora Mae's news. She explained that the mill in Cannelton wasn't hiring, but that she'd found seamstress work that included room and board.

We are safe and fine, she wrote again. *We'll come home to you as soon as we can.*

Ethan passed the letter to Mrs. Stewart, who traced Cora Mae's writing with her finger.

"It's not safe here yet," she whispered. Grooves furrowed her brow as she looked up. "It's not safe for her and June to come home yet, is it, young man?"

"Not with all the fighting around Atlanta right now. Not with the railroads being attacked by both armies, no. And the food being so scarce . . ." Aside from missing her mother, Cora Mae and June were better off where they were, at least for now.

Mrs. Stewart coughed again, then took a careful breath. "Would you set down my words for her, and mail it?"

"Of course." If she hadn't asked him, Ethan would have offered this service to her anyway. But as he pulled the paper and pencil from his haversack, unease rippled through him. Without his dominant hand, he'd make a poor scribe indeed.

Pinning the page to the table with his right elbow, he held the pencil with his left hand in an awkward, curling grip. He wrote the date, and a sound of frustration escaped him at the sight of the childlike scrawl. Shame pricked at the idea of sending this to Cora Mae.

"What's wrong?" Mrs. Stewart asked.

"It's not much to look at, is it?" He hid his embarrassment behind a chuckle. "I used to be better than this. And so much faster."

Her eyes softened. "The marks you're making on that page will tell my girls that I'm alive and well. They'll carry my love across hills and rivers and miles of land I'll never see." She tapped the paper with her fingertips. "That makes this downright beautiful. That it doesn't come easy for you only makes it more so. Understand? It's got nothing at all to do with how tidy your lettering is, and everything to do with you and me working together to send hope to Cora Mae and June."

He felt exposed beneath her steadfast gaze, knowing she'd seen both his pain and his pride. Yet instead of pulling back, she drew closer. This was what mothers did, he recalled, for he'd had a mother once, too. The wonder of it was that Mrs. Stewart bestowed that grace to him, a soldier of the enemy army. If she thought of him that way, it didn't show.

"It will get easier, you know, with time," she added, a fresh gentleness in her tone. "Now, I can take this slow. Can you?"

Chapter Eighteen

CANNELTON, INDIANA
WEDNESDAY, AUGUST 31, 1864

Hemming that gown could wait.

Cora Mae told herself to breathe in and then out again. If Mr. Aldridge had said anything else before he'd taken his leave, she didn't hear it. All she heard was the throb of her heart as she studied the envelope he'd given her.

The handwriting struck her as vaguely familiar, like a memory buried deep. Still standing, she tore the seal and began to read.

Dear Miss Stewart and June,

You may not believe this by the scratches I set to paper here, but this is Ethan Howard. I write on behalf of your mother.

Cora Mae's knees went weak. The letters blurred, and she sat at the worktable once more.

"What is it?" June cried, halting her stitching practice.

"It's from Sergeant Howard."

"Your Yankee got better? He's well again?"

"Give me a minute to read this, and I can tell you. He's fetched news from Mama, too." She'd gotten better at reading since she'd been studying every night the book Ethan had given her. But she took her time with this letter, which explained how it came about that Ethan, and not Chaplain Littleton, had made the trip to Roswell.

Then after my visit, I returned to camp at Marietta, and rewrote this letter so many times I'm too proud to count them up. Though you wouldn't think so to look at it. Before this letter, I hadn't put pencil to paper since I lost my writing hand. It took some doing to get it legible.

I'm humbled by what you're reading now, the result of more practice than I'll admit. But if you'll bear with me, I'll keep on practicing, so long as I have good reason to.

That's you, by the way. The two of you, plus your mother.

Cora Mae reached beneath her apron and withdrew the small book she kept in her dress pocket. She opened to the lines Ethan had written and heard his voice in every one of them. In the early pages, she heard him as a boy reciting a lesson. Then as a young man, grasping for light after hours upon hours in the mine. The poems near the end, written in a firm, bold hand, sounded to her like the confident, beauty-loving man she remembered.

She heard Ethan in this letter, too. The writing wasn't nearly as smooth, the voice broken in places. But it was still him. It was her Yankee, trying and trying again, for her and her family.

From now on, please direct your correspondence to me, and I'll see it gets to Roswell.

My function here is as the conduit between you and your mother. But if you'll permit me to insert myself, I do apologize for speaking to you harshly when you found me in the church hospital. I've regretted it. I have prayed for you and June ever since I heard they sent you away.

Now, if that's all the personal word you care to receive from me, I'll keep these letters strictly to your mother's words from now on.

The rest of the letter was in Mama's voice. Cora Mae drank in every word with the thirst of a body starved for it. She was all right, and she wasn't alone. Mr. Ferguson had escaped capture, as far as they knew.

"What's he say?" June asked. "Is the sergeant fighting? With just the one full arm?"

"I don't think so." Cora Mae had seen injured soldiers and those recovering from sickness acting as nurses in Marietta. She could imagine Ethan among them now, when he wasn't visiting Roswell. "He's helping others get better, though, and learning how to get better, himself."

June nodded. "It suits him. Could you read their talkin' to me?"

Cora Mae read it aloud, glad she'd taken the time to work out some of the words already.

"Doesn't it say to come home yet?"

"No."

"What? Why?" June pointed through the open window to a pair of butterflies, their wings orange and bordered in black. "Look, even the butterflies know it's time to head south."

The real reasons were too grown-up for June to carry. Cora Mae hadn't read aloud the part about food being scarce, battles breaking out here and there, and deserters and guerilla soldiers combing the land.

Instead, she said, "Well, for one, butterflies don't need train tickets."

A small smile bloomed on June's face. "But imagine that. A train full of butterflies. Mamas and papas dragging their babies in cocoons and carrying tiny little satchels." She giggled, and Cora Mae thanked God for the sound.

That night, Cora Mae couldn't fall asleep. Her mind was too busy trying to figure out how to reply to both her mother and Sergeant Howard, and guessing how long it would take for her letter to reach them.

When the case clock in the parlor downstairs chimed midnight, she decided to try a cup of tea. Silently, she made her way to the kitchen by the light of her kerosene lamp and set a kettle of water to boil. While she waited, she sat at the table and reread the letters, which she was halfway to memorizing.

"You're up awfully late, Miss Stewart."

"Mr. Aldridge!" she gasped. Mortified to be seen in her nightdress, she held the letters over her chest and stood to leave. At least the light from the lamp she'd brought was not bright enough to reveal much of anything that was not within its small circle of light. Then again, the shadows between them felt just as inappropriate. "I'm sorry, I'll go."

"Before you've had your tea?" He must have noticed the kettle warming on the stove. "Please, stay. At least until you can have what you came for."

Her pulse raced. At this point, either the tea would be no match for her agitation, or it was more necessary now than it had been two minutes ago.

"I insist," he said. "And I know you wouldn't defy your employer and landlord." His tone of voice held a tease, but Cora Mae had no idea how serious he was.

She sat down again. "I apologize if I disturbed you in any way."

Mr. Aldridge sat opposite her. His side whiskers made dark wedges framing his face. "Please don't be sorry. I was already awake. I'm glad you're here."

"Oh?" She glanced at the kettle, willing it to boil faster.

"What I mean is, your work is excellent, and you've been a great deal of help to my wife and me. I realize she hasn't been easy on you, but there's no denying that you have proven a godsend for us and the shop."

"Oh." Tension fading from her shoulders, she leaned back against the chair. "I'm very glad to hear that." How strange to be talking business in the middle of the night, dressed as they were in their nightclothes. At least, she was. She hadn't the nerve to look at him since he entered, so she had no idea what he was wearing and didn't care to find out.

"In fact, I've decided your trial period is over. Rest easy, Miss Stewart. You and June may stay indefinitely."

"That is a comfort. Thank you." From somewhere inside the kitchen, a lone cricket chirruped.

"Of course. I don't want you thinking that any little mistake may lose the roof over your heads. Whatever your past, I want you to feel secure in your position here. Perhaps it's asking too much for you to feel at ease around Mrs. Aldridge, but I wish you would feel comfortable with me, at least. Quite comfortable."

Steam hissed through the kettle spout. Cora Mae swept from the table and set about fixing a cup of tea. In her haste to pour the hot water, some splashed onto her hand. She sucked in a breath.

"Did you burn yourself?" Bringing the lamp with him, Mr. Aldridge set it nearby.

"It's nothing." She replaced the kettle and stepped back, leaving her cup on the sideboard.

"Let me see." He cupped her arm and slid his hand down until he was holding the hand she'd burned, turning it this way and that in the light.

"Truly, it's nothing," she said again, gently pulling away.

"Miss Stewart. You are allowed to look at me. However low or ashamed my wife has made you feel, you must know I share none of her judgment."

"Yes, sir," she said, then added, "I'm not ashamed of who I am."

"Good. Then look me in the eyes."

When she did, she could not tell what she saw there. Most likely, it was simply the concern of a compassionate employer attempting to compensate for his shrill wife, forsaking propriety for a chance to speak his mind.

"I've made you uncomfortable," he said, putting more space between them. "I am sorry. It was the last thing I wanted to do, and you have every right to be here. I must have had too much drink after dinner not to realize my timing is appalling. You stay, and I'll go. Do remember, Miss Stewart, that your place here is safe. I want you to feel that. You're safe here."

He bade her goodnight and left. Alone with her tea, she wanted to believe him.

Chapter Nineteen

MARIETTA, GEORGIA
THURSDAY, SEPTEMBER 1, 1864

The wounded did not stop coming.

It seemed to Ethan that for every patient sent to Chattanooga's general hospitals for a better chance at recovery, two more arrived from the front to take their place. And that was only in the Methodist Church where Ethan nursed, to say nothing of the hospital tents swollen with sick and wounded all over Marietta.

With those odds, he'd expected soldiers he knew to come into his care.

He had not expected Zeke Aldridge to be one of them.

Wind flapped the canvas stretched on poles outside the church to shield them from the sun. Hoofbeats clopped as horses pulled wagons full of supplies from the depot to the buildings-turned-warehouses surrounding town square. The clamor of trains coming and going were a near constant shriek in the air. But those sounds and all others faded to the edges as Ethan stared at the pale young soldier. Amid the snarl of thoughts that sprang to mind, he wondered what his parents had been thinking, letting him sign up at age fifteen.

Or had he enlisted without permission? Had he run away? Had he reason to?

His skin beaded with sweat, Zeke managed to twitch a smile. "Fancy meeting you here," he rasped. The doctor had already performed the initial treatment for a projectile that had entered his chest and exited the other side. Bandages wrapped tight around his ribs, a crimson blossom marking the wound. "Bet you wish I was one limb the lighter, instead, though." He coughed, a gurgling, airy sound.

"I'm not so barbaric as that," Ethan replied. Kneeling on the thin blanket between ground and patient, he set down his bucket of water, then dipped a rag into it and swiped it over Zeke's face and neck. The stink coming off him was no different than the odor common to all the other wounded, and Ethan liked to think himself immune to it.

But he was not immune to the barbs of regret Zeke's presence brought. The last thing he felt like doing was tending this young man. If he wasn't a nurse attached to this hospital, he'd walk away. If he never exchanged another word with Zeke, he would not consider it a loss. In fact, for the last four weeks or so, he'd been doing his best to forget about this man and move on.

So much for that plan.

Lord, help me, he prayed, and braced himself to do exactly what he had no heart for. As Ethan dipped the rag into the bucket once more, Little Feller picked his way between patients in the tent, licking one outstretched hand and then another, before lying down next to Ethan. His tail wagged, tapping Zeke on the leg, but not hard enough to be bothersome.

While Zeke watched the dog, Ethan washed the young man's arms and as much of his torso as he could reach around the bandages. Telling himself he was just another patient helped some. But what caught him up short was recalling what Cora Mae had told June the day Cynthia was nasty to her. *"It's one thing to show kindness to a friend,"* she'd said. *"Seems to me it's a finer thing indeed to show kindness to one who hasn't been kind to you."*

It would be so easy for Ethan to let other nurses tend this particular patient from now on. But his stinging conscience suggested that it may be better to do it himself. To put into practice loving one's enemies—for Zeke's sake and his own soul's, too.

"I saved your life, you know," Zeke whispered.

"Oh yeah? How do you figure?"

Zeke waited for breath and spoke on the exhale. "Had you been whole, you'd have gone on to battle. Might have been killed. See?"

"I was expecting to be killed for a cause I believe in."

A few more beats passed while Zeke gathered the air to speak. "Like I said, thanks to me, now you get to live for that cause instead."

According to Dr. Wilcox, Ethan had more life ahead of him than he'd ever dreamed he would. Confused by his infrequent coughing spells since July, he had asked the doctor how it was possible if he had the beginnings of the same black lung disease that had killed his father. After an examination, the answer had been a simple one. Ethan didn't have it. He had only assumed he did.

Naturally, he'd coughed as a miner. Likely, his lungs had been somewhat compromised, making him more sensitive to dirt kicked up on army campaigns and in stables or anywhere there was bound to be dust or pollen or campfire smoke. "But stay out of the mines," Dr. Wilcox had said, "and you have as much reason to live a long life as anyone, now that your battle days are over."

"I get to live," Ethan repeated Zeke's words, still getting used to the news. He tried to imagine decades looming ahead of him.

Tears leaked from Zeke's closed eyes, refocusing Ethan's attention.

"Is the pain that bad, soldier?"

Zeke shook his head.

Brow pinching, Ethan scanned Zeke's body and saw that Feller had rested his head in his upturned palm. His thumb stroked the side of the dog's muzzle.

"I'm as useless as my father always said I was," Zeke whispered. "I am sorry, you know, about your arm. Sorry I did that to you." The words were not spoken all at once but in pieces, between wheezing, coughing, gasping. But he'd said it anyway, though it cost him. "I'm sorry for so much."

Zeke's old bravado melted, revealing the vulnerability beneath. He'd surely confronted his own mortality with an injury like this one. Doing that had a way of paring a man down to the marrow of who he was. Not every soldier liked what he saw when he gave a hard look at what he had or had not accomplished in the short life God had given him.

"We all have regrets," Ethan told him. "For your own good, you best not list them now." The blood soaking through the bandage spread wider. Standing, he hailed a surgeon's attention.

"Come back later," Zeke whispered. "Won't you?"

Ethan told him he would.

When Dr. Wilcox made his way toward them, Mrs. Buford came with him, carrying a tray piled high with instruments, bandages, lint, and a bowl and sponge. A new ribbon of silver streaked her jet-black hair. She was working herself too hard, he thought, but she wouldn't listen to reason. And as much as he wanted to look out for a fallen soldier's widow, it wasn't Ethan's job to convince her to stop. Truth was, they needed all the help they could get.

"What do we have here, son?" Weary though he was, Dr. Wilcox began his usual banter while he inspected the wrappings. "Mrs. Buford . . ." He beckoned her closer so he could reach what she carried.

She didn't move, staring at the wound the doctor had uncovered. Her eyelids fluttered, and she began to sway.

"Don't you faint on me." Dr. Wilcox swiveled from Zeke and grasped the listing tray with both hands. "Don't you dare fall on my men."

Ignoring a crass patient's favorable opinion of the possibility, Ethan wrapped his arm around her waist. "Can you walk?" he said. "Let's get you out of here. Fresh air—or fresher, anyway—will do you good."

"And now I've lost two nurses," Dr. Wilcox muttered. "Set her out of the way and get back here, Howard."

Ethan couldn't blame the doctor for his frustration. The sooner he could get her a safe distance from the hospital tents, the better. If she swooned, could he hold her weight with just one full arm? How could he carry her?

He tightened his arm around her waist and felt the stiff corset beneath the black mourning dress. It may not be seemly to notice, but he couldn't help but observe that such trappings had to interfere with normal breathing.

"I'm sorry, Sergeant," she said. "I do believe I'm about to—"

She went limp, her head lolling against his shoulder. There was only one thing he could do. He turned her body to face him, then bent and heaved her over one shoulder, carrying her like a sack of grain.

With her arms dangling behind him, he carried her to the tent she shared with Mrs. Littleton. "Hello? Mrs. Littleton?"

The lack of response didn't stop him from going in. Kneeling at the nearest camp cot, he sat Mrs. Buford on it, then carefully eased her back down until her head rested on the pillow. Wisps of dark hair curled and clung to her neck.

"Mrs. Buford?" He gave her shoulder a little shake. "You all right? Can you hear me?"

"I hear you," she murmured. She blinked her eyes open, then focused on his face.

"Can you drink?" There was some water left in the canteen strapped crossways over his shoulder. After uncapping it, he supported her head with his right arm and brought it to her lips.

She drank, then leaned back and smiled at him. "Thank you. I'm sorry to keep you. I'll do better tomorrow."

He shook his head, wondering at her perseverance.

"You don't believe me?"

"That's not it, ma'am. It's just that I don't think Joseph would like you wearing yourself out for his sake."

"Oh." She closed her eyes as if the sunlight was too much for her. Tiny droplets of sweat dotted her hairline. "And what would he like, pray tell? Are you suggesting he'd like me to forget him? Pretend our brief marriage never happened? Or is it my own mistakes at the end I should deny? My parting words to him were not what I wish they were."

Ethan could have figured as much, especially if he'd re-enlisted without her blessing. He wondered how long Joseph had waited to tell her before leaving again. "He'd want you to mourn him, of course he would. And I've surely found it to be true that helping others helps me, too. But is this work you're insisting on—is it really helping you? Or are you punishing yourself instead?"

To his dismay, a tear rolled free. "How'd you get to be so perceptive, soldier? Have you got a woman of your own at home, dreaming of your return?"

Ethan swallowed. There was a woman at home. But she wasn't his. And the reunion she dreamed of was not with him. It had made him sore before, but now that he knew his life wouldn't be cut short by bullets or black lung, the bruise went deeper. The years ahead could still hold meaning and purpose. But without her, they would not hold love.

Mrs. Buford lifted a delicate eyebrow, waiting for his response.

"No."

She studied him, though he schooled his face to reveal nothing. "I find that exceptionally difficult to believe. Many a girl would swoon for a handsome war hero like you." She tried a smile. "I'm an expert on swooning, you may have noticed."

Chuckling, he stood, taking a swig from the canteen before recapping it and slinging it across his shoulder. "I'm pretty sure you swooned near me, not for me. Besides, I'm no hero."

"I beg to differ."

"Based on what you see? Or rather, what you don't see?" His missing hand ached, a sensation that disturbed him no matter how often it happened. "I wasn't wounded defending our country or the rights of all men and women to be free. I was shot by a fellow soldier who thought I was a Reb. That's why I've been here ever since, keeping wounds moist, emptying bedpans, fetching water and fresh bandages, and fighting a battle against lice on behalf of the men who can't do it for themselves."

Mrs. Buford held his gaze steady. "That's what you did for my Joseph. As I said, a hero like you."

He rubbed the back of his neck, unsure what to do with her praise. It rolled over him but did not absorb, instead landing in a shining puddle at his feet.

A flush stole into her cheeks. Her coloring better, he deemed it safe to take his leave.

Chapter Twenty

CANNELTON, INDIANA
FRIDAY, SEPTEMBER 2, 1864

Mrs. Aldridge didn't like Cora Mae talking to the customers. But Mrs. Aldridge was busy with one herself. So when Mrs. Beasley came in to pick up the yards of wool she'd ordered, Cora Mae met her at the register.

"How are you, Cora Mae?" The elderly woman asked as though she wanted an honest answer. She was plump as a raisin soaked in honey, and in the dress she wore, about the same color, too.

"I'm fine, ma'am, thank you."

June smiled from where she sat behind the counter, practicing stitches on remnants of fabric.

"And how are you, my dear? We've met once before. Now, don't tell me your name, and let's see if an old lady can remember. It's a month of the year, that much I recall. April?"

June shook her head.

"July?" Mrs. Beasley's eyes twinkled with her teasing. "No? Then it must be August. Augustine, that's it. Much better."

While Cora Mae rang up the woman's purchase, June wrinkled her nose and cried, "June!"

The laughter spilling from Mrs. Beasley soon caught hold of June, too. "Yes, that's it." She paid Cora Mae and redirected her full attention to the little girl who slipped from the chair and drew near. "June. I'll remember that now. And I am Mrs. Beasley. What have you got there?"

"Just practice to keep me out of trouble." June stuck the needle through the corner of her scrap of calico and dropped it on the counter. Then she pulled an envelope from her pocket and placed it on the counter. "We're fixin' to—I mean, we're going to mail this to our Yankee in the Union army today. Do you have a Yankee, too?"

"I do! My grandson, Seamus Dooley. He's actually a blacksmith in the army, so—"

"Lt. Dooley?" Forgetting her manners, June interrupted. "We know him!"

"You don't say!" Mrs. Beasley looked at the envelope's address and smiled. "Well, I'll be. Sergeant Ethan Howard. He and Seamus are good friends, which I guess you know. We spent many Sunday afternoons together, telling stories, reading, and writing. Ethan grew into a fine young man. I guess you know that, too."

"Yes, ma'am," Cora Mae agreed. "We surely do."

Smiling, Mrs. Beasley bent down to June's level. "My grandson wrote me all about a little girl he'd picked up from a town square in Roswell and carried on his horse Toledo all the way to Marietta. He said she was sweet as pie, though she did attempt an escape on the road. You don't happen to know her, do you?"

"That's me!" June cried, then ducked her head from Mrs. Aldridge's view. "He wrote about us?"

"He did. And though I'm as loyal to the Union as can be, I think what Sherman did to you mill hands was totally uncalled for. You were doing your jobs and ought not to be punished so severely for it." Her words were laced with a compassion Cora Mae had not felt from another in quite some time.

Mrs. Beasley folded her hands atop the counter, a wedding ring loose between two knuckles. "I'd like to hear more about your experience since Sherman's orders took you from home. Tomorrow's Saturday. This shop closes at noon on Saturdays, I believe. After that, how would the two of you like to join me for a picnic?"

Cora Mae told her they would.

~

SATURDAY, SEPTEMBER 3, 1864

The wind touching Cora Mae's face was the cleanest she'd ever known. It swept through the clearing where June ran barefoot with outstretched arms and a feather tucked into her braid, pretending to be an eagle. It swayed the tops of trees at the edge of the woods, shushing through branches that shivered with silver-bellied leaves. The air carried the scent of crushed clover and warm grass.

From where she sat on the picnic blanket with Mrs. Beasley, Cora Mae drank it all in. The next time she wrote to Mama, she'd tell her of this place where the light lay golden across the flowering meadow as though spilled from the upside-down bowl of a sky. She would tell her of soil that was rich brown instead of red and of grass that felt like silk ribbons, soft and yielding, beneath her feet.

June let out a whoop as she charged toward a tree, scaring blackbirds from its branches.

Laughing, Cora Mae turned to the elderly woman beside her. "She needed this place. So did I. Thank you for bringing us here." The three of them had ridden out with a man who cut wood for Mrs. Beasley and her church. The distant sound of his axe splitting logs traveled across the meadow, a dull percussion to the rippling of the nearby stream.

Mrs. Beasley sipped lemonade from a jar, then smiled. "I thought you might like it. Here now, have a slice." She offered a wedge of gingerbread on a napkin.

Thanking her, Cora Mae broke off a piece and ate it slowly, savoring the way the spices warmed in her mouth.

"This was Ethan's favorite place," Mrs. Beasley told her. "My husband—God rest him—and I brought Seamus, Ethan, and his brothers Sam and Andrew here after church on Sundays. They'd run off their energy, and then when they were worn out enough, I'd read to them and teach them to do the same."

"And you taught them to write?"

"With sticks in the mud, on the banks of this very stream." Mrs. Beasley laughed. "Eventually, they graduated to chalk and slates, pencil and paper. But oh, what a grand time they had drawing letters in the mud. The youngest two were far more interested in digging up worms for their hooks, but Ethan gave his lessons his all."

Cora Mae believed that. "What about his pa? Did he ever come? Did he want his sons to learn?"

Mrs. Beasley took another drink, then dabbed the moisture from her pleated lips. "Mr. Howard didn't put much stock in book learning. He said the mine would take care of them. The mine was all they needed to know, which I'm sure is why Sam and Andrew didn't try harder."

Sadness threaded through Cora Mae to think on it. No wonder Ethan had felt trapped. His pa must have already been sick with coal dust in his lungs by that point and yet could not see a different future for himself or his boys.

The same was true for almost every mill hand in Roswell. The mill paid them. But the mill also made them old before their time. The mill killed them. Now the mill was gone, but she reckoned it would be rebuilt. Cora Mae didn't favor the idea of returning to it.

"Tell me more," she said without thinking whether or not she should.

Meanwhile, June seemed happy as a colt to run free. The child had been cooped up too much. Even in Roswell, she'd spent so much time at the mill, she rarely played in the sun for more than a few minutes at a time.

"After Mr. Howard succumbed to black lung," Mrs. Beasley continued, "the three sons carried on in the mine as before until Ethan was ready for another job elsewhere. He'd found a farmer to hire him on. Oh, that boy was so eager to spend all of his time outdoors and above ground."

"Did his brothers want to go with him?"

Mrs. Beasley shook her head. "They had no interest in leaving the only life they knew. Then, one week before Ethan was scheduled to quit, there was a cave-in at the mine. Ethan pulled his younger brothers to safety in time, but two other miners were killed. It shook Ethan, and yet his brothers refused to leave, insisting they were lucky. So Ethan changed his plans instead and never talked about leaving the mine again. He didn't say so, but I know he gave up his dream to keep watch over them."

Cora Mae sat quiet, feeling the weight of his sacrifice. Loyalty like that was rare. She felt with new depth how Ethan must have grieved that both brothers died in battle while he wasn't with them.

"Did he never think of courting? Marrying?" she asked.

"He wouldn't think of starting his own family when he had Andrew and Sam to lead. Once he does find a woman to make his wife, he'll be devoted to her as long as he lives." Mrs. Beasley ate the last of her own gingerbread slice and sighed. "Now I'm ready to hear about you, my dear. Won't you tell me about yourself and June, and what you've been through?"

Bit by bit, the older woman gently pulled the story from Cora Mae. With the sun on her face and her toes touching grass off the edge of the blanket, a pressure slowly eased inside her. Mrs. Beasley made her feel like everything she said was important, which in turn made Cora Mae feel like releasing more.

She might even have told of Ethan's proposal, were it not for June shouting, "Look! Mama! Look up, look up!" She ran back to the blanket. Butterflies by the dozen, then by the hundreds, winged through a blinding blue sky. "They're too many to count!"

Mrs. Beasley tipped back her head and smiled. "Ah, what a treat to see this. It happens every fall, right around this time."

Cora Mae had never seen so many butterflies in her life. She wondered if any would make it all the way to Georgia. What a very long journey for such small and fragile things.

They were still overhead when it was time to pack up the picnic and climb into the wagon for the ride back into town. As they neared, a great commotion exploded in streets choked full of people. They shouted and sang. Some waved flags. Fireworks rocketed above the rooftops, scattering the monarchs.

June leaned on the edge of the wagon. "It must be a holiday! But it isn't the Fourth of July."

"Folks sure are celebrating something," Cora Mae said, but unease gripped her. These were Yankee folks waving Yankee flags. Something had happened in the war.

Church bells pealed. It struck her that they hadn't been melted down to make ammunition as all of Marietta's had been.

The wagon driver slowed enough to shout a question into the crowd.

"Atlanta has fallen!"

"Are you sure?"

"Read the paper if you don't believe me! Ol' Hood turned tail and ran, and Sherman took Atlanta at last!"

With all the soldiers, horses, and guns she'd seen in Marietta, and with Sherman in charge, Cora Mae wasn't surprised. Just sobered.

Insults arrowed past, branding all Southerners traitors and cowards. Shouts clapped her ears, and sparks spangled the sky. The smell of smoke recalled to mind the day she watched the mill burn down.

"What does this mean?" June asked while Mrs. Beasley called to a newsboy.

It meant no one would stop Sherman from destroying everything in his path as he pressed on. It meant Georgia would never be the same. But to June, she said, "I think it means we're closer to the end of the war than we were before."

A frown flickered over June's face. "That'll be good when it's over. At least then we can go home."

Cora Mae held June close. There was nothing at home for them now except Mama. And possibly Mr. Ferguson.

Chapter Twenty~One

MARIETTA, GEORGIA
SATURDAY, SEPTEMBER 10, 1864

Exhaustion weighted Ethan. It had been a long day's journey to the McGee farm and back at the end of a very long week. The only reason he'd gotten leave for the errand was that his left arm and shoulder were absolutely worn out from lifting men on litters.

Now that Atlanta had fallen, Sherman was culling his army, shedding anyone who would slow him down as he prepared for his next move. That meant sending all who were sick, or likely to become sick, north into the hospital system.

All of them came through Marietta on their way to Chattanooga and beyond. They came by the hundreds and numbered well into the thousands after only one week of transfers. They came with malaria, dysentery, scurvy, pneumonia, debilitation, typhoid, and every other kind of fever. The number of soldiers disabled by disease was more than ten times those wounded in battle. Dr. Wilcox had said that last month, twenty-five thousand of Sherman's 130,000 troops were on the sick rolls. He expected about that many to come through Marietta.

Ethan believed it. Whatever Sherman had in mind next, his army would be fast and fierce.

Crows cawed across a lowering sky. Ethan sat outside his tent near a fire, the wind carrying smoke away from him. Too tired to cook anything at this hour, he resigned himself to the hardtack he had left. He had more than an hour before sunset, which gave enough time to write letters without needing to light a candle. In truth, it would be a relief to set his mind to something besides the steady stream of casualties whose faces he saw in his sleep.

Setting a cracker box across his knees to serve as desk, he began by rewriting in a more careful hand what Mrs. Stewart had dictated. It was shorter this time, most likely due to her coughing.

Dear Cora Mae and June,

We're getting along all right, with many thanks to Sergeant Howard. He's fetched us vittles from his own rations and from what he buys from the sutler. Shannon calls him "Stranger," but I don't think of him as such, except in the way that we all are strangers in this land, as the Bible says, with our true home in heaven. That's a comfort to me, and I hope it's a comfort to you, too.

Mr. Ferguson has called on us, too, laying up firewood while he was here. As long as the Yankees are in Atlanta, he says he must make himself scarce. But as soon as they leave, he'll come back and stay, to do for us what needs doing. Horace was much relieved to hear that you and June fare well but is anxious for the family to be reunited. So am I.

With all the love in my heart,
Mama

Ethan paused and considered that last paragraph anew. Ignoring the twinge it brought to his chest, he reminded himself that his role in the Stewarts' lives was a short-term assignment, like bending those railroad ties had been. And just like with those railroad ties, once the job was complete, the path between him and the Stewarts could not be traveled again.

With this thought pricking the back of his mind, Ethan's letter to Cora Mae was only slightly longer. She'd asked how he was, so he told her he'd done some healing, inside and out, since his last letter. His handwriting had improved, and he'd gotten better at getting on and off a horse, but he thought better of including those details. What he saw as progress might come across as cause for pity.

Grasping for any other news of interest, he mentioned the Littletons and Mrs. Buford, and the fact that among his patients now was the young man who had shattered Ethan's arm. He ended with:

I expect you are glad to hear that Mr. Ferguson has escaped capture and will be ready for your plans to proceed, as soon as may safely be.

The mail is spotty between us and you, with raids on the trains on the regular. Letters going both ways are delayed and sometimes lost. If you don't hear from us for a spell, that's likely why.

I am your humble servant,
Sergeant Howard

P.S. Please see enclosed a separate letter for June.

Dear June,

Little Feller asked me to write and tell you howdy for him. He is healthier than I've ever seen him. Other soldiers admire his permanent wink, so they sneak him little bits of food, and his ribs don't poke up under his skin anymore.

That coonhound has well and truly adopted me as his pet and will not leave my side if he can help it. I am sorry to report that he snores. Would you believe he trotted beside me and the horse I rented all the way to Mrs. McGee's farm and back again on my most recent visit? Mrs. McGee wouldn't let him inside, afraid that he carried fleas. Feller wants me to tell you, June, that he is 100% flea-free. He was afflicted by them for a while, but I used a remedy meant to get rid of lice, and it worked like a charm.

I pray you are doing well in Indiana. I know you're being good for your mama.

Dooley is blacksmithing for the army in Atlanta, but if he were here, I'm sure he'd have me tell you hey.

Your humble servant,
Sergeant Howard

P.S. Please see enclosed a separate letter for Sassy.

Dear Sassy,

Surprise! A big ole Yankee found me tucked under Mama June's mattress and told me about your adventure in Marietta and all the way to a place called Indiana. Or was it Marianna and Indietta? You must have seen some wondrous things, and I hope you'll tell me about them as soon as can be. In the meantime, I am staying at a farm outside of Roswell. I can't wait to see you and Mama June.

Your long-lost sister,
Sissy

MONDAY, SEPTEMBER 12, 1864

"Zeke," Ethan called. "It's time we get some water inside you. What do you say? Can you sit?" A light rain pattered the mildewing canvas above them.

The boy's eyelids fluttered, and his lungs rattled. His long hair had been shorn nearly to the scalp last week, right after Ethan discovered it was infested with lice. With the greasy strands gone, it had been much easier to keep his head clean. It also made him look younger than his eighteen years. That was three years younger than Ethan's youngest brother. Zeke never had an older sibling to knock sense into him, and it showed. What he'd had, to his detriment, was Weston.

Ethan sat beside him, slipping his right arm under his shoulders to help him sit more upright. Zeke's wound had healed, but the doctor had detected pneumonia. They'd tried propping him up with pillowcases stuffed with Spanish moss, but they kept sliding away from him. Zeke needed a general hospital with a real bed, and real pillows, if he was ever going to get well.

"Take a drink now." Ethan brought the dipper to Zeke's lips and tipped it, water dribbling down his chin and neck. "You're headed to Chattanooga today, do you remember that?"

Zeke's eyelids flared open. "Am I that bad off?" In the distance, thunder rolled. Any relief from cooler temperatures was countered by the near-suffocating humidity.

"You'll be that much better off when you get there." Ethan helped him drink some more. Little Feller sauntered over, his fur wet and his paws caked in mud, a winking grin on his face. Zeke petted the dog's head, and Feller did not flinch away.

"Will you send word to my folks?"

"I'll take down a letter if you'd like to dictate it." After giving him one last drink, Ethan eased the boy back down.

"I can't think of what to say," he wheezed. "This is exactly what my mother feared. And my father . . . I couldn't ever please him anyway. Not even a little." From what Zeke had shared, he hadn't tried all that hard to please his father. The exacting standards had been so high, he'd found it easier to rebel against them than to try and fail over and over again. For reasons unnamed, the son had no respect for the father. "But I suppose they should know."

Ethan agreed. He waved his arm in a losing battle to scatter the black flies tormenting the patients.

Zeke rolled to his side and coughed for a spell. He was so spent after the fit, he lay panting before he could speak. "Tell them I'm sick and been moved to Chattanooga. That's enough."

Ethan wrote down the direction Zeke told him for where to send it, then frowned, repeating it back. He'd sent an envelope of letters to that house yesterday. "Is that right?"

"I think I'd know." A dull smile bent Zeke's lips. "Why?"

"Your parents own a dress shop?"

He nodded, eyes drifting closed.

"Two of the mill hands from Roswell are living with them now, working in the dress shop as seamstresses. Well, Miss Stewart is employed, but I doubt little June draws wages. Your parents didn't mention it in any letters to you?"

Zeke's eyes opened again. "Those mill hands live in my house?"

Ethan worried he'd blundered. Maybe Zeke's parents hadn't told him for a reason. But he couldn't take it back now. "Yes. They work for room and board. It sounds like a good fit for all concerned."

"I'll bet." Zeke labored for every breath. "I'll bet that was my father's idea, and my poor mother tolerates it with gritted teeth. As usual."

"What does that mean?" Ethan asked, but Zeke broke into another bout of coughing. The only thing louder was the chugging of trains less than two blocks away. Sherman's sick from Atlanta kept coming.

Dr. Wilcox approached, along with Scipio and Titus. "All right, soldier, time to get you to the depot." The freedmen clasped each other's arms to form a human basket, and the doctor and Ethan lifted Zeke and his haversack into it.

"Forgive me," Zeke exhaled, then coughed again, pointing to Ethan's empty sleeve. Every sentence, every phrase, cost him. "Please. Pretend it's my dying wish." Blood smeared from the corner of his mouth.

Feller ambled to Ethan's side and leaned against Ethan's leg while Scipio and Titus carried Zeke to a wagon lined with hay.

Ethan thought of Mrs. Stewart, who welcomed him as friend and fellow sojourner, even after all the Union army had done to her homeland and her family. Zeke had made a mistake when he'd shot Ethan, but there had been nothing accidental about Ethan's actions and Sherman's orders, and still Mrs. Stewart forgave. She'd taught Cora Mae to love her enemies, and she in turn taught June. Could he do less?

He'd been convinced he'd die for the cause. But the way Ethan died wasn't nearly as important as the way he lived. And he knew how he wanted to live.

Trotting to the wagon, Ethan reached over the side and gripped Zeke Aldridge's shoulder. "I do," he said. "I forgive."

"Thank you," Zeke whispered, and lowered his head back into the hay. The lines on his brow disappeared.

After Titus and Scipio brought another patient to join him, the wagon lurched into motion. The rain stopped and clouds shifted above, but sunlight struggled to break through.

Mrs. Buford approached Ethan, her gown dragging on the earth now that she'd given up her hoops in order to be more practical. The black fabric had faded under the sun, and the hem was rusted with dirt. He hadn't seen her much since she'd fainted, and he hoped that meant she'd kept herself busy well away from the hospital tents.

"I don't know how you did that," she said.

"Pardon?"

"That was the soldier who shot you, wasn't it?" she guessed. "You forgave him."

"By the grace of God."

Her jaw set in defiance. "I've got a long way to go before I can forgive the men who clamored for this entire, cursed war, to say nothing of the Rebels who fought in it. I can barely forgive my husband for signing up not once, but twice."

He believed that. "And can you forgive yourself for wanting to keep him home?"

With a wry curve to her lips, she touched his elbow. "You do surprise me, Sergeant. You're more insightful than Joseph ever was." She colored. "That was wrong of me to say. In truth, we barely had any time together at all before the war took him. I'm on my way to visit him now, as it happens. Care to join me?"

"I would if you'll wait until my shift is over." It wouldn't do to let Mrs. Buford visit the cemetery alone.

~

Joseph had been buried behind St. James Episcopal Church, less than a ten-minute walk northeast of the Methodist Church where Ethan nursed. He and Mrs. Buford skirted the town square to get there, weaving past countless tents and multiple merchant buildings-turned-warehouses for army supplies. Though the bulk of Sherman's army now camped in Atlanta, Marietta remained as active as ever as a hospital complex and main supply depot for sixty thousand men—and their animals. The cemetery was no restful place.

Ethan offered Mrs. Buford his arm as they entered through iron gates, and she took it. Little Feller loped behind them. The Union soldiers buried here were easy to spot among the marble headstones. Besides the more recently turned earth, they were each marked with planks from wooden boxes that had held a thousand crackers before being broken apart for this purpose. Names and details had been written in black ink. Some markers already showed signs of weathering beneath the pitiless Georgia sun and summer rains. Here and there, soldiers roamed, looking for fallen comrades. In the far corner, two men dug another hole in the ground.

When they neared Joseph's grave, Ethan stayed back and let Mrs. Buford go on alone. A widow ought to have privacy.

A single live oak tree canopied one edge of the cemetery, moss draping its branches in thick black veils. A thin breeze feathering his skin, Ethan regarded the patch of land that held a portion of the dead from this campaign, along with folks who had lived and died in Marietta before the war ever began. It would be felt as another degradation to returning townspeople, to have the invading enemy mixed in with their forebears, and in the shadow of a church steeple whose bell had been melted into bullets. Maybe those church bell bullets had felled these men, and now here they were, the logical consequence of that intention.

Marietta had melted all its church bells, in fact, and now Yankee dead filled churchyards, both here and at the First Baptist a block farther down on Church Street. They'd also been buried east of the City Cemetery. Union men were scattered over the city and all over the

South, their final resting places out of reach for most of their loved ones. It gave Ethan an unsettled, wandering feeling. He knew their souls had parted from their bodies, but their bodies would never go home.

More than four thousand Union soldiers had been killed in the monthslong fight for Atlanta, and more than twenty thousand had been wounded, with men dying from those injuries every day. He'd been so sure he'd be among them, moldering in the ground, and yet here he was in the land of the living, beneath a sunset worthy of poetry.

His thoughts winged to the place where he'd left his brothers buried near Chickamauga. He'd left a piece of himself there when he'd had to leave those mounds of earth, especially knowing he'd not be back. He knew Sam and Andrew had gone on to a better place. Even so, guilt had filled his steps with lead when he turned his back on them and walked away. He had broken his promise to keep them from harm.

It was a promise he'd never had the power to keep. Not in the mines. Not in the war. But that hadn't stopped Ethan from feeling like he'd failed them. When they died, so did the purpose that had been driving him ever since he was a child.

It was time to find another one. And thanks to the Littletons, he had.

Feller nosed his palm, and Ethan scratched behind the coonhound's floppy ears. When he looked up, Mrs. Buford was coming back toward them, her gait cautious through the mud.

He reached out to steady her. "Are you finished here?"

Her fingers wrapped around his arm. "That is the question, isn't it?" She motioned to a thick live oak tree branch that bent all the way to the ground before reaching back up. It made a fair bench. "Let's sit."

The evening was fine, so he had no objections. Once seated, she asked, "Have you thought of what you'll do next? After your enlistment is up."

The sound of shoveling filled his ears, and he trained his focus away from the fresh vacancy it represented. "I've been talking to Chaplain and Mrs. Littleton about an idea that's taken root. It's a grand scheme and will take plenty of planning and funding to get off the ground, but I can't get it out of my mind."

"Is it a secret, this grand plan of yours?"

Birds sang. A sparrow splashed in a footprint still full of the afternoon's rain, and Feller's ears pricked up as he watched. "More like too full of question marks and blank spaces yet to be worth sharing."

"I see."

The sparrow hopped out of the footprint and onto a patch of grass, pecking the ground for seeds or insects. It brought to mind a story he'd heard from one of the patients passing through. "I heard that the civilians in Atlanta are so hard-pressed for provisions, they're digging minie balls out of the earth and trading the lead for food." The image of women and children harvesting ammunition to survive was not an easy picture to look at.

Sun pierced the clouds and glinted on the silver in Mrs. Buford's hair, so at odds with her unlined face. "What the civilians of Atlanta do is of no concern to me."

Her reply had come so quickly and was so devoid of sympathy that Ethan was taken aback. He considered the cost of war a price worth paying so that all people might be free. That didn't mean he liked the idea of human suffering on either side.

Then again, it had been a thoughtless comment for him to make, especially so near her husband's grave. She was grieving and likely had no charitable feelings to spare. Anyhow, maybe she'd asked to sit less for conversation and more because she needed to rest. It had to bother her, though, listening to the digging of a grave. It bothered him.

"Ma'am, how long will you stay away from your

home? All due respect, but this work seems to go hard on you. Instead of bringing healing, I do wonder if this place is reopening your wounds."

She wrinkled her nose but said, "Oh, I'm tougher than I look. It's not the work that's hard on me. It's—well. Dr. Wilcox has forbidden me from nursing anymore, so I must decide whether to stay and do something else—launder, or help with cooking, or find some administrative task to do—or go home. The doctor says I can't keep on like this without risking injury to the baby. He lectured me with special vehemence on the dangers of catching sickness from the men passing through. I can't lose Joey, too. Or, if it's a girl, Josephine." Her hands crossed over her middle.

Ethan gaped at her. All this time, he'd thought she was weak, but she'd been carrying a baby. He didn't know the first thing about being with child except that it had to take a toll on a body. He didn't see how she'd done what she had.

"Please take care of yourself, Mrs. Buford." He ached for Joseph, who may or may not have known of the baby, and for Mrs. Buford, and for the little one who would never know his or her father. No wonder she could not be bothered about the plight of Atlanta civilians. "Do whatever you need to do in order to keep you and the baby healthy and safe. That's what Joseph would want," he hastened to add.

"I did what Joseph wanted the entire time I knew him, although not agreeably at the end. He's not here anymore, God rest him. What do *you* think I should do? Am I in the way here? Should I go home? Or can you think of any reason for me to stay?"

The way she looked at him suggested layers of meaning to the question. He didn't trust himself to decipher them.

Mrs. Buford sighed. "I don't mean to shock you, Sergeant Howard. But I must consider my options carefully. Now you know why. I came here for Joseph, truly. But at this point, he's not the reason I would stay. A baby needs a father, and where I'm from, all the men my age are married or killed in the war or about to be. You're done fighting, and I've been watching you for weeks. I admire your character. I'm fond of you. We get along. I'd like to know if you're fond of me, too. Even a little. You did say you aren't courting anyone else. That hasn't changed in the last ten days, has it?"

Thoughts of Cora Mae and June flashed through his mind, but Mr. Ferguson awaited their return. They were betrothed. They were already a family. "That hasn't changed." He pulled a strand of Spanish moss from the bark beside him and crunched the gray fringe between his fingertips.

"Good. And how do you feel about me?"

"I—" In the far corner of the cemetery, the shoveling stopped. Enough quiet passed for a pine box to be lowered into it. Earth sprayed on wood as they began filling in the hole. Ethan tried again. "I admire and respect you. I'm concerned for your well-being and fully agree with Dr. Wilcox's assessment." He couldn't deny that she was an attractive woman, but it felt wrong to say so. She had months of mourning before her, besides.

The pinched corners of her mouth relaxed. "It's as good a start as any, and better than most."

They had not said or done anything wrong. So why did he feel as though he'd betrayed the people he most held dear?

Feelings could change, he reckoned. And after so long pining for another man's betrothed, a change would be welcome indeed. He couldn't hold on to a phantom forever.

Chapter Twenty-Two

CANNELTON, INDIANA
MONDAY, OCTOBER 10, 1864

June could not stop laughing at Sergeant Howard's letters of September 10. They had taken nearly a month to reach Cora Mae, but the wait was more than worth it.

The idea of Little Feller sending his howdies had tickled June's funny bone and made her smile, but the letter written to Sassy from Sissy on a doll-sized piece of paper had set her laughter loose. It tumbled out of her like the waterfall at Vickery Creek, a powerful, unstoppable thing.

Cora Mae laughed, too, her eyes watering from the joy of seeing June's delight set free. Outside, behind the Aldridges' shop, nobody told them to hush, and every detail seemed set in place for pure enjoyment. Freshly fallen leaves carpeted the yard and piled up in golden drifts. Clouds glowed pink with sunset. Even the cold didn't chill her.

At last June's laughter faded. "I guess Mr. Ferguson wants us back."

Cora Mae's smile slipped. "You're not surprised by that, are you? This was always the plan," she reminded herself along with June. She would not, however, study on the feelings that had come with hearing from Ethan—Sergeant Howard—that her betrothed was nearly ready for them. But Mr. Ferguson—she still didn't feel natural calling him Horace—was a man of his word.

And Cora Mae was a woman of hers.

"He wouldn't just leave for good . . ." Her words trailed away as she realized that was exactly what June's father had done. "Mr. Ferguson is an honorable man. Remember how faithful he was while he waited for me to come out of mourning? He didn't have to share his vittles with us, but he did, and he helped with repairs at home, too." When the board in the porch floor cracked, he'd pried it up and replaced it. When the railing felt rough, he sanded the wood. Ever since the first winter after Pap and Wade enlisted, Mr. Ferguson filled in the cracks around the windows and laid up a store of firewood.

"I know we've been waiting on him for some time now," she went on, "but the timing wasn't right. Once the Yankees clear out, it'll be safe to go back."

"And then we'll go home?" June asked.

"Then we'll go back to Mama." But Cora Mae wondered if there was any place left that would truly feel like home.

Unbidden, Ethan's mention of Mrs. Buford came to mind, and Cora Mae felt a sympathy toward the woman who came to visit her husband's grave and then couldn't bring herself to leave. If the widow was delicate, as Ethan judged her to be, he'd be helping her, taking care of her as much as he thought was right. That was what he did. It was who he was. And Mrs. Buford would be grateful to him.

"Your nose is red." June touched the tip of her own. "Is mine?"

"Like a cherry." Cora Mae smiled.

After stuffing all four letters back into the envelope, she slid it into her pocket and ushered June back inside and up to the bedroom they shared. She turned the knob on a kerosene lamp and opened a book called *The Swiss Family Robinson*, which Mrs. Beasley had lent them. Reading the tales of a family far from home had become their favorite part of every day.

A knock at the door interrupted her. Without waiting for her to answer it, the door swung wide, and Mrs. Aldridge filled the frame. "I've had news of my son. He's been sent to a general hospital in Chattanooga—weeks ago—and for some unknown reason, I'm only finding out about it now."

Cora Mae stood. "I'm sorry to hear that."

"I'm leaving as soon as may be. When I bring him home, he'll need his room. He'll recover better in his own bed. You'll need to make other arrangements."

Mr. Aldridge hurried to join his wife at the doorway. "Sarah, there's no call to turn them out yet. You may find you need to stay a mite longer than you plan, if he's not up for traveling. And I can't handle the work here on my own without Miss Stewart's help. She stays. Wire me from Chattanooga before you make the return trip, and I'll make sure his room is ready for him. But let's take this one step at a time, all right? Let's get you packed tonight."

~

Mrs. Aldridge left on the first steamboat out the next morning.

While Mr. Aldridge managed the storefront that day, Cora Mae learned how to use his wife's sewing machine. June pitched in by sewing on buttons, as long as they were already pinned in place.

Hours ticked by. When the shadows stretched long enough to reach the knot on the pine wood floor, Cora Mae heard the click of the front door locking and could picture Mr. Aldridge turning the sign to announce they were closed.

He appeared in the back sewing room, his pallor grave. "One day done." Shadows ringed his eyes.

"Go on," Cora Mae told June. "Run outside and play." Ever since their picnic with Mrs. Beasley, she tried to see that June had time outside every day.

Mr. Aldridge angled to let the girl by, then turned back to Cora Mae. "Join me for dinner tonight. In the dining room."

"Mrs. Aldridge wouldn't like my kind sitting at your table," she protested. "Especially now. She doesn't want me in the house." She figured his wife's ire against Southerners would be even greater now that their son was laid so low. Besides which, she hadn't been alone with Mr. Aldridge since their chance meeting in the kitchen more than a month ago. She aimed to keep it that way.

"Mrs. Aldridge isn't here," he said. "I am, and I don't mind your kind. Please, don't make me eat by myself, alone with my worries. I'm not ready to visit the dark places they'll take me."

Cora Mae swallowed a sigh. She was not without compassion. "June and I both will join you. Will that suit?"

He told her it would.

At dinner, Mr. Aldridge smelled of shaving soap and wore a fresh suit of finely tailored clothes which he most likely had sewn himself. She supposed keeping to his routine would help shore up his troubled mind, even though it was not his beautiful wife sitting with him but the hired help and her daughter. The nick on his neck proved he had shaved with an unsteady hand. He needed to eat. Cora Mae recalled he'd skipped lunch.

Perhaps that was why he forgot to say grace over his meal before taking the first bite. June looked askance. Cora Mae took her hand beneath the table, bowed her head, and said a quick prayer herself to bless the food and ask for mercy for those in need, whether Northern or Southern.

"Forgive me," Mr. Aldridge said. "You must think me entirely without manners. I've been at sixes and sevens ever since we received the news yesterday. Do help yourselves."

"You've had a shock. It's understandable." Cora Mae served June a piece of steaming pot roast and glazed carrots before taking some for herself. Cut crystal bowls of applesauce topped with whipped cream and cinnamon had already been placed at each setting. Never in her life had she eaten off such fine china or in a room papered like this, in a flocked damask pattern the color of red wine. Small flames of light swooned atop candles held in brass sticks.

Surrounded by finery though he was, the man seated at the head of the table looked miserable.

"How did you get started in the tailoring business?" Cora Mae aimed to steer his mind from the shadows gathering there.

He blinked, then launched into his tale while Cora Mae and June quietly ate. By the end of the delicious meal, he'd lost his hollowed-out look.

"How interesting. Well, good night." Cora Mae stood. June's small fingers were sticky in hers. "We'll see you in the morning."

His expression falling, Mr. Aldridge glanced at the clock on the wall, likely tallying how many hours he'd have to fill alone. "Good night, Miss Stewart. Good night, June. Thank you for the fine company." He rose and offered a stiff smile.

That night, sleep did not come easy. Cora Mae hadn't done anything wrong, but she didn't feel purely right, either.

Violet shadows draped everything in the room. A log crumbled in the hearth, and she climbed out of bed to add more wood to the fire. *Had* she done wrong? She returned to the warmth of the bed. Guilt wormed its way in alongside her.

With Mrs. Aldridge gone, had it seemed like Cora Mae was pretending to be her substitute? Mr. Aldridge had practically insisted she join him, and nothing untoward was said or done—other than the fact that she'd joined him at all. Whatever the reason, she had sat in his wife's chair. She had eaten off Mrs. Aldridge's dishes, broken bread with her husband, and kept him company outside of business hours. She'd attempted to relieve his suffering, if only by distracting him with questions she didn't even care to hear the answers to.

Truly, it wasn't her place. It was wrong.

Guilt grew stronger, making it harder to breathe. Memories surfaced of another man who'd invited her into his life. Charles Hampton, the engineer visiting from New York to repair Roswell's factory equipment, had promised to take her away and give her the home and happiness she deserved. The mere idea had given her wings, and she was ready and willing to fly. She'd thought herself in love with him. But that was before she found out he was already married. Before other mill hands found out, too, and spread it about that Cora Mae had been dallying with another woman's husband.

After that, shame nearly consumed her. She never dreamed of romance again. It was dangerous and couldn't be trusted.

She and June couldn't stay here with Mrs. Aldridge gone. They had to go. Tomorrow.

The next morning, Cora Mae broke her fast early in the kitchen, then found Mr. Aldridge going over customer accounts in the shop before it opened.

He smiled at her. "You look fresh as a daisy. Slept well?"

She hadn't, but that didn't seem a fitting topic to discuss. "Mr. Aldridge, June and I are so grateful for the room and board you've allowed us as my earnings. But the time is right for us to move out into our own situation."

His brows drew together. "Now? When I need you more than ever? Have pity, Miss Stewart. I meant it when I said I can't get along without you."

"I'm not quitting my job, mind you," she said. "I'd just like to be paid with wages instead of room and board. We'll move out today, and you can start getting the room ready for your son's return."

Mr. Aldridge scratched through his side whiskers. "I suppose that was inevitable. As long as you come to work every day as usual, we can certainly adjust the terms of your employment. But this is so sudden. Have you had time to make other living arrangements?"

"Mrs. Beasley's boardinghouse will suit us fine. Only—could you possibly give me an advance on my wages so I can afford to rent the room? The money I earned from laundry amounts to next to nothing. I won't be doing that anymore, either."

Color crept into his face. "I never wanted you doing our laundry, anyway. Has it toughened your skin?"

A chuckle threatening, she hid her hands in her pockets. Did he think she hadn't grown up doing laundry for her own household? Did he suppose her hands weren't tough from work already?

"In any case," he went on, "you're quite right. You ought to be paid in cash for your fine work as a seamstress and live wherever you please. I'll visit the bank during a slow spell today. When the shop closes, you'll have your advance. Just promise you won't run off with it and leave me in a lurch. We're heading into the holidays soon, and that's our busiest season."

"I wouldn't leave you alone with the work while Mrs. Aldridge is away. Thank you."

His smile reflected hers and lingered a little too long.

~

The rest of October passed in a swirl of leaves and wind as Cora Mae established a new routine. Living in Mrs. Beasley's boardinghouse proved a blessed relief. The establishment frayed at the edges, but that was understandable for wartime, especially considering the widow did not charge enough rent to cover regular repairs. She couldn't bring herself to ask one more dime of people than she already did, she said. But her personal warmth more than made up for loose doorknobs and drafty halls.

June still came to the shop with Cora Mae. While Mr. Aldridge dealt directly with customers, Cora Mae sewed in the backroom while June worked on reading and writing lessons assigned by Mrs. Beasley. All was above reproach and strictly professional.

Cora Mae continued to improve her reading and writing as well. Mrs. Beasley called penning letters good practice, and Cora Mae reckoned Sergeant Howard might find it diverting that the woman who taught him now tutored her and June. She wondered how he'd feel if he knew Mrs. Beasley often told stories about him. Cora Mae felt like she knew Sergeant Howard better than she'd ever known any man, aside from her brother.

She wrote and mailed letters three times in October, longing for news of Mama's health. Mama might not be honest about that, but she trusted Sergeant Howard would tell her true. He had warned that the mail could be delayed from now on, but unease filled her just the same. By the time the calendar page turned over, she still hadn't received a word from Georgia since the letters he'd written on September 10.

Chapter Twenty-Three

November 2, 1864

Dear Sergeant Howard,

I been reading the newspaper for word of Georgia and learned Sherman cut his own supply line, and that cut off the mail, too. So I won't be wasting money on postage for a letter that won't reach you, but I'm writing anyway. To keep practicing my hand.

I confess I been fretting about Mama's health. I long to see her again.

It's odd to think of how we've switched places, you in my hometown, and June and me in yours. We are both strangers in a strange land, and yet not strangers to each other. When I am sewing at the dress shop, my mind wanders to this puzzle. When I think of home, I also think of you. I wonder if you think of me when you think of your home, too. I also wonder if the widow Mrs. Buford is still there with you, and how she's getting along.

As you'll never read this, it won't shame June for me to say she's still having trouble at night waking up to use the toilet in time. Mrs. Beasley is so good about it. She gave us an India rubber sheet to put between the mattress and the bed linens, so when there is an acci-

dent, it doesn't ruin the mattress. Poor June feels awful every time it happens. I thought she might get better after we moved out of the Aldridge place, but she isn't all the way yet. She has started coughing some, too. I tell myself she'll get over it soon.

We pray for everyone we care about each night at bedtime. That includes you.

~

November 15, 1864

Dear Sergeant Howard,

It has been one month since we first read your last letters, and two months since you wrote them. I try not to worry about Mama, and about you. It has been a while since I've practiced writing, so I best do it.

I'm still working for Mr. Aldridge during the day. His wife tarries with their son in Chattanooga, and some days I wonder if they'll ever get home. I asked Mr. Aldridge if he wanted to go see his son, too, thinking he may not be long for this world. Sadly, he said he doubted if he'd be welcome at the sickbed. Then he reminded me how much work he must do to stay in business.

June still isn't well. We never been this cold before.

I don't know what else to write.

This is madness.

If I'm to practice my writing, I might as well write to the One I know will hear me, even without mail service. Even without me writing a word at all.

Dear Lord, I need You. You know my heart has turned into a briar patch, a tangled, thorny place that I try to ignore, but the truth is, my feelings are a mess. Help me trust You, and not the way I feel.

My worries are a burden to me. I worry I'll never find home again. I worry for Mama and Mrs. McGee, and for June and Mr. Ferguson. I worry for ~~Ethan~~ Sergeant Howard, though I know his silence is more than likely because the mail can't go through. I thank You for all he's done for my family and ask that You bless him for it. Help him keep healing.

Help all of us heal, for we all of us have our wounds.

Chapter Twenty-Four

Wind whistled through the hole in the only window the boardinghouse attic had. Shivering, Cora Mae laid the pencil on the letter she'd been writing, then scooped up the rag that had dropped to the floor and stuffed it back in the gap between the pane and sill.

On the bed, June pulled her quilt to her chin, though it wasn't nearly time to sleep. "Why couldn't we keep our old room?" She sucked the end of a strand of her hair.

"Mrs. Beasley has a full house of paying customers. It wouldn't be right for us to stay in one of those rooms anymore. Besides, this room fits our budget better." Cora Mae wasn't making enough money to afford a nice room and still be able to save for the journey home. "Let's be grateful for the roof over our heads, Junebug. Even if there are holes in it." In the corner, rain leaked into a pail. Surely, the women's prison in Louisville where most of the mill hands remained was far worse than this.

June turned on her side and coughed, then huddled under the covers.

Snatching up a stack of newspapers Mrs. Beasley had given her, Cora Mae returned to the window and felt for drafts. When she found one, she tore the headline of Lincoln's reelection from the newspaper, folded it in half, and wedged it into place to block the cold air from seeping through.

Then she stopped. She brought the paper over to the kerosene lamp and slanted the tiny columns of print into its glow. How had she missed this news before?

Cora Mae started at the beginning of the article.

Sherman's sixty thousand troops evacuated Marietta by November 13. . . . Sherman destroyed the railroad behind him. . . . The Union army set fire to the Georgia Military Institute in Marietta, and to the buildings around the town square. . . The army is now marching south through Georgia.

"What is it?" June asked.

"The Yankees have left Marietta." And they were laying waste to the rest of Georgia.

"Then where is Sergeant Howard? Does that mean it's safe to go back?"

Cora Mae told her she didn't know.

Dropping the news, she picked up the letter she'd written and fed it to the fire, as she'd done with the one she'd written two weeks ago. The pages curled and blackened, and her carefully penned words turned to ash. She watched the flames and saw in them the burning of Marietta, of Atlanta, of everything in Sherman's path.

MONDAY, NOVEMBER 21, 1864

With a sigh of frustration, Cora Mae picked up the seam ripper and bent over the blue taffeta bodice she'd been sewing. Kerosene light winked off the metal with each yank as she snapped the stitches, leaving a line of blue fringe where a neat seam should have been.

She was tired. It wasn't an excuse, but she reckoned it was reason enough to account for her mistakes today. June had stayed in bed back at the boardinghouse after another night full of coughing. Neither of them had slept well. At least being in the attic meant they hadn't bothered other guests as much as they could have if they shared a floor.

Pinching the tiny threads between her fingernails, she ripped them out of the fabric, then lined up the panels beneath the sewing machine's needle and tried again. Even as she concentrated on the task, she managed to fret over June. This was the fifth day she'd stayed home sick while Cora Mae went to work. Last Friday, Mr. Aldridge had invited her to stay for supper, but she'd refused.

In fact, in her haste to return to June last week, she'd not been paid. So when the clock chimed five, she closed up the sewing room and went to find Mr. Aldridge in the storefront.

The accounts ledger was open on the counter, but he wasn't there. He'd already locked the front door and pulled the shades over the windows.

"Mr. Aldridge?" she called.

His voice carried through the door that led into their living quarters. "In here."

Cora Mae turned the knob and opened the door a few inches. "I'm sorry to interrupt, but I forgot to collect my wages last week."

"Of course. Please, come in."

Smoothing her palms on her apron, she entered the Aldridge parlor. A piano stood against one wall, its three-legged stool covered in red damask trimmed in gold braid. Arranged around a handsome polished wood fireplace, a claw-foot sofa and two armchairs were upholstered to match. A little stand with scallop-edged shelves fit into one corner of the room, bearing seashells, framed embroidery samples, and a porcelain shepherdess. She'd never seen its like.

She waited in the doorway. "I'll be going now, sir. If I could just get my earnings, I'll scoot on back to June."

Mr. Aldridge looked up from where he sat at a writing desk, reading a piece of mail. "Your care for her does you credit. Having a child is a marvelous, terrifying thing. Wouldn't you agree?" He lifted a glass tumbler to his lips but found it empty and set it back down again.

"You've had news?"

He wiped a hand over his side whiskers and stared vacantly into the fire. She wondered how long ago he'd closed the shop and retreated here for solace. She wondered how bad the news was. Sympathy swelled. Her fretting over June's cough amounted to so little when held up beside whatever this father felt for his son.

Mr. Aldridge pushed himself up, then walked to the sofa. "Sit with me."

Though impatient to get home, she perched on the opposite end of the cushion from him. There remained enough room for a third person to sit between them.

"Mrs. Aldridge is coming home," he said quietly. "She's bringing Zeke to convalesce here." Yet he did not seem happy.

Cora Mae blinked. "That's good news. I'm sure it will be a comfort to have your family together again."

"Neither of them have been a comfort to me for years. But you are. I could not have carried on these past weeks if it were not for you."

Her fingers knotted together, and she studied them. "I do appreciate the work and the wages." She hoped the gentle reminder would be enough. Now that she knew he was not thrown into mourning, she was ready to leave.

"You have been a comfort to me," he repeated, "and you could be more." He withdrew a stack of bills from inside his pocket and laid it on the cushion between them.

She frowned. "That's more than usual, Mr. Aldridge. I'll take what I've earned, no more."

He slid closer, nudging the cash her way. "Wouldn't that bonus be helpful to you? And to little June?"

"Of course. But . . . are you suggesting I take this as another advance? I don't favor being in your debt, sir." It had taken her weeks to pay off the first advance.

"Must we really play this game, Miss Stewart? Surely you don't miss my meaning. I'm saying that I'm willing to pay you what you're worth. No penny would be unearned. I thought we understood each other. Remember that night I found you in the kitchen, fixing tea?"

She cast her mind back to that evening, replaying the scene in her mind. She licked dry lips. "I recollect it."

"It was soon after my wife called you out for having a child but no husband. I told you to feel comfortable around me, that I carried none of the judgment my wife had. You told me you were not ashamed of who you are, which pleased me greatly. But I knew better than to pursue a liaison with Mrs. Aldridge and June in the house."

Alarm pounded between her ears.

"When I invited you to dine with me that first night she was away, I told you I didn't mind your kind. In fact, I quite enjoy your kind."

"My kind," she choked out. "I reckoned you were talking about us Southerners. Or us poor folk. But all this time, you thought I was—" She could not bring herself to say the word for a woman who sold her body. "I'm not."

The inside of her mouth turned to cotton. But she needed to be paid for the work she'd done in the shop. She made to take the top few bills, but he caught her wrist.

"There's no shame in doing what you must to survive," he whispered. "I sent Cook home shortly after the mail arrived. We're alone. No one will know." His palm felt hot and damp on her skin.

"You would betray your wife in this way? Here, in her own parlor?" She hazarded a glance at his face and watched the dark in his eyes grow larger.

"Sarah and I have an understanding. I have needs. She doesn't always have the energy or inclination to meet them. I'm discreet, and she doesn't ask questions. In turn, I continue to provide for her a good life, a stable income, security."

Cora Mae's picture of Sarah Aldridge convulsed in her mind from a prejudiced, unfair woman to one who lived with a terrible secret. Her bitterness against Cora Mae and June made more sense. For one startling instant, she wondered if Mrs. Aldridge had known it would come to this. Was that why she'd resisted the employment arrangement? Was that why she'd tried to drive them away with harsh words and conditions?

Cora Mae struggled against his grip and felt bruises forming on her skin. "Let me go, Mr. Aldridge." Her racing pulse left her almost dizzy. "I'm not what you say I am!"

In a flash, he transformed into a man she'd not seen before this. "I'm tired of waiting," he said.

Chapter Twenty-Five

It was after five, but Ethan could see that lights were on inside the Aldridge's dress shop. The sign said it was closed, but he tried the door anyway.

Locked. So why were the lights on?

He knocked, waited, and heard nothing. Turning, Ethan blazed a quick trail across the front yard, scanning windows for other signs of life. Moonlight frosted the brittle grass beneath his feet. Shrubs bordering the house looked skeletal without their leaves, the dormant branches the color of cobwebs. A thin ribbon of light shone between the front parlor's curtains.

Upon reaching town not long ago, Ethan had stopped at Mrs. Beasley's to register for a room and drop off his things. There, Mrs. Beasley had told him that Cora Mae and June were staying there now, too. Only Cora Mae hadn't come home from work yet. So unless they had missed each other in passing, she had to be here.

At the front entrance to the private residence, his boot bumped into a brick coming loose from the short wall on the right side of the steps. He nudged it back into place, gained the landing, and lifted his fist to knock.

A woman shouted. *Cora Mae.*

Dread and anger licked through Ethan. He rattled the door, but it wouldn't give. Every sense alert and ready for battle, he bolted back down the front steps, grabbed the loose brick, and hurled it through the glass pane beside the door.

"Miss Stewart!" he shouted, reaching through the opening and unlocking the door. "Mr. Aldridge, I'm coming in."

Ethan burst into the vestibule.

"I will blow your head clean off your shoulders." The slightly slurred voice boomed from the direction of the parlor. The fact that the tailor wasn't already here to face his intruder meant that Ethan had caught him off guard. It would take Mr. Aldridge at least a moment or two to get his gun, unless he always carried it on his person, which Ethan doubted.

It only took an instant to absorb the irony. The last time Ethan entered a house not his own, he'd been shot by this man's son. Now here he was, on the brink of being fired upon by the father. His right hand—the one that wasn't there—cramped as if in warning.

Ethan wouldn't heed it. He'd worried that some danger lurked in this house ever since Zeke had made that comment about Cora Mae's living here being his father's idea. He'd written to her the next time he had a chance, urging her to be wary of her new employer, but the mail hadn't functioned for weeks.

"My name is Ethan Howard," he called out, crossing the vestibule and kicking in the double doors to the parlor. "I'm here to take Miss Stewart home."

With a cry, Cora Mae ran to his side, clutching her collar.

The sight of her after so many months, and the thought that she'd nearly come to harm, threatened to undo him. "Did he hurt you? Did he—dishonor you?"

"No." But bruises bloomed on her wrist. "Nothing more than that, thank God. Thank you."

Mr. Aldridge fumbled to load bullets into a revolver. An empty tumbler squatted on the desk, and an open bottle of whiskey sat the floor beside it. So this was Zeke's role model growing up. His hands shook, and Ethan judged it had less to do with drink and everything to do with the fact that this fastidious tailor was not a killer. He was scared, as his son had been.

Ethan lunged and wrested the gun from Mr. Aldridge's sweaty palm. The tailor's reaction time was terrible, thanks to the whiskey. Ethan backed away, and Mr. Aldridge dropped heavily into the chair, as if relieved to be done with entire business.

"Ethan Howard? One of those miner brothers?" Recognition sparked in his expression, quickly replaced by the same disdain the Howards had felt from most town folk. Town folk who used coal but looked down on those whose labor provided it. "Now what will you do, with only one arm?"

"Apparently more than you think." A mirthless smile twisted Ethan's lips, but he wouldn't reveal it was Zeke who'd shot him.

"You broke into my house. You broke my window, damaged my property!"

"There's the money to repair it, right there." Cora Mae gestured to a pile of money on the sofa. "I don't want the wages anymore—earned or not."

"You're trespassing," Mr. Aldridge said.

"We're leaving. I'll report my own break-in to the police—and why I did it—and you best think about how you'll explain the mess to your wife and son. They'll be here any minute, by the way."

The tailor blanched. "How would you know?"

"Chattanooga happens to be on the way home from Georgia. I stopped there and found them. When I heard they were planning to travel soon, I offered myself as an escort home. It would have been too much for Mrs. Aldridge to manage on her own."

Mr. Aldridge swallowed. "If you traveled together, why aren't they with you?"

"They were waiting to hire a hackney cab. I traveled much lighter, so I had no need of it." Besides, Ethan couldn't shake the urgency he felt to find Cora Mae. He thanked God he hadn't arrived any later.

"Goodbye, Mr. Aldridge," Cora Mae said. "I quit."

Ethan asked her to wait for him in the vestibule. He dropped the bullets from the chamber into a vase full of water and flowers, then tossed the gun into the fire to keep it out of play long enough for a safe exit.

Mr. Aldridge stood but seemed as if he had no idea what to do next.

Ethan did. Placing himself nose-to-nose with the lecher, he grabbed the man's shirtfront and twisted until the celluloid collar popped free. He lowered his voice and growled, "If you come near her or June again, and I mean within twenty yards of either of them, you will find out exactly what a one-armed man can do."

~

Not until they had put a block behind them did Cora Mae stop on the sidewalk and turn to Ethan, convincing herself this was real. "This feels like a dream," she whispered. "Having you here." Her eyes watered, and no more words would come.

He was every bit the man she remembered him to be, but more. Thinner, perhaps, but stronger. More rugged, but also more refined. There was something deeper and more settled about him now.

"It felt like a nightmare," he said. "Hearing you shout. Not knowing if I could reach you in time."

"But you did." She shuddered and wondered what he'd said to Mr. Aldridge at the end. But she didn't need to know. She was through with the Aldridges for good, and the less time spent thinking on what happened tonight—and what could have happened—the better.

"Are you sure he didn't do more than mark your wrist? Would you tell me if he did?"

Heat climbed into her cheeks despite the chill. If Mr. Aldridge had done as he'd intended, she had no idea what she would have done. To speak of it would be so shameful. To have Ethan know another man had taken her . . . she wouldn't be able to bear that.

"I promise you came in time." Small gray puffs appeared and vanished with her breath.

He exhaled, circled a thumb over the back of her hand, then released her. "My enlistment is up. I meant it when I said I'm here to take you home. And I don't just mean to Mrs. Beasley's boardinghouse. I aim to bring you all the way home to your mama."

Tears welled. Overcome, she covered her face and bent her head against his shoulder. Everything in her yearned to embrace him.

His arms went around her, cinching her against him while wind tugged her skirt and pulled strands of hair from their pins. "I won't steal another kiss from you," he said. "But I do want to keep you from falling."

Laughter broke through her sobs, and her shoulders shook as she nodded.

"You still want to go home, don't you?"

"With all my heart." She stepped back and looked at him. His form was veiled in shadows, calling to mind their after-dark talks outside the courthouse in Marietta. "I wrote you letters, but I don't suppose you got many of them."

"I received three. I take it you didn't receive all mine either."

"The last was the bundle of four, dated September 10. We loved them, by the way. Especially the letters to June and Sassy."

A subtle smile hooked his cheek. What she wouldn't give to know every word he'd written to her. The space between them seemed to hum with things unsaid.

Maybe it was better this way. Having more letters from him would not make it easier to say goodbye.

"How's June?" He offered his arm, and she took it, allowing him to escort her back toward the boardinghouse.

"Sick. Her cough is something awful. I don't know if she should travel yet."

"Can I see her?"

"It would do her good."

Once they returned to Mrs. Beasley's, Ethan followed Cora Mae upstairs into the chilled garret. "June, I have someone here who wants to see you."

Ethan grabbed a chair by its back and set it down next to her bed. "Hi there, little lady."

At the sound of his voice, June turned. "Sergeant Howard!" The words caught, and she began coughing again.

He shook his head. "That's too big a cough to come from you."

She reached up, and he leaned down, clasping her to himself before gently releasing her. From inside his jacket, he withdrew her long-lost doll.

"Sissy!" June hugged the raggedy thing, then picked up Sassy and held them both. "Together at last. Thank you kindly, Sergeant. Are you feeling better? Is your arm sore?"

"I'm feeling much better, thank you."

"Where you been all this time?"

He laughed. "Expecting me sooner, were you? I was busy getting healed up and then visiting some special people I think you know, when I wasn't nursing other sick men in Marietta."

"Did you bring Feller with you?"

"He wanted to come something fierce. But I left him with Mrs. McGee and Mrs. Stewart for the time being. He's a fair guard dog, even with only one eye." When she asked if he was going back to the army, he told her his years of service were complete. "That means I'm just a mister now, not a sergeant."

"That means you can do whatever you want instead of always following orders?"

"It means I can do whatever I think is best." He tapped her on the nose. "And do you know what I think is best right now?"

"No."

Ethan stood and walked around the room, feeling the draft come in through the window and roof despite the newspapers and rags stuffed in the cracks and holes. "The best thing we can do is to trade rooms."

"Do you mean it? Mama, did you hear that?"

"I mean it." He crossed the small space to Cora Mae. "She'll never get better in this room, and you're liable to fall ill yourself. I won't let that happen. You take my room, and I'll stay here."

"For how long?" June was already climbing out of bed.

"Until you're well enough to go home."

June clapped, and then fell into a gasping cough once again.

Ethan settled a hand on Cora Mae's shoulder. "I know you're worried."

She cut her voice low so June wouldn't overhear. "My mother sounded like that, and she's dying of brown lung."

"And my father died of black lung. But little June has neither. A body can cough from all kinds of things other than fatal disease. She's sick from the air, and we're changing that."

"I pray that's so," Cora Mae said. "Now please, tell me about my mother. How was she, the last you saw her?"

His hesitation did not bode well. "Worse than my first visit with her. She's getting weaker."

She fought the fear climbing up her throat.

"Why don't you make some tea while I move June to room six and bring my own things up here? I noticed a crack in one of my windowpanes, but it's nothing compared to this."

Cora Mae reckoned that to be polite, she should argue with him. But she was so eager for June to be well again, and it felt so good to be taken care of, that she simply agreed.

By the time she brought a tray of tea up to room six, June was beaming in the bed, her hair in two coppery plaits over her nightdress. Ethan was on one knee, building a fire in the hearth. She set the tray on a small table before joining him at the fireplace.

He stood and rolled his shoulders back. "I'm glad you and Mrs. Beasley found each other."

"So am I." She told him what a gift the older woman had been to her, then brought June her tea. "Sit up, please. It's hot. Little sips."

"Yes, Mama."

"For me?" Ethan pointed to the third cup of tea.

"Please. Sit." In the corner of the room, Cora Mae sat across from him and focused on the steam curling from her cup, suddenly at a loss for what to say. Despite her best efforts, her mind looped back to Mr. Aldridge. She couldn't believe that all this time, he'd thought she was "that kind" of woman. She didn't want to think about it, let alone talk about it, and never in front of June.

Ethan stirred sugar into his tea. Leaning in, he murmured low enough so June wouldn't hear, "How long has she been calling you 'Mama'?"

"Since Marietta," Cora Mae replied, grateful for another place to put her thoughts. "She thought that would make us more likely to stay together. It sounded strange at first, but it seems to fit now. When her step-pa skedaddled, I agreed to take care of June as though she were my own. And now I feel as if she is."

"Of course she is."

She nodded, grateful he needed no convincing. She asked after Chaplain Littleton and Anne, and he told her they were well, last he knew, and that they'd transferred to Nashville. "I don't suppose you have any idea about Venus?" she asked. "I've thought of her often. I pray she found her mother."

He added a little more sugar to his cup, then set down the spoon and sipped. "I know she went south when Sherman's army did, but beyond that, I could only guess. It's good of you to remember her."

"I'm not likely to ever forget her. Her story of being sold away from her mother put my own separation in perspective. And the way she shared that comfrey salve with Little Feller, though dogs like him inspired such fear and pain . . . No. A body doesn't forget a woman like that, now, do they?"

"A woman who repays hurt with kindness? No. A body does not forget." His smile loosened something inside her. She cast about for another topic, another question. Anything to distract from what she felt when he looked at her that way.

"Whatever happened to the widow you mentioned—Mrs. Buford? Did she stay long in Marietta?"

He took a drink before responding. "She did stay long. She stayed until early October, in fact, and only left then because we were running out of food. When Sherman cut his own supply line, that meant we weren't just going without mail. We went without incoming rations, too, and had only what we'd previously stocked, along with what sutlers could find, which wasn't much. We had to survive on less than what was normal for one person, but Mrs. Buford was supposed to be eating for two."

Cora Mae blinked, the implication settling over her. "Oh my. The poor woman." She didn't reckon a young widow with child would find much comfort in Marietta. "You looked out for her?"

"As much as I could."

She didn't doubt that. "And were you friends?"

"As much as we could be, with her in mourning for a husband and so many patients needing care and transfer." He didn't look at her as he said this. He picked at a thread on his sleeve.

"Were you—are you—more?" She wondered if it came across as prying. But they'd shared so much in the last five months, and she hoped he would share this news, too.

"She's still in mourning."

That didn't answer her question, and yet, in a fashion, it did. He could have said no. What he said was that the timing wasn't right. But Mrs. Buford wouldn't mourn forever. The widow had been in Marietta with Ethan long enough to recognize that he would be a devoted husband and father for her baby. And why shouldn't he marry such a courageous woman and have the family he longed for?

A strange mixture of emotions spiraled through Cora Mae. The one she grabbed hold of was relief. He was moving on, as she would with her own betrothed. It was only right that he should.

Reaching across the table, she dared to touch his hand. "If you're saying you'll court her later, I'm pleased for you. I'd count it a comfort to think of you well-matched."

Ethan coughed into his elbow, and she realized it was the first time she'd heard him cough all night. When she remarked on this, he blamed it on irritation from the smoke of the fire.

"What of the coal dust?" she asked.

A wan smile lifted his lips. "As I said, a body can cough for all kinds of reasons other than fatal disease." He told her of the conversation he'd had with Dr. Wilcox after an examination of his lungs.

"Ethan, that's wonderful!" His Christian name slipped from her before she had time to think about it. In their letters, they'd addressed each other more formally, but that wasn't how she thought of him. They'd been through so much. Now, Cora Mae felt like laughing and crying at once, so intense was her joy at this news. "You deserve a long and healthy life, full of happiness with your wife and children. Babies and grandbabies. Great-grands." She felt herself color to speak of it, but this man was made for family, more than any she'd ever met.

He met her gaze. "So do you. Your mother tells me Mr. Ferguson is a good man."

She shifted her thoughts to her betrothed, though the agreement felt so distant. "He was my father's friend. He offered to marry me and provide for me and my mother." Just as Ethan had offered to marry and provide for her. She was about to point out that the two men were not so different but thought better of it. Aside from their sense of duty, they were not at all the same. Glancing at June, she was relieved to find the young girl had set her tea on the stand and settled down to rest. Once Ethan returned to his room, she would put another sheet of India rubber on the mattress.

"Do you love him?"

The fire he'd built hissed and popped while she searched for an answer that would suit. "I respect him. My mother and I owe him a debt for the kindness he's shown in Pap's absence." She traced her finger around the rim of her porcelain cup. "It's a practical arrangement."

"I see."

Maybe he did. If he and Mrs. Buford had an understanding, maybe it was more practical than romantic as well. Even so, she wanted to explain. "Do you recall I told you about a textile engineer who came to Roswell?"

"I remember."

"I didn't tell you that he took a shine to me. Promised to take me up to New York and marry me, then take me every place I had a hankerin' to see."

Ethan's eyebrows rose. "And?"

"He broke his word." She shifted in the chair, mustering the courage to force out the rest. "Because he already had a wife."

He leaned back. "Filthy, lying cheat."

She shrugged, as if she had not been crushed. "He told me I was too common to be his wife, but I could be his—" Her cheeks burned. Her longing for romance and escape had almost cost her honor. And tonight, another married man had almost taken it. Any fear and shame she'd felt before twisted into a hard knot of anger. "I said no, of course, and stayed at the mill. When rumors started about Mr. Hampton and me, Mr. Ferguson is the one who squashed them. He took up for me and wouldn't abide anyone saying a word against my reputation."

She sipped her tea, then warmed her hands on the cup. "He could have let that ugliness with Mr. Hampton put a wedge between him and my family, but he didn't. He's a good man and loyal. I'll not break my promise to him the way Mr. Hampton broke his promise to me. I aim to be honorable. Mr. Hampton and Mr. Aldridge both fancied I wasn't, but as God is my witness, I will not prove them right."

Brow furrowed, Ethan looked far wearier than he had twenty minutes ago. "I'll do my best to help you keep your word. For now, I'll take my leave so you ladies can rest."

Abandoning his unfinished tea, he went to June and tucked the quilt around her body until she couldn't move an inch. "Snug as a Junebug in a rug." He kissed her forehead, and Cora Mae's breath caught at his tenderness.

June stirred and yawned. "You know something? You weren't too bad for a Yankee, but you're even better as our friend. Don't you think so, Mama?"

A bittersweet smile curved her lips. "I do."

Ethan Howard was the best friend she'd ever had.

Chapter Twenty-Six

WEDNESDAY, NOVEMBER 23, 1864

Ethan could hear June coughing from the end of the hall as he made his way toward room six. It was only two days since he'd given up his room, so he didn't expect her to be well yet. But her rasping scraped at him.

He knocked, and Cora Mae opened the door. Sunlight from the west-facing window behind her glinted on the thick braid coiled around her head. "Getting cold in the garret yet?"

He wouldn't admit that his fingers tingled from the attic's chill. "Actually, I've just been to see Mrs. Beasley, who pumped me full of gingerbread and her impressions of you. All good, by the way. I understand you've already talked to her about joining the housekeeping staff here."

"Part-time," she said. "To cover our room and board. If she can afford to pay for more hours, she'll let me know."

From what Ethan had gathered during his conversation with the older woman, she was hard pressed to pay the staff she had. But she was determined to help Cora Mae and June as much as she could.

"She gave me permission to fix the crack in your window." He held up a thin sheet of wood. "So here I am. If you don't mind."

Cora Mae opened the door wider, and he stepped past her. Birch branches shook outside the window, and light and shadow played across her face. He tried not to notice how lovely she was.

Shifting his attention, Ethan strode to where June sat playing with paper dolls cut from newspaper and dropped a kiss onto her silky hair.

"What's that for?" She pointed.

"To cover that pane so wind can't get through anymore." He nodded to the cracked glass.

"Oh, it's just a tiny smidge of wind."

Removing his jacket, Ethan stepped over to the window in his shirtsleeves. "No smidges allowed."

Tucking the plank under his right arm, he drew several nails from his pocket and held them between his lips before unhooking the hammer from his belt. The tool pressed to his palm with two fingers, he grasped the plank and placed it over the glass. Angling his body, he pinned the wood in place with the end of his right forearm—and froze.

Cora Mae appeared at his side. "May I?"

"I think you'd better," he said around the nails poking from his mouth.

She reached up and wiggled a nail from between his lips. "Where do you want it?"

"There." Hammer still in hand, Ethan pointed to a spot on the plank.

Pinching the nail, she held it in place.

"Don't miss!" June piped up from the bed.

Ethan chuckled. He tapped the nail into the wood until Cora Mae could release her grip. Then, with a few solid swings, he drove it into the wooden frame beneath. "Next," he said around the nails.

"Oh, stop it." She laughed, holding out her hand. "Let me have them."

Bending his head, he dropped the nails into her palm. "Thought you'd never ask." He grinned.

Together, they drove several more nails into place all around the pane until the cracked square of glass was completely sealed. Ethan stood back, satisfied. It wouldn't win any beauty contests, but it got the job done.

"Thank you."

"Thank *you*." He couldn't have accomplished the task without her. "And now I have a favor to ask. I find myself in need of a new shirt. If I supplied the material, would you have time to sew it for me?"

The corners of her lips tipped up. "I would."

"And if I should happen to come across a bolt of fine green wool, the kind that makes warm dresses for ladies and girls in the winter—would you know what to do with that, too?"

She smoothed a wrinkle from the thin calico dress he'd seen her wear in Marietta. The lightweight fabric was no good for winter. "I couldn't pay for it."

Moving to the hearth, Ethan knelt and stacked more logs upon the dying flames. "Never mind the cost. You and June need clothing more suited to the weather. And for traveling. And I need to get the fabric out of the attic where it's doing no earthly good."

"You already purchased it?" Her voice was laced with disbelief.

Rising, he turned to face her. "I paid a visit to the Aldridges' dress shop earlier today to see how Zeke and his mother were getting along. I also explained to her what I had in mind for the two of you. She insisted on giving the fabric. She said she noticed you hadn't been paid for your last week of work, and she'd like to settle accounts."

Her complexion paled. "Did you see anyone else?"

"Zeke was resting in his room, so I didn't disturb him. Mr. Aldridge made himself scarce as soon as I entered the shop."

"Do you think Mrs. Aldridge knows what happened?"

"I didn't ask." But he had a hunch she had figured out at least some of it. Enough to be ashamed of her husband, though not surprised. "But let's not change the subject." The less time she spent dwelling on Mr. Aldridge, the better. "Please, make something for yourself. Make a shirt for me, too, and I'll consider it a fair trade. Any extra white linen, you can use for yourselves."

"A new dress? For me, too?" June grinned, accentuating the point of her small chin.

Cora Mae's nose pinked as she looked at the little girl. "Well, then. I reckon I best get busy." The smile she turned on Ethan held far more than a mere thank-you. "Do you know your measurements?"

"Figured you'd do it right." He reached into his pocket and withdrew a measuring tape.

Accepting it, she circled around him and pressed one end of the tape to the back of his neck. A shiver swept over him as her fingertip slid over his spine, stopping at his waist. Next, she held the tape shoulder to shoulder across his back.

"Need to write it down?" he asked.

"I'll remember." She came back to face him. The faint scent of rosewater filled the space between them. "Hold out your arms, please."

Heat flashed over his face as he raised only his left arm. Beyond the partially boarded window, leaves fell in a blizzard of brown and gold.

"Ethan," she murmured gently as she measured to his wrist, "wouldn't you like both your sleeves to fit you properly? It's up to you, of course. But I think you'd be more comfortable with a perfect fit."

He looked at her, his perfect fit. "Yes, I would." He struggled to swallow his longing. Still holding her gaze, he spread both arms wide and felt the weight of the emptiness they held.

Her cheeks bloomed pink.

His eyes closed while her touch trailed to the end of his right arm, where the fabric had grown thin and torn.

"Good," she said, and he lowered his arms. "I just need one more measurement." She lifted the tape over his head and drew it snugly around his neck, her fingertips cool as they brushed his skin and feathered his hair above his collar. The flush in her face matched the heat in his own. She was close enough to hear his heart hammering.

It had been hard to be apart from Cora Mae. But it was even harder to be together.

THURSDAY, NOVEMBER 24, 1864

Mrs. Beasley and her cooks had outdone themselves, providing a Thanksgiving feast that overwhelmed the only Georgian boarders in the house. After living on rations and sutler fare for three years, Ethan's own stomach couldn't handle much of it.

That didn't mean he couldn't be thankful. He was.

With the bustle of the day behind them, Cora Mae and June had joined him and Mrs. Beasley in the older woman's private parlor. June rested on the sofa with her head on Cora Mae's lap while Mrs. Beasley rocked in the corner, her knitting needles clicking a gentle rhythm against the crackling fire.

With a mug steaming on the table beside him, Ethan read to the captive audience from one of his favorite books, *The Three Musketeers*. He and his brothers had called themselves such, years ago. Reading it aloud again gave him the feeling of being with family, of being home. The hollow space in his chest began to fill. He glanced up and caught June's drowsy blinking, the hint of Cora Mae's dimples, and Mrs. Beasley's contented smile.

Careful, Ethan told himself. *This is not your family.*

And yet, Mrs. Beasley had always been as much of a grandmother to him as any he could remember. Cora Mae and June, he could train himself to regard as sisters.

"Ethan." Mrs. Beasley's quiet tone stopped him from turning the page. "We've lost one."

He looked up and saw June sleeping. "Then I'll stop there for the night."

"More tomorrow?" Cora Mae asked. "She'll be eager to learn what happens next." She told him how June begged for more chapters from *The Swiss Family Robinson*, and it warmed him to think of Cora Mae reading from the book that had fed his own love of learning. He wondered if she realized how proud he was of her, how he admired that she'd reinvented herself time and again in order to give June the best situation she could.

Sisters, he reminded himself. They had to be like sisters to him.

"Have you given any thought to what you'll do after your upcoming journey?" Mrs. Beasley asked him.

"As a matter of fact, I have. The last five months have taught me plenty, but what I keep coming back to is how this war has affected the children. June has a family, but other little ones aren't so fortunate. I've been thinking of the other mill hands, too. Most of them are old enough to be on their own or old enough to care for younger siblings, but some are orphaned outright. By the way, I inquired at Louisville after the Roswell workers I knew by name."

Cora Mae's eyebrows lifted. "You went to the female prison?"

"I did. I looked for Cynthia and Fern, to bring them word from their aunt. I also looked for Damaris and Tabby while I was there. No one could tell me what became of them, except to say they likely found prison life too harsh and traded it for domestic service. But there's no record of where they went. I'm sorry I don't have more information. But that prison was full of disease, so if they found a different place, we can be thankful, at least, for that."

She agreed. "Thank you for looking. So what do you aim to do?"

Setting the book aside, Ethan tasted his coffee, savoring the fresh cream that had been absent from his campfire brews. "I wrote a fair share of letters for the patients in my care. I think of the wives and children left behind. Especially the orphans. What kind of role models will they choose? Will they grow up hating the other half of our country? Will they let hostility steal any chance for joy? Who will take an interest in their education, teaching them to read and write, as Mrs. Beasley taught me? Most importantly, who will help them heal?"

The knitting needles fell silent. Mrs. Beasley rested them on her lap, bestowing her full attention on Ethan.

"I had a lot of time to think, especially on my long rides to and from Roswell. So I talked to the Littletons about it, and it turns out they've had a similar burden. They're planning to open a Soldiers Orphans Home, and the funding is already underway. They've asked me to be on staff to shepherd the boys. The home will be in Tennessee, and we expect orphans from families who fought on both sides. Teaching these kids to love their enemies, to love each other, will be one of the most important lessons they can learn. If the country is going to heal after this war, it's a lesson for all of us." It felt strange to describe a future that did not include Cora Mae or June. But it was still a future he believed in.

"Oh, Ethan." Mrs. Beasley's voice warbled. "There is no better man than you for the job."

Cora Mae's eyes shone in the firelight. "I agree. And the need for safe and loving homes for children is so great." She looked down, her lashes dark against her cheeks as she smoothed June's hair. "You said you'd work with the boys. Will Anne Littleton teach the girls?"

"The Littletons see themselves in a more administrative role, with regular chaplain duties, although they'd like to find a southern couple to help shoulder those. They'll hire a woman to shepherd the girls, but it may take some time to find the right one. Formal education is not required because there will be separate teachers for academic subjects. But the shepherdess must have life experience the children can relate to and be willing to love on kids whether their daddies wore blue or gray. She must see the hurt behind poor behavior while keeping a firm hand in training character. She must be able to love children like they were her own."

He took a drink and tried not to look for her reaction. He tried not to dwell on the fact that he had just described Cora Mae.

~

Days marched by. As June improved in health and spirits, Cora Mae stayed busy with housekeeping or sewing while her emotions tumbled about inside her, looking for a safe place to land. Hearing Ethan speak of the future he planned endeared him to her all the more. Watching him interact with June further convinced her of what she already knew. Any children in his care would be truly blessed.

In the two weeks since his arrival, June had not wet the bed. Even as Cora Mae rejoiced in the respite, she wondered how long it would last. She wondered if the next upheaval in the little girl's life would show itself in soiled sheets, in more tears and secret shame.

Every stitch she made on Ethan's shirt seemed to bind their friendship closer, though she knew the end was coming. Eventually, the strands would snap, and whatever they had would unravel.

Snow fell, coating trees in frosty crystals and casting a silvery glow into the room. At last, the dresses were made, the shirt was complete, and June had all but stopped coughing. When Ethan purchased three tickets for the steamboat to Louisville, Cora Mae felt the threads that bound them pull taut.

Chapter Twenty-Seven

WEDNESDAY, DECEMBER 14, 1864

Rain pelted the windows as the train hurtled through the dark. Shadows quivered across the compartment. On the opposite bench, June dozed, curled between Ethan's arm and his side. So close were they seated, the hem of Cora Mae's new wool skirt covered the tops of his shoes.

If there was a way to be near him without missing him already, she hadn't found it. Still, she could keep busy, so she picked up her sewing and began stitching again. If she could concentrate, June's new pinafore would be finished before they reached Nashville.

But the straight seams didn't require much focus, so her thoughts drifted stubbornly away. They weren't a comfort. Sighing, she dipped her needle in and out of the white cotton and then carelessly pricked her finger. She glared at the drop of blood on her fingertip, then wiped it quickly on a scrap of fabric in her basket.

"The light's too dim for that kind of work, maybe," Ethan offered.

She met his gaze. "I see just fine." June didn't wake up, so she spoke again. "I see my little Junebug is quite attached to you."

He smiled down at the little girl. "She is, isn't she? Quite latched on."

"That's not what I meant. She's so fond of you."

"I'm fond of her, too."

Cora Mae stabbed her needle through the corner of June's apron pocket and pulled it through the other side. "If you keep being so wonderful with her, it'll only make it harder when she says goodbye." In truth, it was far too late. He'd won June's heart time and again.

"Should I pinch her?"

She held back the laughter that threatened. "You're impossible." Giving up on her sewing, she tucked it away while one thought alone stitched through her: once they arrived in Roswell, she would not be able to keep June and Ethan both.

"We're stopping," he murmured as the chugging slowed, rousing the little girl from her sleep. "Stay close to me once we get off. Nashville is glutted with Yankees."

"So I recall." The iron wheels screeched to a halt, and steam hissed from the funnel as they climbed down narrow steps. "Button your coat," she told June, wrapping the green-and-red-plaid shawl over the child's head before tying her own tartan flannel beneath her chin.

Ethan offered his arm. "So I don't lose you."

Cora Mae took it, holding June's hand on the other side. Together, they weaved through the crowded platform to the depot where they'd purchase fare for the next stage of the journey.

"Two adults and one child for Chattanooga, please." Ethan's breath steamed against the glass above the ticket counter for the Nashville & Chattanooga Railroad line.

The man behind the counter shook his head. "No passage for civilians."

Dread drizzled over Cora Mae. She rubbed June's hands in her own to keep them warm.

"But I rode this railroad a month ago coming the other way," Ethan pressed.

"A lot's changed in a month."

"Such as?"

"Such as Sherman diving down south and General Hood making a dash at us while he's away. The line between Nashville and Chattanooga is to be kept clear for military use only right now. Sorry."

Cora Mae studied Ethan's face as he led them away from the counter. For a moment he didn't look at her, scanning the crowd instead. Outside the depot, carriages and wagons rattled over the street, and horses stomped and nickered.

"Well?" she tried, tentatively. "What do we do now?"

When he turned to face her, his jaw was set. "We improvise. But first, let's get you two settled in for the night. The Littletons are expecting us and are especially eager to see you."

Cora Mae smiled at June. "They'll be so surprised at how much you've grown."

"Are we going to spend the night in army tents?" June asked.

"Not tonight," Ethan assured her. The Littletons were staying in the home of a local couple who were Union sympathizers. When Ethan had written the reverend that he'd be coming through Nashville, a brief telegram reply held an invitation to stay the night.

Cora Mae was grateful for the chance to see the Littletons again. They'd treated her and June kindly, and she'd left Marietta before she could thank them for that.

Darkness surrounded the horse-drawn cab Ethan hired to take them across the occupied city. The smells and sounds were enough to remind her of Marietta, only Nashville was many times larger and more overwhelming.

When they arrived at the house, Cora Mae had to crane her neck to see the top of it. Six columns supported the portico over the front porch. Not even the founders of Roswell could boast a finer home.

Ethan asked the driver to wait for him, then handed her and June down from the cab before escorting them to the double front doors.

June frowned. "Why do they need two doors when one will do? Aren't Nashville bodies the same size as other bodies?"

Before Cora Mae could reply, one of those doors opened, and a Negro man in a servant's uniform ushered them inside a front hall with a grand central staircase. His hair was almost completely white, his shoulders rounded with age. They followed his shuffling steps across marble tiles and into another room, where four smiling faces greeted them. Both women wore hoops beneath their skirts.

"Cora Mae! June!" Anne Littleton rose from a plush sofa the color of chinaberries and hurried to pull them into her soft embrace. She kissed their cheeks and stood back again. "If I didn't know you were coming, I doubt I'd recognize either of you. How much you've changed since summer."

"How much, indeed." There was so much to tell this woman. But after only the briefest exchange, Cora Mae turned to Reverend Littleton and the couple who had opened their home to them. There seemed to be quite an age difference between the husband and the wife, who looked to be not much older than Cora Mae despite the shining silver streak in her hair.

"May I introduce you to Mr. David Englewood and his daughter, Mrs. Daisy Buford."

Ethan looked as surprised as Cora Mae was. "You're a great one for secrets, Reverend." He shook the men's hands, kissed Mrs. Littleton, and bowed over Mrs. Buford's hand. "I had no idea this was the couple putting you up."

"It would have been too costly to explain in a telegram. But yes, Mr. Englewood and Mrs. Buford are of one accord with our purposes and were only too eager to host you three as well."

"The Littletons have told us so much about you." Mrs. Buford greeted the visitors before settling her attention on Ethan. Her rounded cheeks and figure hinted that hidden beneath the higher waist of her hoop skirt, a baby grew healthy and strong.

This was the woman who would likely make Ethan a husband and father in a matter of months. With the way she looked at him, Cora Mae judged the courtship would be short once it began. Her eyes burned. She summoned a smile for them both.

"I'm so pleased to meet you, Mrs. Buford," she said, and she meant it. "Thank you for inviting us into your fine home."

"You must be weary from your travels," Mr. Englewood said. Gray fanned through hair that shone with pomade. "James will show you to your rooms where you can rest and wash before dinner."

"That sounds fine, sir," Ethan began. "But I'm afraid I've got to go out again and make new arrangements for tomorrow. You all continue with your evening, and I'll return as soon as may be."

"I'd lend you one of my horses for your errand," Mr. Englewood said, "but I emptied my stables to help supply the Union cavalry."

"No need. I left the cab waiting outside for me, but thank you just the same."

Reverend Littleton clapped Ethan on the back. "When you return, we've got some ideas for the Orphans Home we'd like to discuss with you."

"That's right," Mrs. Buford added. "I'm interested in helping with the girls."

The Littletons looked at each other, then at Ethan, as if this was the first time they'd heard of it.

Mrs. Buford smiled at Ethan, one hand covering her middle. "It's perfect, don't you think?"

~

Holding June's hand, Cora Mae followed James to the room that had been prepared for them, questions swirling through her mind. If Mr. Englewood owned slaves, as the presence of James suggested, why had he personally invested in aiding the Union? Why had Mrs. Buford's husband died for the cause of their freedom? There was so much she didn't know, but she couldn't think of a polite way to find out.

In the quiet chamber papered with green country scenes on pale yellow background, the fatigue of the journey caught up with her. Though tempted to skip dinner and surrender to sleep, she and June washed, brushed and re-pinned their hair, and then sponged their dresses as clean as they could.

Two hours later, a soft knock on the door drew Cora Mae to open it.

Ethan smiled, freshly shaven and smelling of balsam and leather. "Hungry?"

"Yes!" June leapt off the bed where she'd been resting.

"How did it go?" Cora Mae asked, because she could not bring herself to ask for his reaction to seeing Mrs. Buford again. "Did you find a way for us to carry on tomorrow?"

He told her he had, then led them downstairs to the dining room, where the others waited.

"I'm sorry, I haven't been clear," Mrs. Buford said. "The child can eat in the kitchen with the servants. Or we can send up a tray to her room. She'll be more comfortable there."

Cora Mae stiffened. Perhaps it was Mrs. Buford or her father who would be more comfortable with that.

"I want to stay with you, Mama. And with Mr. Howard." June held fast to his hand while grasping a fold of Cora Mae's skirt.

"Mr. Howard has things to discuss with the grown-ups, but the two of us can eat in the kitchen," Cora Mae told her, somewhat relieved at the notion. Sharing a table with their hosts suddenly seemed beyond her.

"Oh, nonsense," Anne said. "June will be no trouble."

Mr. Englewood hesitated.

"I don't mean to speak out of turn." Ethan cleared his throat. "It may be irregular, sir, to have children at table, but considering how irregular these last several months have been for these two, I don't suppose it would hurt anything to have them eat together with us right here."

Mrs. Buford flicked a glance at her father before turning her dazzling blue eyes on Ethan. "Your charitable feelings do you credit. No wonder the Littletons speak so highly of you as the perfect shepherd for the orphan boys."

With a look that told June to be on her best behavior, Cora Mae pulled out a chair for her, then scooted her in, while another aged slave—or servant—laid an extra place setting.

After the meal was blessed, Cora Mae told Anne about Mrs. Beasley and the fine dresses she'd worked on at the Aldridges', all the while urging June not to slurp the soup and half-listening to whatever Ethan was saying beside her.

"Tell me more about yourself, Mr. Howard." Mr. Englewood took a roll and passed the basket along. "What did you do before the war?"

"I mined coal, sir. In Cannelton, Indiana. Our family moved there from Kentucky when my mother died, and my father and brothers and I mined coal there since I was twelve."

Mrs. Buford flinched. Had she not known this before? Hadn't she ever asked?

"You don't say." Mr. Englewood looked pointedly at his daughter. He ripped his roll in half, and steam rose from its middle.

"But you'd never know it to look at him now, would you, Daddy? We were all such different people before the war, anyway," Mrs. Buford said.

Cora Mae tried not to simmer, but they made it sound as though mining was something to be ashamed of, a secret to be kept hidden. And what was that supposed to mean, 'you'd never know it to look at him now'? Was she talking about his incomplete arm? Would she define him by what he lacked?

The room seemed to grow warmer, though there was no fire to be seen. In fact, an iron stove with intricate scrollwork and decorative knobs sat in the hearth instead.

"I've never seen a stove like that before," she said. "Does it heat with wood?"

"Of course not, my dear." Mr. Englewood finished buttering his bread and took a bite. "That's coal."

"I see." She'd reckoned as much. "Then how fortunate that miners pull it from the earth." She smiled and caught Ethan's eye, wondering if she'd said too much. But his lips tilted and pressed together, the way they always did when he kept back a chuckle.

"What matters most now is not our past but our future," the widow insisted.

Cora Mae burned her tongue on the soup rather than let herself speak again. No one would be who they were now without the past that formed them. She treasured every story Ethan had shared about his life, as well as what Mrs. Beasley had told her. The future would not be possible without the past. This was true of people, and it was true of the country, North and South. But she wouldn't correct her hostess.

As if reading her dismay, Anne smiled across the table, and the kindness cooled Cora Mae's irritation. "Now, Miss June." The older woman leaned forward. "I heard that Sassy is no longer alone. Is it true? Has she reunited with her sister at last?"

"You heard right!" June pulled from her pockets the two handkerchief dolls, both full of wrinkles, and handed them across the table.

"Dear me," Mrs. Buford whispered. "Are those dusting rags? What on earth?"

Another wave of heat flashed over Cora Mae. Pasting a smile in place, she explained, "These are June's beloved dolls. One of them was made with help from Mr. Howard and with fabric from Anne's own apron. They have traveled a great distance to be here, and I know they look it."

Anne crooned over each one as if they were made of porcelain. "There now, back to your mama," she said, and returned them to June.

Mrs. Buford had the decency to blush at her blunder. "How charming. Looks can be deceiving, can't they? For example, you may wonder at our keeping servants when Johnson emancipated slaves in Tennessee in October."

Reverend Littleton looked up. "Johnson? I understood that Lincoln's Emancipation Proclamation set slaves free in January 1863, nearly two years ago now."

Mr. Englewood touched a linen napkin to his mouth. "Lincoln's Proclamation freed slaves in states in rebellion against the United States. Tennessee, although a seceded state, did not fall under the provisions of the proclamation because it was and is under Union control, with Andrew Johnson serving as Military Governor. So, my daughter is correct. Johnson freed Tennessee slaves two months ago."

"But these servants didn't want to leave," Mrs. Buford added. "Where would they go in their old age? Here, they are fed and sheltered and now paid. They're grateful not to be evicted, and they're free to go whenever they please."

"They've been part of your household a long time?" Ethan asked.

"I should say so. These fifty years and more," Mr. Englewood replied. "They were purchased by my father when I was a boy. This was my father's house. It was only when he died five years ago that I was able to free his servants. So you see, even before Johnson decided the issue, our servants had their manumission papers."

"My late husband, Joseph, grew up with none," Mrs. Buford interjected. "He and his parents were always of one mind with Mr. Lincoln on that score. You'll find a variety of opinions in Tennessee on all kinds of political matters. That's what has made these last few years so volatile here. Neighbors turned against neighbors, brothers against brothers. Fathers against sons. Or sons-in-law."

Silence followed, broken only by the scrape of silver on china. It was a comfort to learn that, despite initial impressions, James and the other servants here were not in bondage. At least, not anymore.

Anne laid down her spoon. "Mrs. Buford has been volunteering with me three days a week."

"Not nursing, I hope, in your condition?" Ethan voiced a concern that was only reasonable.

"Oh no," the reverend assured him. "It wouldn't do to expose her to illness. She and Anne have been watching the children who traveled with their mothers to visit their sick and wounded fathers. They come from all over."

Cora Mae softened at that. "That's very good of you." Children ought to be kept close in such a place. They ought not run loose and see what they shouldn't, as June had.

The main course arrived, and servants brought plates of steak, mashed potatoes, and green beans. The meat was tough, and she wondered if it was something other than beef. The knives were so sharp, Cora Mae watched June closely as she cut the meat. Then a sinking awareness came over her that, in this instance, Ethan could not do what her eight-year-old could.

At the Thanksgiving meal at Mrs. Beasley's, Cora Mae had asked if she could cut his turkey, and he'd been fine with that. But this was not Mrs. Beasley's. Would he welcome her help here or be shamed by it? Would Mrs. Buford offer instead?

There he sat, his meat growing cold, and the widow doing nothing about it.

"May I?" Cora Mae asked him, glancing at his plate.

"If you don't mind."

If he wasn't bothered by it, she certainly wasn't. "With pleasure."

"Miss Stewart has been my right hand." Ethan leaned forward to catch June's eye, one eyebrow raised.

The joke landed, and the little girl clamped a hand over her laughter.

Cora Mae smiled at those two. Back in Cannelton, after every night that Ethan read to them, June would say, "*I wish it could be like this always.*" And every night Cora Mae would tell her, "*It will end.*"

Now the end was closer than ever.

~

Mr. Englewood's parlor was finer than any room Ethan had ever occupied. At least, from what he could see of it. A single kerosene lamp on the nearby tea table was the only one in service, a common economy these days. The fancy coal stove gave off enough heat but didn't add light to the room.

"Please don't assume I require all this," Mrs. Buford said. She sat beside him on a doily-topped sofa, her voluminous black skirts spreading from her waist and brushing against his knee. "I may have grown up here, but as you saw in Marietta, I can get by on far less."

"I recall that," he conceded.

Cora Mae had excused herself at the end of dinner to put June to bed and retire for the night. The Littletons kept company with Mr. Englewood in the adjoining room. That left Ethan and Mrs. Buford alone for the first time since their brief goodbye in Marietta.

"I'm so glad you're here," she said.

"It's good to see you in such fine health." He'd have to be blind not to notice her shining hair, glowing skin, and the fullness of her figure, even in this dim light. She'd be six months along by now. "Is all well with the baby?"

She smiled and told him it was. "I'm sorry, by the way, for any embarrassment you might have felt when the subject of your coal mining came up. I was surprised, that's all, and I was afraid my father wouldn't be pleased. I chose my words poorly. Poorly enough, it seems, for that mill hand you brought to take up for you. Please forgive me."

Her apology carried a sting, but he wouldn't dwell on that. Marietta had been a great equalizer. They'd been too busy working to discover their differences. "Think no more of it."

She exhaled. "Thank you. I declare, forgiveness is one of your best qualities. It's part of what will make you such an excellent shepherd for the boys in the Orphans Home."

"Speaking of which, I was surprised to learn you're applying for my counterpart. Do you feel you'll be ready to love orphans from both Yankee and Confederate families?" It had only been five months since Joseph's passing.

"Love is a strong word."

"Love is a powerful thing."

"It's not necessary," she insisted. "My parents never doted on me, and I'm sure I wasn't spoiled because of it. I can guide children in morals without gratuitous displays of affection."

Ethan hesitated, wondering if allowing June to eat with the adults tonight would qualify as one such display.

How different this home was from the family he'd grown up in. How different it was from Cora Mae's.

"And in your moral guidance, will you be ready to teach the orphans how to love their enemies?" he pressed. "If we don't teach the next generation how to do this, our country has no chance of surviving, even if the Union wins the war."

Mrs. Buford's lips twitched into a placating smile, then settled back into place. "I understand this is another of your specialties, Ethan. You feel some guilt over what Sherman did in Georgia, and this is your way of compensating. That makes sense to me. I understand what you're trying to do, reuniting that mill hand—"

"Miss Stewart. You can call her by her name."

She blinked, frowning, then wiped the lines from her brow. "Fine. You're trying to reunite Miss Stewart and her daughter with their family. But I feel no guilt over any military general's actions. I have no need to compensate."

Ethan rubbed his chin. "You may be right that I've struggled with guilt. But guilt is a poor motivator. Loving our enemies is a Scripture command. It's the way I want to live my life. It's the way all of us running the orphanage ought to live if we're to have any hope of fostering healing among the little ones who come into our care. Based on what you shared at dinner, they'll be coming from vastly different backgrounds, too, from both sides of every issue. They'll be coming to us looking for a safe place. A true home. And they won't get that if we don't love them and teach them how to love each other."

Her eyes flashed in the kerosene glow. "You're very passionate about love. I trust that will extend to your own family. As for me, I'll love my enemies on Sundays from the comfort of a church pew. Monday morning is a different story. I do believe you and I will get along better if you stay with the boys and I stay with the girls. Each of us will do as we think best. Agreed?"

When he didn't reply, she laughed, but it was a brittle thing. "If the position doesn't work out for me, I can take a different one. I'll teach the girls piano lessons or how to paint botanicals. I'm sure it makes no difference to me, as long as I can do something to keep busy."

Ethan shifted on the sofa, widening the gap between them. She wanted to keep from idleness. He wanted to pour himself into his life's work. "So, then, you'd focus your moral guidance on your own child," he prompted. "Your own children."

"My child will have his or her own governess. But don't worry, I wouldn't dream of relegating all teaching to someone else. I will teach my child to look out for himself and his own family and not to fight another man's battles and end up dead. What good is honor and principle if it takes you away from the ones who depend on you? What do I care if the South has its own government, separate from the North? What do I care what laws they choose for themselves?"

What did she care if millions of souls were set free from slavery or held in chains for centuries more? He wouldn't ask. He didn't want to hear her answer.

If Joseph could have heard her speech, he'd be rolling in his grave. Ethan told himself this was raw grief talking and that she would feel differently in time. He wanted to believe that of the woman he had admired and respected, the widow of a fallen soldier.

But he didn't.

There was little left to say.

Leaning back, he let his gaze wander to the palm leaves carved into plaster crown molding. He reached for a word or two to drop into the distance he felt growing between Joseph's widow and himself. It would do nothing to breach the width, but it might sound out how deep the chasm.

But that was pointless. He no longer mined for hope of a future with this woman. The space between them was too vast to bridge. He didn't need more time to know that.

"I'm glad we talked tonight, Mrs. Buford. We didn't have much time to get to know each other in Marietta."

A rueful smile bent her lips. "And now you think you know me. Before our courtship has begun?"

"I know you better than I did before. And you know me better after tonight, too. Enough to realize that you and I would not make for the partners we may have imagined. I do apologize if you feel that I've misled you in any way. I wish you all the health and happiness you deserve. If you do become a teacher of some feminine subject at the orphanage, I hope we can be friendly to each other when our paths cross. But that's as far as my hopes go."

It brought him no pleasure to disappoint anyone, but in this matter, his conscience was clear.

"Do you love her?" Mrs. Buford asked in the same tone she might use if inquiring whether he played dominoes. As if the answer weighed nothing at all.

"I do. I love Miss Stewart and June both." But that wasn't why he'd ended any understanding he had with the woman sitting so near.

"Miss Stewart is betrothed to another," she said. "The Littletons told me all about the situation. The girl is this other man's stepdaughter."

"That's true. And I'd never break a family apart, so I'll trust my confession goes no further than this. But that doesn't change my answer to your question. I do love her, as hard as I've tried to stop. It wouldn't be fair to you to pretend otherwise."

"Well." She pulled a black lace-trimmed handkerchief from her sleeve and balled it in a fist. "Now we're both telling the truth. I predict that the same sense of honor that compels you to deliver those two home will also bring you back. As you said, you won't interfere with her marriage. You and I can set our trifling differences aside and start a new life together. You loved her first, and I loved Joseph first. Neither of us can have our heart's desire. But love isn't necessary for marriage. You're a good man, and I'm still a young woman. We won't grow old alone, and my baby will have a father." She cupped her fingers over his knee. "I can live with that. Can you?"

Ethan took her hand and placed it on the sofa. "I'm sorry," he told her. "I can't."

Chapter Twenty-Eight

SOUTH OF NASHVILLE
THURSDAY, DECEMBER 15, 1864

Ethan had never claimed to be a knight in shining armor. But as he regarded Samson, a worn-out artillery horse he'd procured in Nashville yesterday evening, he couldn't help but feel how far short he fell from the ideal rescuer in so many ways.

Mrs. Buford would be all right. She'd shed a few tears last night, but this morning before they took their leave, she'd confessed that after a good night's sleep, she could see what he'd meant. They were not a matched pair. If he wasn't mistaken, there had been a measure of relief in her countenance. She didn't need to rush into a marriage, anyway. Her father would provide for her as long as need be.

During a quick conference with the Littletons after breakfast, he confirmed he still wanted the job of shepherd. He also shared his impressions of Mrs. Buford's suitability for the various roles available. In this, there was no rush, either. The orphanage would not open for several more months.

The more pressing task now was fulfilling his promise to get Cora Mae and June safely home.

The little girl walked beside him, and Cora Mae sat in the saddle on Samson. Looking over his shoulder at the Union embankments they'd just crossed through, Ethan prayed they wouldn't all need rescuing before the day was through. Those soldiers had been ready for battle. Ethan wasn't. When one of the Yankees tipped him off that Hood's army had gathered to the southeast of town, Ethan had decided to travel west of it in a wide arc before cutting east to the Nashville & Chattanooga Railroad track. They might not be allowed on the train, but they could follow the rails south.

"A little looser with the reins," he called up. "Samson is mouth-sore and won't appreciate pressure from the bit. Remember, reins are for steering, not for balance. Keep your weight squarely in the saddle and stirrups."

Cora Mae nodded, her face tight and pale. The gray cloak he'd bought her draped over the Percheron's black haunches, hiding the moss green riding skirt she wore. The double row of black ribbons she'd sewn to its edge resembled a Confederate officer's stripes.

Walking beside Ethan, June shivered in her knee-length cloak. "Are we going to walk all the way to Roswell?"

"I might," Ethan said. "But you and your mama can share Samson as soon as those two get to know each other better." Samson wasn't up to hauling any more cannons for the Union army, but he could carry both Cora Mae and June at once.

The roads were rutted and glazed with ice, so both man and beast had to choose their path carefully. Ethan called instructions to Cora Mae, content for her to learn some horsemanship while he hoofed it on solid ground.

Thunder rolled. He glanced at the heavens, but there wasn't a cloud in the sky.

"Want some company up there?" Ethan called up to Cora Mae, whose serious eyes reflected the urgency he felt.

"Whoa." She drew rein, and Samson stopped.

Ethan took a knee, and June used him to climb into the saddle in front of Cora Mae. "Careful not to kick your heels into his belly, now, June. He might be ticklish." His smile felt counterfeit. It didn't fool Cora Mae.

"That's . . . some thunder," she said coolly. "What do we do?"

"We keep going. We're headed away from it, if we can trust that Yankee's word. Regardless, we go southwest until it stops. Then we'll turn east and carry on until we reach the Nashville & Chattanooga Railroad. We're going to follow that south and retrace the journey you took north in August. When we come to the place where Sherman had the railroad torn up, we'll follow the ripped-up trail all the way home. Do you understand?"

A boom shook the ground, and the low rumble of cavalry closely followed. Cora Mae scanned the horizon. "Yes. I understand."

The galloping grew louder behind them. Dust rose in billowing clouds. With a jolt, Ethan realized the Union cavalry was flanking Hood and headed straight toward them. *If Hood heads this way, too. . .*

His heart pounded to the rhythm of distant hoofbeats. "You need to get out of here."

June twisted around to see him. "What about you?"

"Remember the plan. Ride until you can't hear it anymore; then head for the tracks."

"No!" June wailed. "Mama, we can't leave him here!"

"Hush!" Cora Mae scolded, but her face was pale as cotton, her knuckles white on the reins.

Ethan slapped Samson's flank. "Git!" The horse loped into a trot, kicking up icy mud behind him.

~

Pulse rushing in her ears, Cora Mae rose up in her stirrups and clucked her tongue to Samson.

"Ow!" June bounced, clutching the pommel. "Slow down!"

She didn't dare.

Cold penetrated her fingers that were wrapped around the reins. The shawl slipped down the back of her head, and wind knifed through her hair.

Thunder crescendoed behind them. *It's only the cotton mill clanging and banging,* she thought, trying to lie to herself. But the truth was too obvious to deny. The war was right here, right now.

Movement flashed, and she turned her head, careful not to turn the horse as well. A current of bluecoats flowed over the road Samson had trod mere minutes ago. Thousands upon thousands of them poured by. Cavalry ate up the earth on sleek mounts. The sky-blue trousers of the infantry marched together, the sunlight bouncing off their rifles and the brass buttons of their dark blue coats.

June turned to see them, too. "They're like water over the Vickery Creek dam!"

They were too many to count. Too powerful to stop. Too purposeful to change their course—unless the battle turned and they were driven back.

They couldn't be here if that happened. Cora Mae urged Samson into a quicker trot, and they continued their path. Minutes later, from some place unseen, a bugle sounded, and then the chilling Rebel cry split the air. Musketry rattled, and the ground shook with cannon fire. Smoke knit together in a blanket of haze that smelled like eggs gone bad, obscuring the view but not the sound.

The air cracked, over and again, with a force she'd never imagined possible. But worse than that were the cries of men hurling themselves into the fray and of men struck down. Artillery smoke carried on the wind, and she coughed at the terrible smell of battle. She looked left and saw the cloud of smoke light up in snatches but could only guess at the carnage that lay beneath.

Minutes dragged as she prodded Samson along the road and away, she hoped, from danger. The sun held no warmth as it peered down on the fighting below. June no longer looked anywhere but right between Samson's ears. Reaching down, she patted his neck with one hand.

Wary of the shredded road ahead, Cora Mae steered him away from the worst ruts. Suddenly, his foot faltered in a mud puddle, and June swung to the right. Cora Mae dropped a rein and lashed her arm around the girl's body, pushing her back up straight again. Samson wheeled left, off the road.

"Mama!" June yelled over the roar of battle.

Frantic, Cora Mae looked over her shoulder and saw the road shrink to a dingy ribbon behind her. Smoke rose from the ground to her left, but the air was clear to the right. If she was lucky, she'd already passed the edge of the battle, though the clamor still rang in her ears. If she waited until she could no longer hear it, she'd ride miles away from where she wanted to be.

She dug her heels into Samson's flanks, and he broke into a gallop. It was all she could do to stay upright and keep June from vaulting off Samson's back. With all her might, she squeezed her legs around the horse's middle and urged June to do the same.

A single set of hoofbeats gained on them. She looked left, and felt herself blanch. A mounted soldier in a pitiful excuse for a uniform headed straight for her.

"Halt!" he cried and thrust his thin gray horse in front of Samson.

Muskets popped, cannons boomed, and the air shuddered in cold waves. Cora Mae drew rein, but Samson only turned, skirting the Confederate horseman.

The ragged rider came alongside them and grabbed Samson by the bridle, forcing him to slow. "What on God's green earth are you doing here, miss? Don't you know you're on the edge of a battlefield?" Large eyes rounded above sunken cheeks. "Where are you trying to get to?"

"Home!" June cried. "We want to get home to Roswell!"

"Mill workers, eh? I heard tell about that. But you're not going anywhere if you don't get off this field lickety-split."

The high-pitched Rebel yell pierced the air from somewhere beneath the smoke, sending a chill down Cora Mae's spine. "We're headed for the railroad to follow to Chattanooga."

"Traveling alone? All the way to Roswell? It don't seem fitting. There's rogues everywhere. You got a gun, at least?"

She didn't, but she felt uneasy admitting it. "I thank you for your help." Heels to her horse, she urged Samson onward.

"My name's Colbert, and I'm a Confederate scout. I'll escort you a piece, to make sure you get shed of this field." He positioned his horse between the fighting and Samson and led the way on a horse so scrawny she marveled that it bore a rider.

One mile followed another as they covered fields where the grass had turned to jelly. Icy water splashed Cora Mae's ankles as Samson plunged into and out of shallow creeks. Overhead, clouds brocaded a blue silk sky. But artillery and gun smoke blotted the sky to the north, and the smell of sulfur thickened.

At last, Colbert turned to face her. "That's the end of the field, I reckon. Head another four or five miles straight that way, and you'll run smack-dab into the tracks you want. Godspeed!"

"Thank you!" She watched him ride west again and sent a prayer heavenward for his safety.

After she'd put three more miles between them and the battlefield, she slipped down from Samson and led him while June occupied the saddle alone. For stretches of time, the child sat directly on Samson's haunches, drawing heat from his body. The sounds of battle grew dimmer, but every crack and roar shook Cora Mae.

Two miles later, they came to the tracks.

Leaning forward, June buried her hands in Samson's mane. "Mr. Howard will get here soon. He'll get here."

Pine trees standing sentinel cast shadows as long as city streets. Wind scraped Cora Mae's cheeks raw and buffeted her ears through her shawl. After leading Samson to a stiff patch of faded grass, she helped June down, picketed the horse, then placed the feed bag over his head.

"We'll camp here for the night." Cora Mae unstrapped the bedroll from Samson's back and brought it closer to the pines, where fallen needles softened the cold ground. After she unfurled the India rubber sheet and wool army blanket, June scrambled between them. It had been more than a month since she'd soiled the rubber sheet, but they needed it now to protect them from the damp earth. June's teeth chattered as she folded herself into a ball.

Hands almost numb with cold, Cora Mae broke hardtack and opened a tin of meat for their dinner. Purple twilight melted into silver, and stars poked through like saber points. As night descended, she coaxed a small fire to life. With several handfuls of pine needles and a few pinecones, the flames lapped higher into the dark.

June stared listlessly at the pluming smoke. "I wish Mr. Howard would hustle."

The fire snapped and writhed, and sparks turned to ash in the air. "Why don't I read to you? It'll pass the time."

"Yes!" Throwing her blanket back, June sprang from the ground and fetched an old metal bottle Ethan had tucked into the saddlebag. It contained the only reading material they had, other than the little book of verses they'd both practically memorized. Packing light meant they hadn't brought any novels with them. By the time

June skipped back to the fire, she had popped off the cork and tipped the scroll out. "Here you go!"

"Thank you." Cora Mae took the booklet and the bottle both, slipped the cork inside her pocket, and burrowed the bottle under the fire's ashes. "We'll heat it up while I read, and then we can take turns warming our hands on it."

Firelight glowed on the open pages of the *Soldier's Prayer and Hymn Book* as she turned to Hymn 177. "'Guide me, O thou great Jehovah, pilgrim through this barren land.'" Recognizing the hymn from church, she recited the rest from memory. "'I am weak, but thou art mighty; hold me with thy powerful hand. . . . Feed me with the heavenly manna in this barren wilderness; be my sword, and shield, and banner; be the Lord my righteousness.'"

June yawned beside her, then tucked herself under the wool blanket. "That's a mighty good prayer for us this night, isn't it?"

"I reckon it is." Cora Mae dug the bottle from the ashes, wiped it clean with a flannel rag, and wrapped it in the fabric before passing it to June to hold.

Hoofbeats sounded, riveting their attention. A deserter? A guerrilla? Ethan?

Cora Mae stood and waited.

Chapter Twenty~Nine

Ethan's pulse pounded faster than the Confederate horse that carried him alongside the railroad. The danger of the battle was behind him, but guerrilla raiders might yet be between him and Cora Mae. They roamed Tennessee and northern Georgia, plundering homes, burning houses, and brutalizing anyone they pleased. A woman alone with a child would be far too easy a target for such men to resist.

A small fire beckoned him, and he rose up in his stirrups as he charged toward it. Easing back into the saddle, he pulled back on the reins as evenly as he could. "Cora Mae? June?"

"We're here!" Cora Mae called out.

"Whoa, Johnny." Halting the gaunt Kentucky Saddler, he awkwardly dismounted, then rushed toward the fire whose glow had been his guiding light. "Are you hurt? You're all right? Both of you?"

"We're fine." Stepping forward, Cora Mae reached out to him, then just as quickly pulled back, crossing her arms instead.

"Thank God." Ethan knelt, and June clambered onto his lap. He draped his arm protectively around her.

"Don't you leave us again, Mr. Howard! Not ever!" June took Ethan's face between her small hands.

"Why aren't your hands cold?" he asked in wonder.

Cora Mae's cloak fanned about her as she sank to the ground beside them. She pressed his bottle into his palm. "We warmed it in the ashes." As he wrapped his fingers around it, heat flowed into his skin.

Ethan bowed his head and studied June's earnest face, from her brown velvet eyes to the determined set of her little chin. Then she nestled against him again, her hair snagging on his stubbled jaw. He held her close, and would not release her before she was ready.

At last, she shifted, and he relaxed his embrace.

Cora Mae wiped at the tears making tracks down her cheeks. "How did you manage?"

"Stayed out of the way, mostly." And felt for all the world like a cowardly skulker as Union troops defended Nashville without him. He pointed to his pitiful new mount. "Found Johnny Reb there caught in a bramble at the edge of the battlefield. His rider no longer had need of him." The Confederate cavalry officer had stared up at Ethan from the bloodied ground, unseeing, his expression frozen in death. He shook his head to dislodge the image from his mind. "I'd have been here sooner, but it took Johnny and me a while to get used to one another." The horse was fifteen and a half hands high. Mounting him had been a challenge.

Freezing raindrops pattered through the branches above them, spitting and sizzling into the fire. He rose, listening for thunder. "We can't stay here tonight."

After packing up the bedroll, the metal bottle, and the feed bag, Cora Mae helped June into the saddle and then seated herself behind her. Ethan took Johnny's reins and a thatch of mane, and with an ungraceful, lopsided heave, mounted the horse and took the lead.

Lightning stabbed the night. The rain drove harder, its icy chill spilling down his neck and between his shoulder blades. Beneath the flashing sky, he found what he was looking for. Wrapped in shadows, the abandoned cabin leaned drunkenly like others he'd come across on the Chickamauga campaign through Tennessee to Georgia. It offered some protection, however scant. A barn loomed behind it, too.

Ethan dismounted and secured the horses in the barn. Rain blew between warped wooden planks, but it was far drier in here than outside. He fed Johnny Reb a few ears of corn and an apple, then gave one to Samson, too, before pouring feed he'd procured in Nashville into a trough. As he slung his haversack over his shoulder and slid the saddlebags from Samson, June pulled the bedrolls from their backs, and Cora Mae set about unbuckling their saddles. Once the saddles and blankets were off the animals, she and Ethan brushed them down, working in tandem with no need of words. When they finished, they shoved the door closed behind them and prayed that both horses would be there in the morning.

Inside the cabin, twenty yards from the barn, Ethan pulled a lucifer and candle from the haversack before letting the bags drop to the ground. They nested in his hand, mocking him, just as the battle had. "I can't hold this candle and light it, too." Though he'd confronted his limitations before, the confession cost him.

The walls shuddered. Cora Mae's silhouette was barely visible as she reached for him. "Let me." She swept her hand over his jacket to find his sleeve, then ran her fingers down his arm to his palm. She could not know the emptiness she left in her wake.

When she took the candle, he struck the match and watched the wick dip into its flame. As she held the light, Ethan shoved the door back into its frame and scanned the barren space. Not a stick of furniture remained. He spread out the bedroll, and June caught the end of it to help lay it on the floor, away from the rain that sprayed through the walls.

"Can't we have a fire?" June pointed to the fireplace. Wind moaned through its chimney, stirring ashes and leaves over the dirt floor.

"Wood's too wet," Ethan explained.

June scuttled under the blanket. "It's so dark and scary."

"We'll let this burn a while." He took the candle from Cora Mae. Stooping, he burrowed the taper into the dirt floor until it stood upright, and then lowered himself to sit. "I'm not tired, so I'm going to stay up anyway. You get some rest. But before you retire. . ." He motioned for her to sit next to him and then wet a handkerchief with water from his canteen.

Hesitantly, she accepted the linen and used it to wipe her face clean before giving it back to him. "We've done this before," she said, and memory washed over him, bringing him back to that red-hot day in July when he first met her.

"Ah, yes. And you told me we wouldn't be friends. Not that I blamed you."

A raw, wet wind swirled about them and around June, asleep under the blanket. Cora Mae held his gaze. "I was wrong."

"Excuse me?"

Rain pummeled the cabin, sharpening the sweet smell of rotting wood. "I reckon you're missing that right hand of yours, and I'm sorry for the pain and trials losing it has caused you. But you have what's more important by far. The last time I saw Mama, she told me to love my enemies. It was a bitter pill to swallow to even say I'd try after what Yankees did to me and my town. But you—" She pressed her lips together.

He braced himself, even as cold began to numb his senses. The candle's flame struggled to stay alive.

"I know you had your orders to follow," she went on, "like every soldier on both sides. I don't know exactly what you were like before I met you—though Mrs. Beasley has painted a picture—but it sure seems to me you've been getting better ever since. You loved your enemy when you told me how to stay in Georgia. You loved your enemy when you chased after those scoundrels invading that lady's home. You loved your enemy by visiting and bringing food to my mother and Mrs. McGee, and by fetching our news between us. You hate what that injury did to your body, and rightly so. But you forgave Zeke anyway. When I see you, I see a man who knows how to love his enemy. You're still doing it, every step of this journey back to Roswell."

The truth sat on his tongue until it burned, and he had no choice but to admit, "You were never my enemy."

She shivered, chafing her arms. "Then what am I?" she whispered. The tip of her nose was pink with cold.

He couldn't tell her that she was the keeper of his heart, not while she was betrothed to another. She believed he had an understanding with Mrs. Buford, and he'd not disabuse her of that notion, for fear it would tempt her—tempt them both—away from the honor she most wanted to preserve. "You're the best friend I've ever had," he admitted instead. "My right hand. Truly."

Her composure crumbled. A tear traced her cheek as she drew a ragged breath.

Rain battered the cabin with a low roar. "I'm sorry if I've said too much." He never meant to make her cry. Worse, he had no idea how to help her feel better.

"You don't have a single thing to be sorry about."

The break in her voice lanced him. He wiped the tear from her face with the pad of his thumb, then let his fingers slide into her hair. "If I could take your sorrow away, I would. Every trouble, every care. Gladly would I shoulder each burden you bear."

"I know." She covered his cheek with her hand in a gesture so tender, he could barely hear his conscience over the drumming of his heart.

Wind churned through the cabin from between the chinks in the wall, snuffing out the candle, leaving only the scent of melted wax behind. Darkness blanketed Ethan and the woman he loved.

Stifling a groan, he denied his impulse to claim her with a kiss that would heat them both. Instead, he said, "Come here." He guided her to sit in front of him on the floor. She leaned back, and he wrapped his arms around her shoulders to warm her shaking body.

Shifting slightly, Cora Mae rested her head on his shoulder, her forehead against his jaw. The weight of her body warmed him.

"I can't do this." Nor should he. He released her, and rain gusted into the space between them. "You aren't mine to hold."

A rustling sound told him that she was already moving away. As Cora Mae curled up next to June under the blanket, Ethan settled on the dirt floor near the door with nothing but cold to cover him.

~

When dawn came, Cora Mae still ached with a longing she could not—would not—name. Her heart was as divided and ravaged as the land they traveled, one portion loyal to the South and to the promise she'd made Mr. Ferguson, June, and Mama. The promise Pap himself had wanted her to keep. The other portion beat only for Ethan.

It would never do. It wasn't fair to Mr. Ferguson or to Mrs. Buford, or to herself. Telling herself to ignore her emotions had stopped working miles ago. But by the grace of God, she didn't have to act on them, either. She refused to be "the other woman," as Mr. Hampton and Mr. Aldridge would have had her be.

The days were bitter and short as they traveled deeper into the South. Near Chattanooga, mountains rose in bristly mounds, their trees a delicate black embroidery on the hem of a slate blue sky. The city itself was too overrun and bustling to be pretty, but the Union army camp gave them a safe place to rest their horses and replenish provisions.

As they crossed the state line, snow powdered horses and travelers alike, but the flakes melted as soon as they landed, so that Georgia was laid bare.

It was desolate. Sherman's destruction blighted the land beyond what Cora Mae could have imagined. The Union armies had scorched fields of wheat and cotton to nothing but blackened stubble. Poor folk who gave her, Ethan, and June a place to sleep warned of nationless bushwhackers claiming to be Wheeler's Confederate cavalry. Also called guerrillas, they'd ransacked neighbors' homes—looking for deserters, they'd said. But the scoundrels ravaged women and stole their last pigs before setting their houses aflame.

Iron rails ripped from the railroad tracks lay forlornly on the ground, looped and crossed like neckties. The scars left in the landscape made the trail they followed to Roswell, where their journey began and would end.

All sense told Cora Mae she should not even be friends with a man who'd helped ruin the South, even if she hadn't promised to marry Mr. Ferguson. But as she rode in the wake of destruction, the thought of the coming separation carved a hollow inside her that threatened to swallow her whole.

Time rebelled against its boundaries. Days became impossible to track, so quickly did they slip away. The pacing of this journey seemed all wrong. After months of waiting to return home, the plodding path now gained a startling momentum. She and June and Ethan made a cord of three strands, but every day that passed, she felt the unraveling.

Chapter Thirty

Shadows cast from loblolly pines stretched long and thin across the road. With Kennesaw Mountain at their backs, they weren't far north of Marietta now. But with the sun going down soon, they needed to find shelter for the night.

Shifting in the saddle on Johnny Reb, Ethan peered at Cora Mae, seated behind June on Samson. "I'm sorry we couldn't make it all the way home today." These poor horses had needed more time to rest these past few days than he'd accounted for. "But tomorrow, for sure."

She nodded, expression solemn. "Tomorrow. It hardly seems real."

"And then we'll finally be done traveling?" June asked. "It's been forever since we left Cannelton."

Ethan chuckled. It had been less than two weeks, but half a month on the road was a long journey for a child. For all of them. Cora Mae was no doubt eager to reach her destination, and while Ethan was less so, he'd rejoice to deliver them safely.

There were too many risks on this journey for him to feel easy, especially since passing through Chattanooga. If Mrs. Stewart hadn't been so bad off the last time he'd seen her, he'd have put off this trip a little longer. But the older woman didn't have much time left. She ought to be with Cora Mae and June for what remained of it.

Twisting in the saddle, Ethan glanced back at Kennesaw Mountain. Memories of the battle there had surged to mind at the first glimpse of that hill and clung to him still. The entire path through northern Georgia had conjured ghosts of war. Ringgold Gap had been the gateway through which Sherman had led his troops to begin the campaign, and every small town where they'd had to stop for the night had been a site of battle. Resaca. Adairsville. Allatoona. Kennesaw. In most towns, folks had been sympathetic to returning millworkers and let them sleep in the house. Last night, the hospitality had reached only so far as the barn.

In the distance, smoke plumed from a chimney. "There's a likely spot." Maybe tonight they'd be warm and dry.

Maybe tonight he would finally solve the riddle of how to say goodbye.

The sun lowered, and with it, the temperature. By the time they reached the humble cabin, the chill had turned sharp and biting.

Ethan dismounted, then helped June and Cora Mae down. Before they reached the porch, the sound of crying came through the door.

Lines grooving Cora Mae's brow, she climbed the few steps and knocked. "Hello?" she called. "We're passing through, seeking shelter, but can we help?"

"We got nothing to spare, missy," came the broken reply. "We ain't in no position."

"I understand." She caught Ethan's eye and pointed to a scatter of cornmeal caught in hoofprints in the front yard, not made by Johnny Reb or Samson. They could not yet be a day old. "But is there some way that we can help you? Seems you've had trouble."

Trouble, indeed. Shards of pottery stuck to the porch in a puddle of frozen molasses. Some distance from the cabin, the barn door squeaked on broken hinges. The smells of hay and livestock floated out, but the silence from within did not bode well. There'd been devilment here, and not long ago.

After a muffled conversation inside the cabin, the door opened to reveal a wizened old couple, and a little girl peeking out from behind the woman's calico skirts. The man eyed Ethan from under wiry gray eyebrows, his thumbs hooked into suspenders. His watery gaze relaxed on the shortened arm before drifting to Cora Mae and June.

"Did you have a run-in with some lawless men?" Ethan asked, urgency mounting. At their answer, he asked, "How long ago? Which way did they go from here?"

"An hour ago, maybe." Wet streaks lined the woman's face. "They went that way." She pointed to the blazing sun dropping behind the trees. It was the opposite direction of Mrs. McGee's farm, which was almost five hours east of here. That brought relief. If danger had been headed for Mrs. Stewart and Mrs. McGee, Ethan couldn't have stayed here, and he wouldn't bring Cora Mae and June with him on the chase.

"My brother's hurt bad." The little girl spoke up from behind a tangle of blonde hair, two fingers stuck in her mouth.

"Is that right?" Ethan looked beyond them, and saw a boy laid out on a table, shaggy straw-colored hair fanning the pillow beneath his head. Bloody rags were bunched up near his thigh. "My name is Ethan Howard, this here is Cora Mae, and this is June. We'd like to help, if we can. The two of us are trained in nursing."

The woman's eyes widened. "Is that God's truth? Then come in!"

Her husband explained that they were the O'Donnells, and that he and his wife were raising their grandchildren, Clay, age fourteen, and Penny, age five. Cora Mae took a saddlebag off Samson, Mr. O'Donnell promised to see to the horses, and June whisked Penny to a far corner of the cabin to show her Sissy and Sassy.

"This boy has too much bravery for his own good." Mrs. O'Donnell clasped her grandson's hand. He looked to be in and out of consciousness. "Them devils came a-thundering up, went right to our barn, and slayed our hog and chickens without so much as blinking. One of them tossed the animals over their horse, and the other started raiding our stores. They run off with the cornmeal we been saving, a slab of salt pork, and broke our last jug of molasses right there where you come in. But Clay, he put up a fight. Didn't you, son?"

As she relayed the tale, Ethan moved the rags and inspected the wound. "Gunshot?" he asked.

"Through and through."

"You're sure?" Cora Mae asked. "I can sew him up, but if there's a bullet inside, it will have to come out first."

In reply, Mrs. O'Donnell shuffled to the mantel above the fireplace and plucked from a small bowl the bullet.

"Good." Ethan bent Clay's knee and found the exit hole on the other side of his thigh. "It missed the bone, thank God."

While he asked Mrs. O'Donnell for clean water and fresh bandages, Cora Mae ripped off a portion of the black ribbon trimming her cape. "Silk makes the nicest stitches," she explained, and set about pulling off a thread. Ethan reckoned the doctors had always been the ones to stitch patients when she was a nurse, but she'd watched plenty, as he had, and he warranted she was a better hand with a needle than most.

"Do you have any flannel?" Ethan asked the older woman. "If you could scrape some lint from it, that would help us." It would also give her something to do.

"Can you hear me, Clay?" Cora Mae found her sewing kit in the saddlebag and threaded the needle. "That was a brave thing you did, protecting your family from those outlaws."

Mr. O'Donnell entered, his hands stained with the blood of his grandson. "I told him not to. By God, I begged him to stay out of it. We didn't keep him hidden from the conscription officers just to let him get shot dead in our home."

Ethan accepted the fresh rags and pitcher of water from Mrs. O'Donnell and brought it all to Cora Mae. "But he's only fourteen."

"That don't matter none. Governor Brown is so desperate for warm bodies after all them desertions, they'd as soon add Clay to the front lines as they would look at him. That's why we hid him good. But when these bandits came today, he wouldn't stay hid for nothin'."

Clay moaned when Cora Mae made the first stitch.

"I'm sorry," she said but didn't hesitate in her task. "I don't have anything for the pain. It'll be over soon." She continued speaking in low, soothing tones, even after the boy passed out again.

Ethan held the rags to the wound, soaking up the blood so she could see her way to sew. Soon, she tied the knot, and Ethan helped her turn Clay over so she could stitch up the exit wound, too. By the time Mrs. O'Donnell was done scraping lint, he was ready to pack it between the wounds and a fresh layer of clean bandages.

"I'll strip the bed," Mrs. O'Donnell announced, heading for the corner where the girls played. "We can cut bandages from the ticking."

"Ethan," Cora Mae murmured, "don't let her do that. She tears into that ticking, she'll be forced to sleep on cornhusks with nothing in between. It won't do." She flipped up the hem of her skirt and began cutting a strip from her new petticoat.

He went after the older woman and assured her they had bandages enough without her ruining her bed.

"Thank you," Mrs. O'Donnell said. "I don't know

what we would have done if you and your wife hadn't come. Your sweet daughter is so good to Penny, too."

An unmanly lump formed in his throat, but he muscled it down. "We're happy to help, ma'am. We're only sorry you had need of it."

Once Clay was cleaned up and bandaged properly, they laid him on a pallet close to the fire, where Mrs. O'Donnell covered him with blanket and song. Meanwhile, Mr. O'Donnell brought sand to throw on the stains on table and floor, and Ethan scrubbed them as clean as they could get.

With June and Penny chattering where they played, Cora Mae brought out their provisions and set about making a meal for everyone.

"I hate them," Clay muttered through clenched teeth. "I hate those sons of guns."

Ethan figured he would. But before he could find any right words to offer, the boy had slipped back into a fitful sleep.

Dinner was a quiet affair, but satisfying. After the washing up that followed, Ethan gestured to Cora Mae and leaned his head toward hers. "I was saving this to give you tomorrow." From inside his jacket, he pulled *The Swiss Family Robinson*. "I want you and June to have this. But what would you think of my reading some tonight, for everyone?"

"I had no idea you brought that. Are you sure you want to give it up?" Her eyes shone with her smile when he said yes. "Please do read to us, if you can by the light of the fire. The least 'uns would enjoy it, and the elder O'Donnells might favor the distraction, too. This family has endured more than they ever should have needed to. I can't imagine the terror of a grandchild being shot."

Ethan fully agreed. And so, with resounding approval from all quarters, he sat by the fire and read aloud from his favorite book of a family far from home. He read until the girls fell asleep in the bed Penny shared with June, and until the grandparents both were snoring, and the only listener left was Cora Mae, her attention never faltering.

He closed the book for the very last time and placed the story in her hands.

"Thank you." She hugged it to her chest. "You have no idea how precious this is to us. To me."

He nodded and offered her a smile. "I'll watch Clay tonight," he told her, keeping his voice low so as not to disturb the rest of the family.

She finished spreading their bedrolls on the floor, one on each side of their patient. "You're not going to sleep?"

"I doubt it." He watched her settle into her bedroll and brush out her hair, as she did every night, before braiding it. Tomorrow they would part ways. He would not shorten his remaining hours with her by sleeping them away. "I'll keep an eye on Clay, in case he develops a fever."

A small smile brought the dimples to her cheeks, just enough for the firelight to catch them. "You were wonderful today. You've been wonderful this whole time. I hope Mrs. Buford knows how fortunate she is. I hope she doesn't mind overmuch that you're making this journey with us. Soon enough, you'll be with her again, and you'll make her happy to the end of her days." She tied a ribbon at the end of her braid and tossed it behind her shoulder.

He climbed into the bedroll she'd laid out for him. "She doesn't mind," was all he was willing to say on that score. Leaning forward, he checked Clay for fever and felt only the warmth of the fire. Ethan glanced at Cora Mae. "I do believe we missed Christmas. That was yesterday, now that I think of it. I'm sorry I didn't get you anything."

She held up the novel.

"Oh." He chuckled. "That wasn't for Christmas. More like a going-away present, and more with June in mind. But there's nothing else."

Her smile lifted like a sunrise. "How can you say that? You're bringing us home. There's no greater gift than that. We'll never be able to thank you enough."

"Even though I took you from Roswell to begin with?"

"Even though. I won't forget you, Ethan Howard."

He placed a hand over the pocket where he kept a lock of her hair. The empty space throbbed where his right hand used to be. "I will never stop missing you."

Chapter Thirty~One

OUTSIDE ROSWELL, GEORGIA
TUESDAY, DECEMBER 27, 1864

Cora Mae should have been prepared for the barrenness surrounding Mrs. McGee's farmhouse, especially after what they'd seen all through northern Georgia. At least the disrepair spoke more of neglect than of a raid like the O'Donnells had suffered. Here the fence was gone, and with it all sense of order. Weeds choked former gardens, climbed the walls of the smokehouse, and reached into the pebbled drive pitted with puddles and slush. With June walking beside her, Cora Mae led Samson by the reins, and Ethan led Johnny Reb.

She had tried to imagine this reunion and pictured herself running into her mother's arms. But this didn't feel like home, and for some reason, she didn't feel like running. Beneath her woolen cape and skirts, her knees had gone soft.

A dog barked from the front porch, then bounded down the steps and ran toward them.

"Little Feller!" June ran to meet him, wrapped her arms around his neck, and laughed over his sloppy kisses. Feller soon made his way to greet Cora Mae, and then nearly tackled Ethan with his reckless adoration.

Then she heard coughing.

Hustling to the porch, she took the stairs and found herself face-to-face with Shannon McGee. The older woman rested her sawed-off shotgun against her hip. "Well, I'll be. Never thought he'd really do it, but I reckon I ought not be so surprised. Welcome back, Cora Mae."

"Mrs. McGee. Thank you so much for taking in my mother while I was gone. I can't tell you what your kindness means to me."

She shrugged. "No need to tell me. I guess I already know. I don't suppose you have word from my girls?"

Cora Mae told her what she knew, then added, "It's good they've found a better situation for themselves."

Mrs. McGee spit on her gun barrel and rubbed it to a shine with her thumb. "They know how to take care of themselves. They know where to find me, once they can. Now get on in there and see your ma. She's in the bedroom at the top of the stairs."

Cora Mae rushed into the unfamiliar house. "Mama, I'm here! We're home!" Holding her skirts out of the way, she climbed the stairs and burst into the first bedroom, tearing the shawl from about her head.

"Darlin'?" Mama gasped from a rocking chair. She dropped the mending she'd been doing and spread wide her arms.

Cora Mae fell into them, weeping. "Oh, how I missed you!"

Footsteps sounded heavily on the stairs before stomping into the room behind her. "What the devil?"

Rising, Cora Mae wheeled around. Each heartbeat was a blow against her breastbone.

Dust motes spun and hovered in the sunbeams streaming between the window's homespun curtains. Striped with light, Mr. Ferguson gaped, and the mismatched teacup and saucer he carried listed to one side.

Quickly, she rushed to take it from him and set it on the table beside the rocker, just as June entered the room.

"You've come home to us." He kissed his stepdaughter on the head and engulfed Cora Mae in a father's embrace for a prodigal child. She could feel his ribs through his back. Mama had grown more frail, too, but that didn't keep her from gathering June onto her lap.

Cora Mae stood back and tried not to show pity for how Mr. Ferguson had changed. Both body and hair had thinned since July. His posture was pressed down with cares, and worries carved seams on his face.

"My lands." He returned her stare. "You look so hale and fine."

He seemed as shocked at her appearance as she was with his. While folks here struggled to keep body and soul together, she had eaten her fill in the North. The toll of the journey aside, she and June were healthier than they'd ever been. Guilt nipped at her heels, but she wrestled it back. They had done nothing wrong. All of them had done the best they could.

"I appreciate what you did for Mama," Cora Mae said, ready to shift his attention elsewhere.

Mr. Ferguson widened his stance and crossed his arms. "As soon as the bluebellies moved south, I came back just as I said I would. But there's no work for me in Roswell with the mills burned down, so I found a job in my widowed sister's town, a day's journey from here. I come here regular to see Matilda has enough food. It's been a stretch, I'll tell you, especially because of the no-accounts who came by and cleaned out our stores. Been working on Matilda to come live with me and Opal, but she insisted on staying with Mrs. McGee to wait for you."

"Have any other mill hands come back yet?" Cora Mae asked.

"You're the first we know of." Mama hugged June again, as if convincing herself they'd really returned.

"Our Yankee, Mr. Howard, brought us back," June quipped. "Same one as took us away."

Mr. Ferguson frowned, calling out every line on his face. "A bluebelly?"

Mama waved the term away. "You already know about this one, Horace. He's the one that fetched us news and vittles while our girls were away. That's his dog yapping outside."

June skipped toward the door. "He's not a bluebelly anymore, he's just Mr. Howard. I'll fetch him here and stay with the horses myself. Mr. Howard's worried about horse thieves," she added.

Moments later, Ethan entered the room alone and doffed his cap, tapping it against his thigh. Mr. Ferguson eyed him.

"Mr. Ferguson, this is Ethan Howard, the man who brought me home," Cora Mae said. Finality weighted the statement. He had done what he set out to do. It was over. Tears bit her eyes. "Mr. Howard, you know my mother, and this here is—this is Mr. Horace Ferguson. He's been looking after her as he could."

"Pleasure to meet you." Ethan bowed slightly to Mr. Ferguson, his face a mask of good manners. "Ma'am, it does me good to see you again."

"Come here, son."

Striding toward Mama, Ethan tucked his hat under his arm and filled her outstretched right hand with his left. But that wasn't enough for Mama. She tugged him into an embrace, and he took a knee as he folded her into his arms.

"God bless you, Mr. Howard." She released him, tears tracing her cheeks. "I been praying the three of you home again. Thank you for my daughter and for June. Thank you."

"It was my pleasure." Ethan opened his mouth as if to say more before pressing his lips flat. Blinking in the slanting rays, he simply bowed again and replaced his hat on head. "I'll take my leave. Miss Stewart, one last word, if you please."

She met him in the hall. "Ethan, I—" Speech abandoned her.

"I have something for you."

"I can't take anything more," she whispered. He had given and given, and it pained her fierce that she had nothing to offer in return.

"Please. It would mean so much to me." From inside his jacket, he drew his beat-up metal bottle, the housing for his prayer book. He tapped the scrollwork on its neck. "Did I ever tell you this word is Latin for 'hope'?"

She told him he hadn't.

"I want you to have it."

"Hope?" She tried to memorize the sweep of hair across his brow, the green of his eyes, the faint lines that fanned from them when he smiled. Her vision blurred.

"Yes. Hope. The bottle. All of it." He held it out to her, and she grasped the cold metal. "If you should feel hopeless, look inside." At that, he tipped his hat to her and whispered, "It's time for me to go."

He disappeared down the stairs.

~

The screen door banged behind Ethan. "Well, June . . ." He scanned the front yard. "Where did Mrs. McGee go?"

"She said it seemed a fine time to hunt rabbit or squirrel. She thought our family might could use the privacy for our reunion. She took her gun and Feller and said she'll be back in a couple hours."

Ethan would miss that one-eyed coonhound, but it was better for all of them if the dog stayed here. He hated what he had to say next. "Then I guess it's time—"

Hoofbeats cut him off. A cloud of dust rose from the road beyond a row of pine trees. Dread snaked through his middle.

June hurried to him. "Comin' fast," she whispered. "Who do you think it is?"

"Get inside," he told her, and she immediately obeyed.

The horse pounded over the hill, barreled up the drive, and halted right in front of Mrs. McGee's porch. Long black hair streamed from beneath the rider's hat and over the shoulders of his oiled deerskin cloak. When he dismounted, the sun glinted on the pistol at his hip and on the musket in his hands.

"Can I help you, Mister . . ?"

"Walker." The man spit syrupy brown juice on the bottom porch step, then grinned, a tobacco plug bulging inside his cheek. "And I aim to help myself." In one leap, he topped the stairs.

Ethan splayed his hand against Walker's chest. "No, you won't." Whether he was a deserter, a guerilla, or a garden-variety bandit, he was a vulture come to pick the land clean. Based on the description Mr. O'Donnell had given them last night, this wasn't one of the rogues who'd raided their home and shot Clay. It didn't matter. There were enough to go around. "There's nothing for you inside."

Before Walker could shoulder the musket, Ethan shoved him off balance, and he crashed down the steps. Pushing himself up from the weed-snarled ground, Walker aimed his rifle at Ethan. "If you was a deserter, I'd have every right to kill you where you stand."

"I'm not." Ethan met him on the ground, planting himself between Walker and the porch.

"You sound like a Yankee." The gleam in his eye was the devil's own as he lit upon Ethan's shortened right sleeve. "Even better."

"I'm a civilian. You have no business here." Ethan's pulse quickened. In his mind, he rehearsed lunging, dodging, disarming Walker. Saw himself fumbling the musket with just one hand and a nub of a forearm. He could not hold it, aim, and fire it. But could he use it like a club if he had to? Would that be enough to stop Walker? Sweat beaded and chilled his skin.

The door burst open behind Ethan, and two sets of footsteps sounded on the porch.

"We haven't got much. Take it and leave." Mr. Ferguson and Cora Mae descended the steps and passed Ethan as they approached the bandit. Each of them held a sack of food. They'd go hungry without provisions.

"Don't give him a kernel," Ethan advised. "He's a thief." Alarm licked through his veins. He could barely defend himself, let alone two more souls.

"And you ain't?" Walker sneered. "What do you call what Sherman's army's been up to all the way through Georgia? I'm through with Yankees." He cocked the hammer.

"No!" Cora Mae jumped in front of Ethan.

A shot blasted the air, and then another, and one more.

Cora Mae fell back at an angle, corn spilling from a hole in the burlap sack she held. Instinctively, Ethan lunged to catch her with his right arm, in vain. With a sickening crack, her skull hit the corner of the porch step.

Horror seized him as he knelt and scooped her head onto his lap. *Not this, not now. Not after everything we've been through.*

Vaguely, he was aware of Walker dropping his gun and collapsing, of blood pouring from two holes in his chest. Mr. Ferguson bent over his betrothed, face ashen, with a smoking pistol in his shaking right hand and the sack of peanuts he'd hid it behind in his left.

"Cora Mae," Ethan called, her name bittersweet on his lips.

Her eyelids fluttered, and her grip released. The corn slid off her waist, golden pebbles pooling in the gray folds of her cloak. A frayed hole next to the buttons sent a shock coursing through Ethan.

"Give her to me." Mr. Ferguson's voice quaked. "You've done your part. I'll take it from here."

Chapter Thirty~Two

A throbbing headache pulled Cora Mae awake to the sound of her mother's coughing. She scanned the bare white room. "Where's Ethan?"

Sitting in the chair by the bed, Mama tucked a handkerchief out of sight as Mr. Ferguson came in. "She's awake, thank God."

Mr. Ferguson peered at her. "You took a nasty spill." His words smelled of coffee. Ethan must have left some here.

Holding her breath, she reached under the quilt to sweep her hand over her middle and found it miraculously whole. "Wasn't I shot?"

"Yes, darlin'." Mama gave her Ethan's bottle.

She took it, the cold metal drawing the heat from her skin. A few inches below the neck, the thick, aged bronze was dented in the shape of a bullet. With a prayer of thanks and wonder for the treasure she'd tucked into her cloak, her fingertip dipped into the space.

"I shot that rat first, and it turned his aim so it wasn't dead on," Mr. Ferguson explained. "He fired at an angle, and the corn slowed the bullet some before it came to rest in that tin. Then I finished him, but you fell and hit your head."

"You been sleeping since all that happened yesterday," Mama told her. "You been calling for Ethan."

"Delirious," Mr. Ferguson insisted. "She ain't well yet."

"I'm not delirious. Where is he?" Cora Mae clutched the bottle in her lap.

"Mr. Howard's fine, likely thanks to you," Mr. Ferguson said. "He's gone on his way."

Mama wheezed, then cleared her throat. "He refused to leave until he knew you'd be all right. Only when he saw the bullet hadn't entered your body could he be persuaded to leave. Although, I'd have been pleased for him to stay on, and told him so."

"And I told him different," Mr. Ferguson said. "Weren't no cause for the Yankee to stay, now that you're with kin."

As though in a fog, Cora Mae's gaze moved from his face to Mama's. Wincing, she touched the ache at the base of her skull, but the searing in her chest could not be reached.

"Now that you're home, we'll all go and live with my sister Opal," Mr. Ferguson said.

Mrs. McGee came into view, passing a cup of tea to Mama. "I'm not going anywhere, Horace. My Cynthia and Fern are out of prison and may be coming back to me any day now. I'm staying."

"But all alone, Shannon?" Mama coughed, and the fit grew violent, staining her handkerchief red.

Cora Mae beheld it with dread and sorrow. She tried to sit up, but the room spun, pushing her back down.

Mr. Ferguson scratched behind his ear. "Looks like you're not up to more travel yet, which is a shame, since we've got the entire day ahead of us. Tomorrow, if you can, we'll go."

Too much was happening all at once. Cora Mae closed her eyes against the tilting walls and ceiling. "What happened to Walker's body?"

"Horace and I buried him," Mrs. McGee said. "We've been keeping watch in case any more scoundrels come poking around. That coonhound is on duty now while I rustle up breakfast."

"We've got his horse, though," Mr. Ferguson added, "so between that one, mine, and Samson, we'll have a mount for each adult, and June can ride with you. Opal's town has a preacher, so we'll take care of that business soon's we get there."

Cora Mae couldn't leave so soon. She couldn't stand before a preacher tomorrow night and pledge her body and life to Mr. Ferguson. She could barely think around this pounding in her head.

"I need more time than that," she said.

The silence that followed turned heavy.

"Cora Mae," Mr. Ferguson said, "it's been eighteen months since you and I made our arrangement to get hitched, to fulfill the promises I made to your Pap and to Mavis. You need a man, and June needs a mother. You were all set to marry me that terrible day the Yankees came to town, and that was more than half a year past. If you ain't ready now, when will you be?"

She had no idea how to answer. Maybe she'd never be ready.

Pushing herself up on her elbows, she looked around the room, then beyond Mr. Ferguson and into the hall. "Where is June? Is she sleeping?"

"June?" Mr. Ferguson shrugged.

Why didn't he know? Had he talked to his stepdaughter at all since Cora Mae had been shot, a man had been killed, and Ethan had left for good?

Mrs. McGee crossed to the window behind Mama and pulled back the curtain. "Well, I'll be. I never told her to do that. Whoever heard tell of laundering bedsheets after one night?"

A stone dropped into Cora Mae's gut. Ignoring the pain in her head, she left the bed to see.

June was bent over a washtub, scrubbing, her little face red and wet with tears.

~

That afternoon, after Cora Mae had spent a good long time talking to June and reading to her from Ethan's book, there was something else she had to do. Mr. Ferguson insisted on coming with her to make sure she didn't faint after knocking her head so hard and to protect her from possible bandits. She didn't argue.

The clamor of the waterfall filled her ears at Roswell's Vickery Creek dam. The bare trees were a black net against gray sky. The air was cold and damp and heavy, and the spray from the falls felt like ice. While Mr. Ferguson waited with their two horses, she took a small shovel and pushed the point of the blade into the earth.

The ground was hard but not frozen. Her head swelled with pressure made worse from the noise. A short, slippery walk from here would take her to the ruins of the mill that had been her entire world until six months ago. With no desire to see it, she confined her energy to a single purpose. Putting her boot on the shovel, she bounced her entire weight on the tool until the earth gave way.

Minutes later, she brought out the cigar box she'd bound in oiled paper, aware that the woman who had buried it in July was not the same one who dug it up. Sitting on her heels, she unwrapped the box and opened the lid to find the valuables she'd tucked inside. Silverware, Pap's pocket watch, Mama's jewelry. And the ruby ring from Mr. Ferguson. The ring Mavis had worn first.

Woodenly, she slid the ring over her finger, and it spun between her knuckles. It would fall off with the slightest shake. Taking it off again, she closed it into the box and indulged in a long exhale.

"Was that my ring?" Mr. Ferguson asked. The sound of the waterfall had covered his approach.

"It doesn't fit anymore," she told him.

"Too big?"

She nodded.

"We'll fix that," he declared. "A strip of cloth wound around the band will see that it stays in place."

Cora Mae handed him the shovel, tucked the box into the saddlebag, and mounted Samson. No strip of fabric would make that ring fit again.

Once they were far enough away from the falls that they could be heard without shouting, Mr. Ferguson began telling her more about his sister and the house they'd be sharing with her.

"Will she mind four more people in her home?" Cora Mae asked.

"It'll be a squeeze, but she could use the help with housekeeping, I reckon."

"What about children? How do you think she'll get along with June?"

He shrugged. "June doesn't seem to be much trouble. Before she went to live with you, I barely noticed her. She's a good worker, as I recall. It may not be millwork, but we'll find her a job, and Opal will not turn up her nose at those wages."

Cora Mae's forehead ached from frowning. "It's been good for June not to go to work every day, Horace. She's learned to read and write, and she's had time to play. You can see how much she's grown since July."

"Has she?" His slight body swayed in the saddle. "I never had much use for book-learnin'. Sounds like June's had a bit of a holiday. Well, now it's time to work."

A holiday. Cora Mae clenched her teeth to trap the anger inside. She watched Samson's ears flick forward and backward, felt his flanks move as he walked. Doubt surfaced in her mind, bobbing into view. She knew June needed her. But did June need Mr. Ferguson? "Do you even consider her your stepdaughter anymore?" she asked. "Your daughter?"

"She's never been my daughter." Then he rubbed his chin, considering. The pause grew long and wide enough to fall into. "A stepchild is one born to the person you married," he said at last. "And as Mavis has passed on to glory, I am no longer married to her. So, no, I don't think on June as my stepdaughter, either. But I did make a promise to Mavis that she'd be cared for, and I aim to keep that promise."

"But how can you care for a child without caring for the child?" she asked. Wind ruffled the edge of her cape. "Do you take pleasure in having her around? Do you love her?"

A puff of air blew through his nose. "Young 'uns ain't for pleasure, Cora Mae. They're the natural result of two bodies coming together. When they can work and contribute to the family, that's a help. I expect any children we have to bring in wages as soon's they're able. I'll do right by 'em, but I don't need to be fond of 'em, too."

For the rest of the ride, Cora Mae sat in dumb and distant silence. Her pulse throbbed in her veins. How had she not known this was how he felt about June, about children?

Fear sprang up from her belly, but she pushed it back down, where it became a flutter of nausea. All she had wanted to do was the right thing, but now everything felt wrong.

At Mrs. McGee's farm, she dismounted and handed him the reins, trusting him to see to the horses.

"You feelin' poorly?" he asked.

"Yes."

"Then it's good we won't leave 'til tomorrow. Take to your bed, Cora Mae. We ride at dawn."

The door slammed behind her as she entered the house and strode into the parlor. Mama's coughing tumbled down the stairs. June looked up, wide-eyed, from where she read Ethan's book. She rested on the floor, using Little Feller's willing body as a pillow.

Cora Mae sank to her knees, gathered her child into her arms, and held her tight. "I love you," she told her. "I love you so much it hurts. You are mine, and nothing will change that. I'm so glad I get to be your mama."

~

That night, Mama's coughing didn't allow for much sleep, but Cora Mae didn't feel restful anyway. When the case clock downstairs chimed four times, she gave up on slumber altogether.

"Mama, I'm going to fix us some tea, all right?" She didn't bother whispering, as Mama was clearly awake.

"I'll come down, too, darlin'. We need to talk."

Cora Mae lit a candle, helped Mama into her robe, then supported her as they took the stairs to the kitchen. Once a fire was lit in the stove and a kettle sat on top, she sat with Mama at the table, the single candlestick flickering between them.

"Talk to me," Mama said. "The truth. You can't feel that miserable and hope to hide it from your mama. Don't tell me it's just your head that hurts, either."

"It's not." While the water worked its way to a boil, Cora Mae confessed every emotion she'd so long denied in the name of honor, until she'd laid bare everything that had happened between her and Ethan. "I tried to do right, but it feels like a mistake that can't be corrected."

"It's never right to cheat on a person, plain and simple. You did right where that's concerned. But now that you're here, there's nothing to stop you from releasing Horace from a promise he made out of obligation. He does his duty. But he doesn't love you. And I know someone else who does."

Cora Mae wished it were that simple. "It's too late. Ethan has an understanding with another woman, a war widow who's with child. I met her, Mama, and she's beautiful. I wouldn't have guessed the two of them would make a match, but war has a way of changing things. I won't get in their way."

"Are they married yet?"

"Not yet."

"Neither are you." Mama winked. "I know Horace, and I know your Ethan. It's for you to make up your own mind, but I know which man loves you."

"He might have, but that was before Mrs. Buford. Feelings change. I missed my chance. And I will miss that man to the end of my days." She pushed back from the table and took the kettle off the heat.

"Surely it's not as hopeless as all that."

Hopeless was exactly how she felt.

Snatches of her last conversation with Ethan came back to her. "*If you should feel hopeless, look inside,*" he'd told her. He'd been referring to that banged-up metal bottle that saved her life. The one with *Spero* etched around its neck.

"I'll be right back." Forgetting to steep the tea, she hurried to the bedroom and returned with the bottle.

After pulling the cork, she upended it, and the prayer book slid out. Around the scroll was wrapped another piece of paper. A note. With every nerve on edge, Cora Mae read:

Dear Miss Stewart,

I pray that your new life with Mr. Ferguson and June brings you great joy and peace and that you will both be loved the way you deserve. I'm returning to Nashville, but first I'll stay with the O'Donnells a few days. I want to talk to Clay about what happened to him and make sure he comes through all right. You'll forgive me for thinking of you when I pass through

Marietta on the way, for I have thought of little else since we rode into it together. But know that with each thought, I'll say a prayer for your family.

Goodbye,
Your Yankee

Longing wrenched her. "He's still nearby," she whispered. "If it weren't for Mrs. Buford, I could go to him today."

June wandered into the kitchen, rubbing her eyes. "Mr. Howard doesn't love that fancy lady."

Mama opened her arms to the little girl, and June climbed onto her lap. "What do you mean?"

"I heard him say so, after you got shot and hit your head."

Cora Mae's pulse thudded. "What did he say? Do you remember exactly?"

Nestling against Mama, June played with the end of her braid. "He said, 'Cora Mae, you wake up and be well. I love you.' And then he said he could never marry Mrs. Buford or anyone else after knowing you. But the *best* part was when he said, 'You're the keeper of my heart, and I don't want it back.'"

A charge jolted through Cora Mae. "Are you sure? Are you sure that's what he said?"

"Sure as I've ever been, honest. A girl doesn't forget a thing like that. Only, he caught me listening and told me that if you did get well, I was not to tell you what I heard. Unless you changed your mind about Mr. Ferguson. Did you? Please, please say you did."

Decision resounded within her.

"What's all this?" Horace entered the kitchen, pulling his suspenders up over his shoulders. "Getting ready to travel? Y'all are up earlier than I expected, but that suits fine. I wouldn't mind some of that coffee before we go, seeing as the sun's not catching up with us for a spell."

"Horace." Cora Mae looked from June to Mama to the man still waking up. "I've got somewhere else to be."

Mr. Ferguson frowned. "What in tarnation are you talkin' about?"

Cora Mae grasped her mother's hand, feeling her support in its grip. "You always been good to us. Pap couldn't have asked for a better friend. So I'm real sorry, but I need to break our agreement. I belong with Ethan Howard."

Mr. Ferguson's face darkened. "Did that bluebelly violate you? You in the family way, Cora Mae?"

"No, no. We never—no," she said. "I love him with all I am. I been bottling it up, trying to do what's honorable by my family. But he's my family, or could be. So is June."

"I want to come!" June cried. "Mama, take me with you!"

"'Mama'?" he repeated.

Tears lined her lashes as Cora Mae absorbed Mr. Ferguson's bewildered stare. "I love her as my own. Since neither of us are her blood relatives, don't you think we ought to let June choose who she stays with?"

Confusion carved his brow. "That's a mighty big choice for a child to make."

"Horace," Mama said. "The child has been in Cora Mae's care almost as long as she was in yours. You and Opal never did fancy having children underfoot. Let her go with the young folks."

June rested her hand on Cora Mae as she turned toward Mr. Ferguson. "I'm going with Mama."

He sighed, and his shoulders slumped. "I'm supposed to provide for you all. I promised Mavis. I promised Asa."

Mama laid a gentle smile on him. "You have done. But Shannon and I can take care of each other, and the Lord has provided for Cora Mae."

At this, Mrs. McGee ambled into the kitchen, carrying her own candle. "Y'all having a going-away party without me?" She propped a fist on her slim hip. "Maybe you didn't hear, with all the excitement that's happened since. But when I went hunting for rabbit two days ago, I found that our nearest neighbors have returned, and them not two miles from here. If we need anything, they'll be there. It makes a heap more sense than you coming and going with a day's journey on each side. We'll be fine now. Truly."

Doubt dimmed his eyes. "It don't suit. Asa wouldn't have stood for her taking up with a Yankee, and I don't need to spell out why."

Mrs. McGee harrumphed. "Howard is not like any Yankee you ever saw before. Even his dog warmed up to me."

He rubbed a hand over his whiskered jaw.

Cora Mae pulled her robe tighter about her. "Pap would have wanted me to be well cared for and well loved."

"Ain't I got a plan to care for you?" Dismay cracked his voice.

Compassion surged for this weary man, loyal to Pap to the end. "I've got to go. And June is coming with me."

Mama stood and enfolded Cora Mae in her soft arms. "Go on, darlin'," she whispered in her ear. "If there's a way, take it. I'll be fine, knowing you are. You give my new son my love, you hear?"

"I'm coming back. I didn't come all the way home just to leave you again." Cora Mae hugged the woman who'd raised her, and embraced, too, the memory of Pap and Wade, things familiar, and the life that had disappeared when the mills burned to the ground.

And then, she let go. For now.

Chapter Thirty-Three

MARIETTA, GEORGIA
FRIDAY, DECEMBER 30, 1864

Samson was lathered with sweat by the time Cora Mae and June galloped into Marietta's town square. Horace Ferguson rode beside her on his thin chestnut bay, having insisted on escorting them. They'd gone first to the O'Donnells' cabin, but Mr. O'Donnell had said that Ethan had just left for Marietta.

Reins firm in her hands, Cora Mae trotted Samson around the square's perimeter. This place had changed the shape of who she was and altered the course of her life. She barely recognized it now. The Cobb County Courthouse, her old prison, was mere rubble, along with most of the other buildings skirting the square. An expanse of fire-charred ground showed no sign of the thousand army tents it once held.

"Are we too late?" June cried. "Did he go without us?"

"I don't know. We'll keep looking." Cora Mae's voice held steady though she felt as exposed and raw as the square laid bare.

"Mr. Howard!" June began shouting. "Mr. Howard!"

Mr. Ferguson shook his head but clucked to his mount to keep apace with Samson.

Wind nipped Cora Mae's nose and cheeks. Her throat ached as she scanned the square again. A few men were scattered among the buildings that remained, but they paid her no mind, consumed instead with the rubble.

Cora Mae knew how that felt. Since the war had begun, all that she'd known had fallen down around her. She'd been haunted by what she'd lost. But out of the ruins, God had brought her Ethan. She could only pray He would bring them together again.

Crossing into the rail yard, they passed the once-grand Fletcher House, now soot-stained and missing its fourth floor. With no trains in sight and tracks torn asunder, the yard was eerily silent. Gone were the soldiers and sutlers, horses and wagons, the patients and doctors, the freed men and women, the mill hand prisoners.

Gone was Ethan.

Wisps of cloud rolled by like ghosts of engine steam. Weariness and memory pressing down on her, Cora Mae dismounted and helped June down as well, while Mr. Ferguson stayed in his saddle.

June leaned on her, looking into the distance. "Maybe he's gone on to Nashville already. Will we follow?"

"That wouldn't be safe for us to do," Cora Mae admitted, knowing Mr. Ferguson would escort them no farther.

"Then we send him a letter?"

"We could try." But Cora Mae didn't think the mail reliable yet. Her mind whirred to find a suitable plan. It had only been a few days since she'd seen him, and the distance between them may be a matter of mere miles. But when and how could she reach him? Would he be safe on the journey alone? The gap separating her from Ethan seemed to widen with every thought.

She was homesick, again. For him.

In the next moment, June took off running at full tilt, her shawl slipping from her hair to her back. At the end of the platform, a figure knelt, and the girl threw herself against him, clinging with all her might.

Cora Mae's breath stalled in her lungs.

"Well, I'll be." Mr. Ferguson's voice drifted to her. "Go on, then."

All the obstacles that had kept them apart finally fell away. Leaving them behind, Cora Mae approached, and Ethan stood, his attention fixing on her alone. In his earnest face she saw the soldier who had swooped into her life and caught her up on his horse, carrying her out of harm's way. She saw the guard under moonlight with a canteen full of blackberries and a book full of wonder for her, a prisoner. The patient who suffered but found healing in helping others, and in forgiving the one who hurt him. The Yankee who cared for his enemies. Above all, she saw the man who had loved her and loved her still.

Ethan met her gaze with eyes the very color of promise, of everything fresh and new. They held worlds of hope she longed to live in.

"Thank God." He closed the final distance between them. "I saw that the bullet didn't penetrate, but I didn't know when you'd wake up."

"It took me a while." She swallowed the catch in her voice. "But I did wake up. I ended the engagement with Mr. Ferguson. It was never love for him that kept me from you. It was commitment to honor and honesty, the same commitment I know you hold dear. I've loved you, Ethan, more than I could bring myself to admit out of respect for Mr. Ferguson and Mrs. Buford. But if I can believe what June has told me, you're not tied to her."

His eyes misting, a smile unfurled. "You can believe it."

The knot in Cora Mae's chest slipped free. "Then I'm yours. If you'll still have me."

Before she had finished speaking, Ethan drew her to himself, erasing any doubt, their togetherness a completion she'd never known. He cradled her head as she melted into him, and swayed his warm lips against hers in an answer more eloquent than any words could be.

When at last she remembered June, Cora Mae pulled back from the kiss that promised more to come. She laughed at the girl's wrinkled nose, a thin disguise for the happiness shining behind it.

Astride his horse, Mr. Ferguson ambled over to them, and Ethan reached up to shake his hand. "Good to see you, sir."

Mr. Ferguson tipped his hat and grunted. "Matilda vouches for you, and in her way, Mrs. McGee did, too. Cora Mae here says she loves you, and you love her and can take care of her and June both. That so?"

Ethan took off his hat, dark blonde hair glinting in the winter sun. "Yes, sir."

"You gonna ask her to marry you?"

Memories of Ethan's first proposal—near this very spot—rushed at Cora Mae. How bewildered she'd been, how upside down she'd felt. Here, she had refused him. He thought he'd lost her. Here, they had found each other again.

Ethan's eyebrows arched, and a hint of a grin flickered. "All due respect, sir, I'll take it from here." Bending on one knee, he took her hand with the same tenderness and strength that marked his character. "Cora Mae Stewart, I love you. I love your integrity, your faith, your resilience. Will you do me the honor of becoming my wife? Would you build a life with me, and partner with me as we build a home for this war's orphans? I'm not saying it will be easy, but if we're together, well—" A lump shifted in his throat. "I'll do right by you, Cora Mae. You are my perfect fit."

Joy shuddered deliciously through her. "Yes," she whispered. "Yes."

June whooped with glee, and Ethan stood, wrapping them both in an embrace. "And you, Junebug, would you do me the honor of being my daughter?"

"Yes, Papa." Her chestnut hair shimmered in the sunlight as she beamed up at him, nearly glowing with the surety of belonging. "Where will we go next?"

He smiled. "Seems to me there's a lovely woman who would sorely miss you both if I were to take you away again so soon. The orphanage won't be ready for quite some time yet. It would do us all good to spend that time with Mrs. Stewart, don't think?"

"And when the war's over, and the orphanage is ready for us, maybe she can come too?" June asked.

"She'd be welcome," Ethan told her.

Cora Mae didn't know if Mama could hang on that long. But what mattered most was that Cora Mae could hang on to her, for as long as the Lord would grant them.

With her beloved's arm about her shoulders, she regarded Mr. Ferguson. "You're the best friend Pap ever had. Thank you for caring for Mama, and for Mrs. McGee too, when you could." Gratitude thickened her voice.

Mr. Ferguson bobbed his head. "Be well, all of you." He turned his horse and softly plodded away.

As the hoofbeats faded, Ethan laid his hand on June's head and kissed Cora Mae once more. Though surrounded by ruins, her heart was whole. War had taken her from Roswell, but it had not destroyed her home. Her home was made new, and it was here, with the man and child she held most dear.

Author's Note

"Are you serious?" I gaped at the museum curator and asked her to repeat the story. What she shared stunned me in the most delightful way.

I was visiting the Kennesaw House Museum (now Marietta History Center) in Marietta, Georgia, the summer of 2014. I was there to give a program related to my novel, *Yankee in Atlanta*, which is the third book in my Heroines Behind the Civil War series. We had some time before the program, so Amy Reed, the curator, ushered me around the museum, showing me the highlights. While we were chatting, she brought up the plight of the mill workers who had been evacuated north by Sherman in 1864. I was already intrigued by this, having discovered this event in my research for *Yankee in Atlanta*. But since I was unable to connect it to the plot of the story I was writing, I had to let it go.

Then she told me about a Yankee soldier who proposed to a Georgia mill worker on her way through Marietta—right on the train platform. I was hooked.

Years passed before I had the opportunity to write a fiction inspired by this proposal, but the original version of *A River Between Us* was published as a novella in *The Message in a Bottle Romance Collection* in 2017.

More years passed. That book went out of print. I purchased the rights to have the story back and decided to tell a more complete version, now that I wasn't limited by a novella's word count. I wanted to more fully explore the themes of hope, reconciliation, and finding home when it seems like home is lost forever. Cora Mae, June, and Ethan, deserved a lot more pages than I first was able to give them. I'm so glad to fix that with this book you hold in your hands!

For further reading about the history behind *A River Between Us*, check out *The Women Will Howl: The Union Army Capture of Roswell and New Manchester, Georgia, and the Forced Relocation of Mill Workers* by Mary Deborah Petite and *North Across the River: A Civil War Trail of Tears* by Ruth Beaumont Cook. Both of these volumes were immensely helpful to me. Eagle-eyed readers may notice that according to these sources, Roswell workers were imprisoned at Marietta's Georgia Military Institute (GMI) along with the mill hands from Sweetwater and New Manchester. However, since these books were published, historian Brad Quinlin found primary sources—letters written by soldiers camped in Marietta—describing Roswell workers cramped inside Cobb County Courthouse while the others filled GMI. My thanks to Brad for sharing his research with me.

One other difference you may notice: after the mill hands were rounded up in the Roswell town square, they were actually moved into the surrounding streets to make room for army tents to shelter soldiers in the square. For the sake of streamlining the story, I confess to skipping this location move.

Aside from those two details, I tried to keep as closely to the history as possible. The characters are fictional, but they all represent people who really lived and breathed. I don't know what happened to the particular couple who inspired Ethan and Cora Mae in *A River Between Us*, but we do know there was at least one marriage between a Georgian and a Union soldier stationed in Marietta.

After the war, the Roswell founding families returned and rebuilt the mill, which opened again in 1867. Some Georgia mill hands relocated to work at the mill in Cannelton, Indiana. (An 1870 census shows more than forty Georgia-born mill hands on the payroll there, at least thirty of whom could be traced back to Roswell or New Manchester.) Some mill hands returned to Roswell or the surrounding area. But many simply disappeared from historical record. This novel is my attempt to honor their memory.

Thank you so much for reading *A River Between Us*—especially those of you who already read the novella first! I pray that within these pages you found hope and light that you can carry with you on your own journey, wherever it may lead.

Acknowledgments

I'm so grateful to the following people for the roles they played in the development of this book:

Amy Reed, who is, at the time of this printing, the director at the Marietta History Center. Thank you, first of all, for your support of *Yankee in Atlanta*, for allowing me to speak at Kennesaw House, and for that tour of your museum. If you hadn't told me about that Union soldier proposing to the Georgia mill worker, I would not have written this book.

Brad Quinlin, Civil War historian, author, and expert on Marietta's Civil War hospitals, among other things. It was Brad who told Amy about the proposal before she had a chance to pass that along to me. Brad also answered countless email queries from me over the span of years, and spent a few hours on the phone with me besides. Thank you, Brad, for your invaluable insights and information.

Steve Dacus, Civil War re-enactor with the 11th Ohio Volunteer Cavalry. Thank you for answering all my cavalry and horse-related questions.

Elaine Deniro and Juliette Johnson of the Roswell Historical Society, who fielded all kinds of questions from me as I shaped this story.

My friend Carrie Albright, who helped identify which horse breeds would work for all the different horse characters.

The four other authors from *The Message in the Bottle Romance Collection*: Amanda Dykes, Joanne Bischof, Heather Day Gilbert, and Maureen Lang. I loved being part of that collection with you talented ladies! Thank you for allowing me an outlet for the original "A River Between Us." (Dear reader, if you haven't already, please check out these authors' works. They are all such wonderful storytellers.)

My agent Tim Beals of Credo Communications, for helping me publish this novel independently. I truly would not have attempted this without your support and guidance.

My readers! When I first floated the idea of turning the novella into this full-length novel, your enthusiasm was overwhelming. You're the reason I dusted off this story and tried again. Special thanks to Linda Attaway, Jeanne Crea, and Christin Faber, for proofing on a deadline!

Last and most important, I'm so grateful to God for being my reason to hope, for adopting me as His child, and for the promise of an eternal home with Him in heaven.

About the Author

Jocelyn Green inspires faith and courage as the award-winning and bestselling author of numerous fiction and nonfiction books, including *The Metropolitan Affair, The Mark of the King*, the HEROINES BEHIND THE LINES CIVIL WAR series, and THE WINDY CITY SAGA. Her books have garnered starred reviews from *Booklist* and *Publishers Weekly* and have been honored with the Christy Award, the gold medal from the Military Writers Society of America, and the Golden Scroll Award from the Advanced Writers and Speakers Association. She graduated from Taylor University in Upland, Indiana, and lives with her husband, Rob, and their two children in Cedar Falls, Iowa. She loves tea, pie, hydrangeas, Yo-Yo Ma, the color red, *The Great British Baking Show,* and reading on her patio. Visit her at jocelyngreen.com. Stay up to date by subscribing to her e-newsletter through her Web site.

More Civil War Fiction from Jocelyn Green

HEROINES BEHIND THE LINES

Wedded to War

*2013 CHRISTY AWARD FINALIST (HISTORICAL FICTION AND FIRST NOVEL CATEGORIES)

It's April 1861, and the Union Army's Medical Department is a disaster, completely unprepared for the magnitude of war. A small group of New York City women, including 28-year-old Charlotte Waverly, decide to do something about it, and end up changing the course of the war, despite criticism, ridicule and social ostracism. Charlotte leaves a life of privilege, wealth-and confining expectations-to be one of the first female nurses for the Union Army. She quickly discovers that she's fighting more than just the Rebellion by working in the hospitals. Corruption, harassment, and opposition from Northern doctors threaten to push her out of her new role. At the same time, her sweetheart disapproves of her shocking strength and independence, forcing her to make an impossible decision: Will she choose love and marriage, or duty to a cause that seems to be losing? An Irish immigrant named Ruby O'Flannery, who turns to the unthinkable in the face of starvation, holds the secret that will unlock the door to Charlotte's future. But will the rich and poor confide in each other in time?

Wedded to War is a work of fiction, but the story is inspired by the true life of Civil War nurse Georgeanna Woolsey. Woolsey's letters and journals, written over 150 years ago, offer a thorough look of what pioneering nurses endured.

Widow of Gettysburg

When a horrific battle rips through Gettysburg, the farm of Union widow Liberty Holloway is disfigured into a Confederate field hospital, bringing her face to face with unspeakable suffering-and a Confederate scout who awakens her long dormant heart.

While Liberty's future crumbles as her home is destroyed, the past comes rushing back to Bella, a former slave and Liberty's hired help, when she finds herself surrounded by Southern soldiers, one of whom knows the secret that would place Liberty in danger if revealed. In the wake of shattered homes and bodies, Liberty and Bella struggle to pick up the pieces the battle has left behind. Will Liberty be defined by the tragedy in her life, or will she find a way to triumph over it?

Inspired by first-person accounts from women who lived in Gettysburg during the battle and its aftermath.

Yankee in Atlanta

When soldier Caitlin McKae woke up in Atlanta after being wounded in battle, the Georgian doctor who treated her believed Caitlin's only secret was that she had been fighting for the Confederacy disguised as a man. In order to avoid arrest or worse, Caitlin hides her true identity and makes a new life for herself in Atlanta.

Trained as a teacher, she accepts a job as a governess to the daughter of Noah Becker, a German immigrant lawyer, who enlists with the Rebel army. Then in the spring of 1864, Sherman's troops edge closer to Atlanta. Though starvation rules, and Sherman rages, she will not run again. In a land shattered by strife and suffering, a Union veteran and a Rebel soldier test the limits of loyalty and discover the courage to survive. Will honor dictate that Caitlin and Noah follow the rules, or love demand that they break them?

Spy of Richmond

Richmond, Virginia, 1863. Compelled to atone for the sins of her slaveholding father, Union loyalist Sophie Kent risks everything to help end the war from within the Confederate capital and abolish slavery forever. But she can't do it alone.

Former slave Bella Jamison sacrifices her freedom to come to Richmond, where her Union soldier husband is imprisoned, and her twin sister still lives in bondage in Sophie's home. Though it may cost them their lives, they work with Sophie to betray Rebel authorities. Harrison Caldwell, a Northern freelance journalist who escorts Bella to Richmond, infiltrates the War Department as a clerk-but is conscripted to defend the city's fortifications.

As Sophie's spy network grows, she walks a tightrope of deception, using her father's position as newspaper editor and a suitor's position in the ordnance bureau for the advantage of the Union. One misstep could land her in prison, or worse. Suspicion hounds her until she barely even trusts herself. When her espionage endangers the people she loves, she makes a life-and-death gamble.

Will she follow her convictions even though it costs her everything—and everyone—she holds dear?

For more fiction from Jocelyn Green,
visit JocelynGreen.com.

Printed in the USA
CPSIA information can be obtained
at www.ICGtesting.com
LVHW041945220923
758953LV00008B/72

9 781625 862556